THE TRUE CONFESSIONS OF
Charlotte Doyle

Avi

THE EMC MASTERPIECE SERIES

Access Editions

SERIES EDITOR

Laurie Skiba

EMC/Paradigm Publishing
St. Paul, Minnesota

Staff Credits:
for **EMC/Paradigm Publishing**, St. Paul, Minnesota

Laurie Skiba
Editor

Paul Spencer
Art and Photo Researcher

Lori Coleman
Associate Editor

Chris Nelson
Editorial Assistant

Brenda Owens
Associate Editor

Kristin Melendez
Copy Editor

Jennifer Anderson
Assistant Editor

Sara Hyry
Contributing Writer

Gia Garbinsky
Assistant Editor

Christina Kolb
Contributing Writer

for **SYP Design & Production**, Wenham, Massachusetts

Sara Day
Partner

Charles Bent
Partner

Library of Congress Cataloging-in-Publication Data

Avi. 1937 –
    The true confessions of Charlotte Doyle / Avi.
        p.   cm. -- (The EMC masterpiece series access editions)
    Summary: As the lone "young lady" on a transatlantic voyage in 1832,
Charlotte learns that the captain is murderous and the crew rebellious.
    ISBN 0-8219-1983-0
    [1. Sea stories.] I. Title. II. Series.
PZ7.A953Tr 1999
[Fic]--dc21   99-33702
                                                                          CIP

ISBN 0-8219-1983-0

Copyright © 2000 by EMC Corporation

Published by EMC/Paradigm Publishing
875 Montreal Way
St. Paul, Minnesota 55102
800-328-1452
www.emcp.com
E-mail: educate@emcp.com

Printed in the United States of America.
    4 5 6 7 8 9 10 xxx 05 04

Table of Contents

APPENDIX

Avi

Avi (1937–) is an award-winning author whose books are popular with young people in many countries. Although he has written many books, Avi struggled with writing in school. His teachers discouraged him from pursuing a career in writing, but he stubbornly followed his dream.

Avi

Avi was born on December 23, 1937, in New York City. His father, Joseph, was a psychiatrist and his mother, Helen, was a social worker. Avi grew up in Brooklyn with his twin sister, Emily, and his brother, Henry. His sister began calling him "Avi" when they were about a year old, and the name stuck. When writing, this is the only name he uses. Avi came from a line of writers and other artists. His great-grandparents and one of his grandmothers were writers, and both of his parents wrote. His twin sister became a poet and a critic as well.

Growing up, Avi was surrounded by books and a love of reading, which greatly influenced his decision to become a writer. He enjoyed stories told by his grandparents and learned to read at age five. Avi read picture books, then novels and comic books, and listened to a lot of children's radio. Instead of being interested in sports, he enjoyed reading and playing imaginative games.

Avi struggled with school. He did well in science, but had trouble with writing and especially dreaded Friday spelling tests. He later learned that these difficulties were caused by dysgraphia, a learning disability that caused him to rearrange words and turn letters around. In fact, he flunked out of his first high school before his parents enrolled him in a small school that focused on reading and writing. Avi also got help from a tutor, a person Avi credits with helping him decide to become a writer. During his senior year of high school, Avi decided to become a writer and recorded this momentous event in his journal.

After high school, Avi attended the University of Wisconsin, where he majored in history and theater. Avi began writing seriously while in college. With a love of theater, he began as a playwright but did not have much success. Avi moved back to New York after college. There, he continued to write plays and also combined his love of theater with his love of books in a job at the New York Public Library's theater collection. Enjoying his library work, he began taking night classes and earned a degree in library science. Avi worked as a librarian for twenty-five years.

During his years as a librarian, Avi began to write for children. He was inspired by the stories he created to tell his own children. His first books for children were *Things That Sometimes Happen* and *Snail Tales*, two books for very young readers. Since then, Avi has written for a variety of ages. He said that for a while, he adapted his writing to the ages of his children, but at some point they continued growing and he continued writing at a reading level that he enjoyed.

Avi's writing spans a wide range of genres. He has published historical fiction novels and other works of fiction such as adventures, comedies, mysteries, adventures, fantasies, ghost stories, and short stories. Many of his books fall into more than one of these categories, such as *The True Confessions of Charlotte Doyle*, which is both historical fiction and adventure.

In all of his books, Avi tries to convey complex issues in a thoughtful and interesting way. His books are usually rich with emotion and imagery and full of suspense. Above all Avi likes to tell a compelling story, one that engages his readers and makes them want to "race to the end."

Reading has been one of the greatest influences on Avi as a writer, and he encourages young writers to read as a way to improve their writing. Avi also encourages writers to pay attention to the world around them and try to understand why things happen. He also suggests questioning answers given by others and thinking things through for yourself.

Avi says that writing is hard work even though he does so much of it. He writes and rewrites his stories many times and takes about a year to write a book. When he needs a break from writing, he enjoys photography as a hobby.

BOOKS BY AVI

Abigail Takes the Wheel
The Barn
Beyond the Western Sea
Blue Heron
Bright Shadow
Captain Grey
City of Light/City of Dark
Devil's Race
Emily Upham's Revenge
Encounter at Easton
Ereth's Birthday

Time Line of Avi's Life

1937	On December 23, Avi and his twin sister Emily are born in New York City.
1959	Avi graduates from the University of Wisconsin.
1962	Avi earns a master's degree in drama from the University of Wisconsin.
1962–70	Avi works at the New York Public Library Performing Arts Research Center, as library staff for the theater collection.
1963	Avi marries Joan Gabriner. They have two sons, Shaun and Kevin.
1964	Avi earns his master's of library science degree from Columbia University.
1970	Avi becomes a professor and humanities librarian at Trenton State College in New Jersey, where he teaches courses in research and children's literature. He will hold this position until 1986. *Things That Sometimes Happen* is published.
1972	*Snail Tales* is published.
1975	*No More Magic* is published.
1977	*Captain Grey* is published.
1978	*Emily Upham's Revenge* is published.
1979	*Night Journeys* is published.
1980	*Encounter at Easton* and *The History of Helpless Harry* are published. *Man from the Sky* wins a Children's Choice Award.
1981	*A Place Called Ugly* and *Who Stole the Wizard of Oz?* are published.
1982	*Sometimes I Think I Hear My Name* is published.
1983	*Shadrach's Crossing* is published.
1984	*The Fighting Ground, S.O.R. Losers,* and *Devil's Race* are published.
1985	*Bright Shadow* is published.
1986	Avi gives up being a librarian and becomes a full-time writer. *Wolf Rider* is published.

Romeo and Juliet—Together (and Alive!)—at Last is published. | 1987

Something Upstairs is published. | 1988

The Man Who Was Poe and *The True Confessions of Charlotte Doyle* are published. | 1990

Nothing But the Truth and *Windcatcher* are published. *The True Confessions of Charlotte Doyle* receives the Horn Book-Boston Globe Award and is named a Newbery Honor book. | 1991

Blue Heron and *"Who Was That Masked Man, Anyway?"* are published. *Nothing But the Truth* is named a Newbery Honor book and a Horn Book-Boston Globe Honor book. | 1992

City of Light, City of Dark and *Punch with Judy* are published. | 1993

The Barn and *The Bird, the Frog, and the Light* are published. | 1994

Poppy and *Tom, Babette, and Simon: Three Tales of Transformation* are published. | 1995

Avi moves to Colorado. *Beyond the Western Sea* is published. *Poppy* receives the Horn Book-Boston Globe Best Fiction Award. | 1996

Finding Providence and *What Do Fish Have To Do With Anything?* are published. | 1997

Avi marries Linda Wright. *Poppy and Rye* and *Perloo the Bold* are published. | 1998

Midnight Magic, *Ragweed*, and *Abigail Takes the Wheel* are published. | 1999

The Good Dog and *Ereth's Birthday* are published. | 2000

The True Confessions of Charlotte Doyle

The True Confessions of Charlotte Doyle takes place aboard a ship called the *Seahawk* in 1832. The *Seahawk* is a brig, a two-masted ship, owned by the company for which Charlotte's father works. Through the seventeenth, eighteenth, and nineteenth centuries, sail structures continued to evolve, leading to faster voyages. Charlotte knew little of life on a ship when she left England, but in the course of her journey, she learned much about the ship itself and about a sailor's life.

Getting Oriented on a Brig

A brig was one of many types of sailing vessels used for transportation and commerce during the nineteenth century. It is a two-masted ship. The mast to the front of the boat is called the foremast and the other mast is the mainmast. The foremast rises behind the forecastle deck and the mainmast rises between the ship's waist, at its center, and the quarterdeck. For a more detailed look at the set-up of a brig, see the illustration in the appendix.

Such a ship has many sails, the names of which are often taken from the piece of rigging on which it is set. The sails on a brig were usually square on the foremast and some combination of square and fore-and-aft sails on the mainmast. Square sails are set across the width of the ship, while fore-and-aft sails are set along the length. Fore-and-aft sails, unlike square sails, can propel a ship forward with wind on either side.

Because the ship is powered by wind, the timing of a crossing depended on the weather. If the ship hit a calm, the crew might lower small boats and row to pull the ship along to avoid being set too far off schedule. If the ship hit a storm, it might propel the ship quickly, but it could be very dangerous for the crew and cause great damage to the ship. The most powerful storm a ship might hit is a hurricane. Characterized by winds of 73 or more miles per hour, a hurricane is a violent storm often accompanied by torrential rains and high seas. A hurricane moves in a circular motion. A period of calm often occurs when the eye, or center, of the storm passes by.

Captain and Crew

The captain of the ship is responsible for the safe and timely passage of the ship and its goods. The captain makes decisions about the ship's course and is the leader of the crew. In *The True Confessions of Charlotte Doyle,* the captain of the ship *Seahawk* is Captain Jaggery, who is assisted by his mates. Mr. Hollybrass is the first mate and Mr. Keetch is the second mate. They deliver the captain's orders and oversee the watches of the crew. Watches are groups that work as teams. The term also applies to periods of time aboard the ship. Each day is broken into seven watches. Bells are rung each half hour to mark time. A more detailed explanation of ship's time is given in the appendix on page 172.

In the shipping world of 1832, the crew was usually made up of experienced sailors who signed articles, or contracts, for their positions. The articles spelled out what the sailors were to do, how they would be compensated for their work, and how they would be punished for misconduct. The worst offense a crew could commit was mutiny, or revolt against their captain and other officers of the ship.

Life on the Ship

Quarters on the ship were tight, or without much space to move about. The captain had his own cabin, which was more spacious than the crew's quarters. The crew usually bunked together, sleeping in hammocks. Paying passengers, like Charlotte, might have private cabins, but they were small and confined.

Meals on a ship were cooked in the galley. It was difficult to keep food on the long voyages. Charlotte complains of meals made of food that has begun to spoil. Hardtack, a tough biscuit, was a popular choice because it was durable, if not edible. Because of the lack of fresh fruits and vegetables, many sailors suffered from scurvy, a disease caused by lack of vitamin C.

The crew kept busy with tasks such as keeping watch, adjusting sails, mending equipment, and keeping the ship clean. Sailors often passed the time telling yarns, or stories about their previous voyages. Sea chanteys, or sailors' songs, were also a popular way to pass the time.

Divided by Class, Race, and Gender

Because of the limited company on the ship, Charlotte ends up spending time with many members of the crew. This is surprising because on land it would be unlikely for a young lady of Charlotte's social class to interact with a sailor. Charlotte sees the captain as a gentleman and someone on the same social standing as herself.

Charlotte's family is well off, part of the upper class. Charlotte has attended a school that prepares her for a role as a lady of this class. She has been brought up to pay attention to such things as appearance, manners, and the social standing of others. At the time, there was a sharp distinction between the classes. Servants and other laborers were expected to show respect to those of upper classes.

When Zachariah, the cook on the ship and a black man, is friendly toward Charlotte, she thinks he is acting inappropriately. Her reaction is based both on his class and on his race. In the United States at the time, slavery was still in effect in many states. Zachariah has found a free life on the sea, but he still finds that, in many ways, his race is still an issue.

Charlotte's experience as the only woman on the ship is also unusual. At the time the story takes place, women did not travel unless their husband, father, or a suitable companion accompanied them. Charlotte dressed in the typical clothes for women of her day: long skirts, a bonnet to cover the head, and white gloves. Fair skin, untanned by the sun, and soft hands showed a person to be of a class that did not have to work. Charlotte begins the voyage with these trappings of her class.

These three distinctions, which were very clear to Charlotte on land, begin to blur throughout her journey as she becomes accustomed to life at sea.

Characters in
The True Confessions of Charlotte Doyle

Main Characters

Charlotte Doyle. Charlotte Doyle, the narrator and protagonist of this story, tells the story of her ocean crossing as a thirteen-year-old girl. As she tells in the introduction, she is accused and convicted of murder. At the beginning of her sea voyage, she is respectful of her elders, does as she is told, and takes pride in being good and maintaining a pretty appearance.

Zachariah. Zachariah is an old sailor who has been hired as the cook, surgeon, carpenter, and preacher. He has been a sailor for many years. The oldest man on the ship, he is also the only black man. Zachariah is the first person to befriend Charlotte on the ship.

Captain Jaggery. Captain Jaggery runs a tight, orderly ship. Before Charlotte boards the *Seahawk,* she encounters two porters who will go nowhere near a ship headed by Captain Jaggery. The captain leads a ship owned by Charlotte's father's company. Charlotte's first impression of Captain Jaggery is that he is a gentleman who reminds her of her father.

Mr. Keetch. Mr. Keetch is the second mate. He welcomes Charlotte aboard the ship because the captain and first mate are not aboard when she arrives.

Minor Characters

Mr. Grummage. Mr. Grummage is hired by Charlotte's father to accompany her to the ship.

Hollybrass. Mr. Hollybrass is the first mate.

Barlow. A member of the crew.

Dillingham. A member of the crew.

Grimes.
Morgan.
Foley.
Ewing.
Fisk.
Johnson.
} members of the **Seahawk's** crew

Cranick. Cranick had been a member of the crew of the *Seahawk* on its prior voyage. He was injured on the voyage and did not join the crew this time.

Mr. and Mrs. Doyle. Mr. and Mrs. Doyle are Charlotte's parents. They returned to Rhode Island earlier than Charlotte did, because of Mr. Doyle's promotion.

Albert and Evelina Doyle. Albert and Evelina are Charlotte's siblings.

Bridget. Bridget is a maid in the Doyle household in Providence, Rhode Island.

Echoes:

On Avi's The True Confessions of Charlotte Doyle

Expections of Nineteenth Century Females

"Never be seen in the street without gloves. Your gloves should fit to the last degree of perfection."
>—*Collier's Cyclopedia,* 1883

"Your shoes and gloves should always be faultless."
>—*Collier's Cyclopedia,* 1883

"A young man or woman upon first entering into society should select those persons who are most celebrated for the propriety and elegance of their manners."
>—*Manners, Culture and Dress of the Best American Society,* 1891

"I place the education of domestic duties first, as essential and indispensable."
>—George W. Burnap
>from *The Sphere and Duties of Woman,* 1848

"Boys are expected to have more or less of the bear in their natures but girls are born and bred to modest and lady-like behavior, and a saucy, pert and selfish girl is simply beyond endurance. . . . Clothes should always be neat and pretty. It is within the reach of everyone to be graceful and genteel in manner."
>—*The Manners That Win,* 1880

The Call of the Sea

"I must down to the seas again, for the call of the running tide
Is a wild call and a clear call that may not be denied."
>—John Masefield
>from "Sea-Fever"

"I know not why I yearn for thee again,
  To sail once more upon thy fickle flood;
I'll hear thy waves wash under my death-bed,
  Thy salt is lodged forever in my blood."

—W. H. Davies
from "Dreams of the Sea"

"Those trackless deeps, where many a weary sail
Has seen, above the illimitable plain,
Morning and night, and night on morning rise"

—Percy Bysshe Shelley
from "Those Trackless Deeps"

"They that go down to the sea in ships, that do business in
    great waters;
These see the works of the Lord, and his wonders in the deep."

—Psalm CVII

"Down on your knees, boys, holystone the decks,
Rub 'em down, scrub 'em down, stiffen out your necks,
For we're gettin' near t' home, lads, gettin' near t' home,
With a good stiff breeze and a wake o' shining foam."

—Charles Keeler
from "Cleaning Ship"

Spirit of Adventure

"A ship in port is safe, but that's not what it is built for."

—Grace Murray Hopper

"Please know that I am aware of the hazards. I want to do it because I want to do it. Women must try to do things as men have tried. When they fail, their failure must be but a challenge to others."

—Amelia Earhart

(top)
Black Lion Wharf
by James Abbott McNeil Whistler

(opposite)
Rotherhithe
by James Abbott McNeil Whistler

An Important Warning

Not every thirteen-year-old girl is accused of murder, brought to trial, and found guilty. But I was just such a girl, and my story is worth relating even if it did happen years ago. Be warned, however, this is no *Story of a Bad Boy*, no *What Katy Did*. If strong ideas and action offend you, read no more. Find another companion to share your <u>idle</u> hours. For my part I intend to tell the truth as *I* lived it.

But before I begin relating what happened, you must know something about me as I was in the year 1832—when these events <u>transpired</u>. At the time my name *was* Charlotte Doyle. And though I have kept the name, I am not—for reasons you will soon discover—the *same* Charlotte Doyle.

◄ What will you discover about Charlotte Doyle?

How shall I describe the person I once was? At the age of thirteen I was very much a girl, having not yet begun to take the shape, much less the heart, of a woman. Still, my family dressed me as a young woman, bonnet covering my beautiful hair, full skirts, high button shoes, and, you may be sure, white gloves. I certainly wanted to be a *lady*. It was not just my ambition; it was my destiny. I embraced it wholly, gladly, with not an untoward[1] thought of anything else. In other words, I think that at the time of these events I was not anything more or less than what I appeared to be: an acceptable, ordinary girl of parents in good standing.

◄ What did Charlotte want to be when she was thirteen?

Though American born, I spent the years between my sixth and thirteenth birthdays in England. My father, who engaged in the manufacture of cotton goods, functioned as an agent for an American business there. But in the early spring of 1832, he received an advancement and was summoned home.

My father, an <u>ardent</u> believer in regularity and order, decided it would be better if I finished out my school term rather than break it off midyear. My mother—whom I never knew to disagree with him—accepted my father's decision. I would follow my parents, as well as my younger brother and sister, to our true home, which was in Providence, Rhode Island.

Lest you think that my parents' judgment was <u>rash</u> in

---

1. **untoward.** Improper

| **Words For Everyday Use** | i • dle (id´'l) *adj.*, inactive, useless
tran • spire (tran spīr´) *vt.*, happen, take place
ar • dent (ärd´'nt) *adj.*, passionate, | intensely enthusiastic
rash (rash) *adj.*, reckless |

► Why did Charlotte's parents decide she should travel to Rhode Island separately from them?

► How is it that Charlotte is able to remember all the details of the trip?

allowing me to travel without them, I will show you how reasonable, even logical, their decision was.

First, they felt that by my remaining a boarder at the Barrington School for Better Girls (Miss Weed, eminent and most proper headmistress) I would lose no school time.

Second, I would be crossing the Atlantic—a trip that could last anywhere from one to two months—during the summer, when no formal education took place.

Third, I was to make my voyage upon a ship owned and operated by my father's firm.

Fourth, the captain of this ship had acquired a reputation—so my father informed me—for quick and profitable Atlantic crossings.

Then there was this: two families known to my parents had also booked passage on the ship. The adults had promised to function as my guardians. Having been told only that these families included children (three lovely girls and a charming boy) I had looked forward to meeting them more than anything else.

So when you consider that I had but dim memories of making the crossing to England when I was six, you will understand that I saw the forthcoming voyage as all a lark. A large, beautiful boat! Jolly sailors! No school to think about! Companions of my own age!

One more point. I was given a volume of blank pages—how typical of my father!—and instructed to keep a daily journal of my voyage across the ocean so that the writing of it should prove of educational value to me. Indeed, my father warned me that not only would he read the journal and comment upon it, but he would pay particular attention to spelling—not my strongest suit.

Keeping that journal then is what enables me to relate now in perfect detail everything that transpired during that fateful voyage across the Atlantic Ocean in the summer of 1832.

| Words For Everyday Use | em • i • nent (em´ə nənt) adj., distinguished, outstanding |
| | lark (lärk) n., merry time |

PART ONE

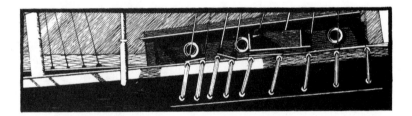

Chapter One

ust before dusk in the late afternoon of June 16, 1832, I found myself walking along the crowded docks of Liverpool, England,[1] following a man by the name of Grummage. Though a business associate of my father, Mr. Grummage was, like my father, a gentleman. It was he my father <u>delegated</u> to make the final arrangements for my passage to America. He was also to meet me when I came down from school on the coach, then see me safely stowed aboard the ship that my father had previously selected.

Mr. Grummage was dressed in a black frock coat with a stove pipe hat that added to his considerable height. His somber, <u>sallow</u> face registered no emotion. His eyes might have been those of a dead fish.

"Miss Doyle?" he said as I stepped from the Liverpool coach.

"Yes, sir. Are you Mr. Grummage?"

"I am."

"Pleased to meet you," I said, dipping a curtsy.

"Quite," he returned. "Now, Miss Doyle, if you would be so good as to indicate which is your trunk, I have a man here to carry it. Next, please oblige me by following, and everything shall be as it is meant to be."

"Might I say good-bye to my chaperon?"

"Is that necessary?"

"She's been very kind."

"Make haste then."

In a flutter of nervousness I identified my trunk, threw my arms about Miss Emerson (my sweet companion for the trip down), and bid her a tearful farewell. Then I rushed after Mr. Grummage, who had already begun to move on. A rough-looking porter, laboring behind, carried my trunk upon his back.

Our little parade reached dockside in good order. There I became instantly agog[2] at the mass of ships that lay before us,

> ► *What attitude does Mr. Grummage show toward Charlotte?*

---

1. **Liverpool, England.** Seaport in northwest England
2. **agog.** In a stare of eager anticipation

Words For Everyday Use

del • e • gate (del´ə gāt) *vt.*, appoint as a representative
sal • low (sal´ō) *adj.*, having a sickly, yellow complexion

masts and spars thick as the bristles on a brush. Everywhere I looked I saw mountains of rare goods piled high. Bales of silk and tobacco! Chests of tea! A parrot! A monkey! Oh yes, the smell of the sea was intoxicating to one who knew little more than the smell of the trim cut lawns and the fields of the Barrington School. Then too, the surging crowds of workers, sailors, and merchants—all rough-hewn, brawny men—created an exotic late afternoon hubbub. All in all it was a most delicious chaos, which, while mildly <u>menacing</u>, was no less exciting because of that. Indeed, in some vague way I had the feeling that it was all there for me.

◀ How does Charlotte feel about her experience on the docks?

"Mr. Grummage, sir," I called over the din. "What is the *name* of the ship I'm to sail on?"

Mr. Grummage paused briefly to look at me as though surprised I was there, to say nothing of asking a question. Then from one of his pockets he drew a screw of paper. Squinting at it he pronounced, "The *Seahawk*."

◀ What is the name of the ship on which Charlotte will travel?

"Is she British or American?"

"American."

"A merchant ship?"

"To be sure."

"How many masts?"

"I don't know."

"Will the other families already be on board?"

"I should think so," he answered, exasperation in his voice. "For your information, Miss Doyle, I received word that departure was being put off, but when I checked with the captain directly he informed me that there must have been some misunderstanding. The ship is scheduled to leave with the first tide tomorrow morning. So there can be *no* delay."

To prove the point he turned to move again. I, however, unable to <u>quell</u> my excited curiosity, managed to slip in one more question.

"Mr. Grummage, sir, what is the *captain's* name?"

Mr. Grummage stopped again, frowning in an irritated fashion, but all the same consulted his paper. "Captain Jaggery," he announced and once more turned to go.

"Here!" the porter exclaimed suddenly. He had come up close and overheard our talk. Both Mr. Grummage and I looked about.

| Words For Everyday Use | **men • a • cing** (men´əs iŋ) *adj.,* threatening |
| | **quell** (kwəl) *vt.,* quiet, put an end to |

► How does Mr. Grummage react to the porter's question?

"Did you say Captain *Jaggery?*" the porter demanded.

"Are you addressing me?" Mr. Grummage inquired, making it perfectly clear that if so, the porter had committed a serious breach of <u>decorum</u>.

"I was," the man said, talking over my head. "And I'm asking if I heard right when you said we was going to a ship mastered by a certain Captain *Jaggery.*" He spoke the name Jaggery as if it were something positively <u>loathsome</u>.

"I was not addressing you," Mr. Grummage informed the man.

"But I hears you all the same," the porter went on, and so saying, he swung my trunk down upon the dock with such a ferocious crack that I feared it would snap in two. "I don't intend to take one more step toward anything to do with a Mr. *Jaggery.* Not for double gold. Not one more step."

"See here," Mr. Grummage cried with <u>indignation</u>. "You undertook . . ."

► Why does the porter leave before getting Charlotte's trunk to the ship?

"Never mind what I undertook," the man retorted. "It's worth more to me to avoid that man than to close with your coin." And without another word he marched off.

"Stop! I say, stop!" Mr. Grummage called. It was in vain. The porter had gone, and quickly at that.

Mr. Grummage and I looked at each another. I hardly knew what to make of it. Nor, clearly, did he. Yet he did what he had to do: he surveyed the area in search of a replacement.

"There! You man!" he cried to the first who passed by, a huge laboring fellow in a smock. "Here's a shilling[3] if you can carry this young lady's trunk!"

The man paused, looked at Mr. Grummage, at me, at the trunk. "That?" he asked disdainfully.

"I'll be happy to add a second shilling," I volunteered, thinking that a low offer was the problem.

"Miss Doyle," Mr. Grummage snapped. "Let me handle this."

"Two shillings," the workman said quickly.

"One," Mr. Grummage countered.

"Two," the workman repeated and held his hand out to

---

3. **shilling.** Former monetary unit of the United Kingdom

| Words For Everyday Use | **de • co • rum** (di kō´rəm) *n.,* propriety and good taste in behavior
 loath • some (lōth´səm) *adj.,* disgusting, detestable | **in • dig • na • tion** (in dig na´shən) *n.,* anger or scorn in reaction to injustice |

Mr. Grummage, who gave him but one coin. Then the man turned and extended his hand to me.

Hastily, I began to extract a coin from my reticule.[4]

"Miss Doyle!" Mr. Grummage objected.

"I did promise," I whispered and dropped the coin into the man's upturned palm.

"Right you are, miss," said the porter with a tip of his hat. "May the whole world follow your fashion."

This <u>commendation</u> of my principles of moral goodness brought a blush of pleasure that I could hardly suppress. As for Mr. Grummage, he made a point of clearing his throat to indicate disapproval.

"Now then," the porter asked, "where does the young lady require this?"

"Never mind where!" Mr. Grummage snapped. "Along the docks here. I'll tell you when we arrive."

The money pocketed, the man <u>lumbered</u> over to my trunk, swung it to his shoulder with astonishing ease—considering the trunk's weight and size—and said, "Lead on."

Mr. Grummage, wasting no more time, and perhaps fearful of the consequence of more talk, started off again.

After guiding us through a maze of docks and quays,[5] he came to a stop. With a half turn he announced, "There she sits," and gestured to a ship moored to the slip before us.

I had hardly looked where he pointed when I heard a thump behind. Startled, I turned and saw that the new man—the one we'd just engaged—had taken one look at the *Seahawk*, set down my trunk in haste, and, like the first, run off without any word of explanation at all.

◄ *What happens when the second porter realizes what ship Charlotte is traveling on?*

Mr. Grummage barely glanced over his shoulder at the hastily departing worker. In exasperation he said, "Miss Doyle, you will wait for me here." And with rapid strides he took himself up the gangplank and onto the *Seahawk* where he disappeared from my view.

I stood my place, more than ever wanting to get aboard and meet the delightful children who would be my traveling companions. But as I waited on the dock for something like

---

4. **reticule.** Small handbag
5. **quays.** Wharves

| Words For Everyday Use | **com • men • da • tion** (käm ən dā´shən) *n.,* act of recommendation or praise, compliment |
| | **lum • ber** (lum´bər) *vi.,* move heavily or clumsily |

half an hour—all but unmoving in the <u>waning</u> light of day—I could only gaze upon the ship.

To say that I was unduly alarmed when I examined the *Seahawk* would be nonsense. I had not the remotest superstitious notion of what was to come. Nothing of the kind. No, the *Seahawk* was a ship like countless others I had seen before or for that matter have seen since. Oh, perhaps she was smaller and older than I had anticipated, but nothing else. Moored to the dock, she rode the swell[6] easily. Her standard rigging, tarred black for protection against the salt sea, rose above me, dark ladders to an increasingly dark sky, and indeed, her royal yard seemed lost in the lowering[7] night.* Her sails, tied up, that is, reefed, looked like sleeves of new-fallen snow on lofty trees.

Briefly, the *Seahawk* was what is known as a brig, a two-masted ship (with a snow mast behind the main), perhaps some seven hundred tons in weight, 107 feet stern to bow, 130 feet deck to mainmast cap. She was built, perhaps, in the late eighteenth or early nineteenth century. Her hull was painted black, her bulwarks white, these being the ordinary colors. Her two masts, raked slightly back, were square-rigged. She had a bowsprit too, one that stood out from her bow like a unicorn's horn.

Indeed, the one unique aspect of this ship was a carved figurehead of a pale white seahawk beneath the bowsprit. Its wings were thrust back against the bow; its head extended forward, beak wide-open, red tongue <u>protruding</u> as if screaming. In the shadowy light that twisted and distorted its features I was struck by the notion that this figure looked more like an angry, avenging angel than a <u>docile</u> bird.

> ► What does Charlotte think of the ship the first time she sees it?

> ► What does the figurehead look like to Charlotte?

*I shall of necessity use certain words during my account that might not be readily familiar—such as *rigging, royal yard,* or *reefed.* They were not words I knew when I first came to the ship, but rather terms I learned in the course of my voyage. Since many people today have no such knowledge, I have included a diagram of the *Seahawk* in the appendix at the end of this account. You may consult it from time to time so as to better understand what I refer to. The diagram will, as well, spare me unnecessary explanations and speed my narrative.

Regarding time aboard a ship, a fuller explanation may also be found in the appendix.

---

6. **rode the swell.** Moved up and down easily on the rise and fall of the water
7. **lowering.** Dark, overcast

Words For Everyday Use	**wan • ing** (wān´iŋ) *adj.,* grow less in extent
	pro • trud • ing (prō trōōd´iŋ) *adj.,* jutting out, projecting
	doc • ile (däs´əl) *adj.,* easy to manage, obedient

The dockside was deserted and growing darker. I felt like taking myself up the gangplank in search of Mr. Grummage. But, alas, my good manners prevailed. I remained where I was, standing in a dreamlike state, thinking I know not what.

But gradually—like a telescope being focused—I began to realize I was watching something clinging to one of the mooring ropes on the ship's stern. It reminded me of a picture I once had seen of a sloth, an animal that hangs upside down upon jungle vines. But this—I gradually perceived—was a man. He appeared to be shimmying himself from the dock up to the *Seahawk*. Even as I realized what I was seeing, he boarded the ship and was gone.

◄ What does Charlotte see on the side of the ship while waiting for Mr. Grummage?

I had no time to absorb that vision before I heard angry voices. Turning, I saw Mr. Grummage appear at the topgallant rail, engaged in an argument with someone I could not see. My gentleman repeatedly looked down at me, and, so I thought, gesticulated[8] in my direction as if I were the subject of a heated discussion.

At last Mr. Grummage came down to the dock. As he drew near I saw that his face was flushed, with an angry eye that alarmed me.

"Is something amiss?" I asked in a whisper.

"Not at all!" he snapped. "All is as planned. You have been expected. The ship's cargo is loaded. The captain is ready to sail. But . . ." He trailed off, looked back at the ship, then turned again to me. "It's just that . . . You see, those two families, the ones you would be traveling with, your companions . . . they have not arrived."

◄ What problem has Mr. Grummage encountered?

"But they will," I said, trying to <u>compose</u> myself.

"That's not entirely certain," Mr. Grummage allowed. "The second mate informs me that one family sent word that they could not reach Liverpool in time. The other family has a seriously ill child. There is concern that she should not be moved." Again Mr. Grummage glanced over his shoulder at the *Seahawk* as if, in some fashion, these events were the ship's fault.

---

8. **gesticulated.** Gestured

| Words For Everyday Use | **com • pose** (kəm pōz´) *vt.*, put one's mind at ease, calm, allay |

Turning back to me, he continued. "As it stands, Captain Jaggery will accept no delay of departure. Quite proper. He has his orders."

"But Mr. Grummage, sir," I asked in dismay, "what shall I do?"

"*Do?* Miss Doyle, your father left orders that you were to travel on *this* ship at *this* time. I've very specific, *written* orders in that regard. He left no money to arrange otherwise. As for myself," he said, "I'm off for Scotland tonight on pressing business."

"But surely," I cried, frustrated by the way Mr. Grummage was talking as much as by his news, "surely I mustn't travel alone!"

"Miss Doyle," he returned, "being upon a ship with the full complement of captain and crew could hardly be construed as traveling *alone.*"

"But . . . but that would be all *men,* Mr. Grummage! And . . . I am a girl. It would be *wrong!*" I cried, in absolute confidence that I was echoing the beliefs of my beloved parents.

Mr. Grummage drew himself up. "Miss Doyle," he said loftily, "in *my* world, judgments as to rights and wrongs are left to my Creator, *not* to children. Now, be so good as to board the *Seahawk.* At once!"

► *Why does Mr. Grummage insist that Charlotte must travel on this ship?*

► *Why does Charlotte think that she should not travel on this ship?*

Chapter Two

ith Mr. Grummage leading the way, I stepped finally, hesitantly, upon the deck of the *Seahawk*. A man was waiting for us.

He was a small man—most seafaring men are small—barely taller than I and dressed in a frayed green jacket over a white shirt that was none too clean. His complexion was weathered dark, his chin ill-shaven. His mouth was unsmiling. His fingers fidgeted and his feet shuffled. His darting, unfocused eyes, set deep in a narrow ferretlike face, gave the impression of one who is constantly on watch for threats that might appear from any quarter at any moment.

◄ *What impression does Charlotte have of Mr. Keetch?*

"Miss Doyle," Mr. Grummage intoned by way of introduction, "both Captain Jaggery and the first mate are ashore. May I present the second mate, Mr. Keetch."

"Miss Doyle," this Mr. Keetch said to me, speaking in an unnecessarily loud voice, "since Captain Jaggery isn't aboard I've no choice but to stand in his place. But it's my strong opinion, miss, that you should take another ship for your passage to America."

◄ *What warning does Mr. Keetch give Charlotte?*

"And I," Mr. Grummage cut in before I could respond, "can allow of no such thing!"

This was hardly the welcome I had expected.

"But Mr. Grummage," I said, "I'm sure my father would not want me to be traveling without—"

Mr. Grummage silenced my objections with an upraised hand. "Miss Doyle," he said, "my orders were clear and allow for no other construction. I met you. I brought you here. I had you placed under the protection of this man, who, in the momentary absence of Captain Jaggery and the first mate, fulfilled his obligation by signing a receipt for you."

To prove his point Mr. Grummage waved a piece of paper at me. I might have been a bale of cotton.

"Therefore, Miss Doyle," he rushed on, "nothing remains save to wish you a most pleasant voyage to America."

Putting action to words he tipped his hat, and before I could utter a syllable he strode down the gangplank toward the shore.

"But Mr. Grummage!" I called desperately.

Whether Mr. Grummage heard me, or chose not to hear me, he continued to stride along the dock without so much as a backward glance. I was never to see him again.

A slight shuffling sound made me turn about. Beneath a

lantern on the forecastle deck I saw a few <u>wretched</u> sailors hunched in apelike postures pounding oakum[1] between the decking planks. Without doubt they had heard everything. Now they threw hostile glances over their shoulders in my direction.

▶ What attitude do the sailors have toward Charlotte?

I felt a touch at my elbow. Starting, I turned again and saw Mr. Keetch. He seemed more nervous than ever.

"Begging your pardon, Miss Doyle," he said in his awkward way, "there's nothing to be done now, is there? I'd best show you your cabin."

At that point I remembered my trunk of clothing, as if that collection of outward fashion—still ashore—had more claim to me than the ship. And since it was there, so should I be. "My trunk . . ." I murmured, making a half turn toward the dock.

"Not to worry, miss. We'll fetch it for you," Mr. Keetch said, cutting off my last excuse for retreat. Indeed, he held out a lantern, indicating an entryway in the wall of the quarterdeck that appeared to lead below.

▶ Why does Charlotte follow Mr. Keetch?

What could I do? All my life I had been trained to obey, educated to accept. I could hardly change in a moment. "Please lead me," I mumbled, as near to fainting as one could be without actually <u>succumbing</u>.

"Very good, miss," he said, leading me across the deck and down a short flight of steps.

I found myself in a narrow, dark passageway with a low ceiling. The steerage, as this area is called, was hardly more than six feet wide and perhaps thirty feet in length. In the dimness I could make out a door on each side, one door at the far end. Like a massive tree rising right out of the floor and up through the ceiling was the mainmast. There was also a small table attached to the center of the flooring. No chairs.

The whole area was frightfully <u>confining</u>, offering no sense of comfort that I could see. And a stench of rot <u>permeated</u> the air.

"This way," I heard Mr. Keetch say again. He had opened

---

1. **oakum.** Loose, stringy fiber made by taking apart old ropes and mixing them with tar to form a caulking material

Words For Everyday Use

wretch • ed (rech´id) *adj.*, miserable
suc • cumb (sə kum´) *vt.*, yield, submit
con • fin • ing (kən fīn´iŋ) *adj.*, restricting

per • me • ate (pʉr´mē āt) *vt.*, penetrate and spread throughout

a door on my left. "Your cabin, miss. The one contracted for." A gesture invited me to enter.

I gasped. The cabin was but six feet in length. Four feet wide. Four and a half feet high. I, none too tall, could only stoop to see in.

"Regular passengers pay a whole six pounds[2] for this, miss," Mr. Keetch advised me, his voice much softer.

◄ How does Mr. Keetch try to comfort Charlotte?

I forced myself to take a step into the cabin. Against the opposite wall I could make out a narrow shelf, partly framed by boarding. When I noticed something that looked like a pillow and a blanket, I realized it was meant to be a bed. Then, when Mr. Keetch held up the light, I saw something *crawl* over it.

◄ What does Charlotte see when she peers into the cabin? How does she react to what she sees?

"What's that?" I cried.

"Roach, miss. Every ship has 'em."

As for the rest of the furnishings, there were none save a small built-in chest in the bulkhead wall, the door of which dropped down and served as a desktop. There was nothing else. No porthole.[3] No chair. Not so much as a single piece of polite ornamentation. It was ugly, unnatural, and, as I stooped there, impossible.

In a panic I turned toward Mr. Keetch, wanting to utter some new protest. Alas, he had gone—and had shut the door behind him as though to close the spring on a trap.

How long I remained hunched in that tiny, dark hole, I am not sure. What aroused me was a knock on the door. Startled, I gasped, "Come in."

The door opened. Standing there was a shockingly decrepit old sailor, a tattered tar-covered hat all but crushed in his gnarled and trembling hands. His clothing was poor, his manner cringing.

"Yes?" I managed to say.

"Miss, your trunk is here."

I looked beyond the door to the trunk's bulky outline. I saw at once how absurd it would be to even attempt bringing it into my space.

The sailor understood. "She's too big, isn't she?" he said.

---

2. **pounds.** Previously the basic monetary unit of the United Kingdom; until 1971, a pound was equal to 20 shillings
3. **porthole.** Opening in the side of a ship to let in air and light

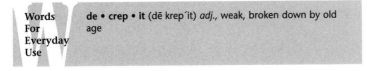

| Words For Everyday Use | de • crep • it (dē krep´it) *adj.,* weak, broken down by old age |

"I think so," I stammered.

"Best put it in top cargo," he offered. "Right below. You can always fetch things there, miss."

"Yes, top cargo," I echoed without knowing what I was saying.

"Very good, miss," the man said, and then pulled his fore-lock[4] as a signal of obedience and <u>compliance</u> to a suggestion that he himself had made. But instead of going he just stood there.

"Yes?" I asked miserably.

▶ What warning does Barlow issue?

"Begging your pardon, miss," the man murmured, his look more hangdog than ever. "Barlow's the name and though it's not my business or place to tell you, miss, some of the others here, Jack Tars[5] like myself, have deputized me to say that you shouldn't be on this ship. Not alone as you are. Not this ship. Not this voyage, miss."

"What do you mean?" I said, frightened anew. "Why would they say that?"

"You're being here will lead to no good, miss. No good at all. You'd be better off far from the *Seahawk.*"

Though all my being agreed with him, my training—that it was wrong for a man of his low station to presume to advise me of *anything*—rose to the surface. I drew myself up. "Mr. Barlow," I said stiffly, "it's my father who has arranged it all."

"Very good, miss," he said, pulling at his forelock again. "I've but done my duty, which is what I'm deputized to do." And before I could speak further he scurried off.

▶ What did Charlotte want to do? Why didn't she do this?

I wanted to run after him, to cry, "Yes, for God's sake, get me off!" But, again, there was nothing in me that allowed for such behavior.

Indeed, I was left with a despairing <u>resolve</u> never to leave the cabin until we reached America. Steadfastly I shut my door. But by doing so I made the space completely dark, and I quickly moved to keep it ajar.

I was exhausted and desired greatly to sit down. But there was no place to sit! My next thought was to *lie* down. Trying to put notions of vermin out of mind, I made a move toward

---

4. **forelock.** Lock of hair growing just above the forehead
5. **Jack Tars.** Sailors

| Words For Everyday Use | com • pli • ance (kəm plī´əns) *n.*, giving in to a request or demand |
| | re • solve (ri zälv´) *n.*, firm determination, fixed purpose |

my bed but discovered that it was too high for me to reach easily in my skirts. Then suddenly I realized I must relieve myself! But where was I to go? I had not the slightest idea!

If you will be kind enough to recollect that during my life I had never once—not for a moment—been without the support, the guidance, the *protection* of my elders, you will accept my words as being without exaggeration when I tell you that at that moment I was certain I had been placed in a coffin. *My* coffin. It's hardly to be wondered, then, that I burst into tears of <u>vexation</u>, crying with fear, rage, and humiliation.

◄ Where does Charlotte feel that she has been put?

I was still stooped over, crying, when yet another knock came on my cabin door. Attempting to stifle my tears I turned about to see an old black man who, in the light of the little lantern he was holding, looked like the very imp of death in search of souls.

His clothing, what I could see of it, was even more decrepit than the previous sailor's, which is to say, mostly rags and tatters. His arms and legs were as thin as marlinspikes.[6] His face, as wrinkled as a crumpled napkin, was flecked with the stubble of white beard. His tightly curled hair was thin. His lips were slack. Half his teeth were missing. When he smiled—for that is what I assumed he was attempting—he offered only a scattering of stumps. But his eyes seemed to glow with curiosity and were all the more menacing because of it.

"Yes?" I managed to say.

"At your service, Miss Doyle." The man spoke with a surprisingly soft, sweet voice. "And wondering if you might not like a bit of tea. I have my own special store, and I'm prepared to offer some."

It was the last thing I expected to hear. "That's very kind of you," I stammered in surprise. "Could you bring it here?"

The old man shook his head gently. "If Miss Doyle desires tea—captain's orders—she must come to the galley."

"Galley?"

"Kitchen to you, miss."

"Who are you?" I demanded faintly.

"Zachariah," he returned. "Cook, surgeon, carpenter, and

---

6. **marlinspikes.** Metal tools for separating strands of a rope

Words For Everyday Use

vex • a • tion (veks ā´shən) *n.*, being distressed

► What is Zachariah's role on the ship?

preacher to man and ship. And," he added, "all those things to you too, miss, in that complete order if comes the <u>doleful</u> need. Now then, shall you have tea?"

In fact, the thought of tea *was* extraordinarily comforting, a reminder that the world I knew had not entirely vanished. I couldn't resist. "Very well," I said, "Would you lead me to the . . . galley?"

"Most assuredly," was the old man's reply. Stepping away from the door, he held his lantern high. I made my way out.

We proceeded to walk along the passageway to the right, then up the short flight of steps to the waist of the ship—that low deck area between fore- and quarterdeck. Here and there lanterns glowed; masts, spars, and rigging vaguely sketched the dim outlines of the net in which I felt caught. I shuddered.

The man called Zachariah led me down another flight of steps into what appeared to be a fairly large area. In the dimness I could make out piles of sails, as well as extra rigging— all chaotic and unspeakably filthy. Then, off to one side, I saw a small room. The old man went to it, started to enter, but paused and pointed to a small adjacent door that I had not noticed.

"The head, miss."

"The what?"

"Privy."

My cheeks burned. Even so, *never* have I felt—secretly—so grateful. Without a word I rushed to use it. In moments I returned. Zachariah was waiting patiently. Without further ado he went into the galley. I followed with <u>trepidation</u>, stopping at the threshold to look about.

From the light of his flickering lantern I could see that it was a small kitchen complete with cabinets, wood stove, even a table and a little stool. The space, though small, had considerable neatness, with utensils set in special niches and corners. Knives placed just so. An equal number of spoons and forks. Tumblers, pots, cups, pans. All that was needed.

The old man went right to the stove where a teapot was already on, hot enough to be issuing steam.

He pulled a cup from a niche, filled it with fragrant tea, and offered it. At the same time he gestured me to the stool.

Nothing, however, could have <u>compelled</u> me to enter fur-

---

Words For Everyday Use

dole • ful (dōl´fəl) *adj.*, full of sorrow, mournful

trep • i • da • tion (trep´ə dā´shən) *n.*, fearful uncertainty

com • pel (kəm pəl´) *vt.*, force

---

ther. Though stiff and weary I preferred to stand where I was. Even so, I tasted the tea and was much comforted.

As I drank Zachariah looked at me. "It may well be," he said softly, "that Miss Doyle will have use for a friend."

Finding the suggestion—from him—unpleasant, I chose to ignore it.

"I can assure you," he said with a slight smile, "Zachariah can be a fine friend."

"And I can assure you," I returned, "that the captain will have made arrangements for my social needs."

"Ah, but you and I have much in common."

"I don't think so."

"But we do. Miss Doyle is so young! I am so old! Surely there is something similar in that. And you, the sole girl, and I, the one black, are special on this ship. In short, we begin with two things in common, enough to begin a friendship."

I looked elsewhere. "I don't need a friend," I said.

"One always needs a final friend."

"Final friend?"

"Someone to sew the hammock," he returned.

"I do not understand you."

"When a sailor dies on voyage, miss, he goes to his resting place in the sea with his hammock sewn about him by a friend."

I swallowed my tea hastily, handed the cup back, and made a move to go.

"Miss Doyle, please," he said softly, taking the cup but holding me with his eyes, "I have something else to offer."

"No more tea, thank you."

"No, miss. It is this." He held out a knife.

With a scream I jumped back.

"No, no! Miss Doyle. Don't misunderstand! I only wish to give you the knife as protection—in case you need it." He placed a wooden sheath on the blade and held it out.

The knife was, as I came to understand, what's called a dirk, a small daggerlike blade hardly more than six inches in length from its white scrimshaw[7] handle, where a star design was cut, to its needle-sharp point. Horrified, I was capable only of shaking my head.

"Miss Doyle doesn't know what might happen," he urged, as though suggesting it might rain on a picnic and he was offering head covering.

"I know nothing about knives," I whispered.

"A ship sails with any wind she finds," he whispered. "Take it, miss. Place it where it may be reached."

---

7. **scrimshaw.** Carving of bone, especially whale bone

◄ *What, aside from tea, does Zachariah offer Charlotte? How does she react to his suggestion?*

◄ *What do Charlotte and Zachariah have in common?*

◄ *What happens to a sailor who dies aboard ship?*

◄ *Why does Zachariah give Charlotte a knife?*

So saying, he took my hand and closed my fingers over the dirk. Cringing, I kept it.

"Yes," he said with a smile, patting my fingers. "Now Miss Doyle may return to her cabin. Do you know the way?"

"I'm not certain . . ."

"I will guide you."

He left me at my door. Once inside I hurriedly stowed the dirk under the thin mattress (resolving never to look at it again) and somehow struggled into my bed. There, fully dressed, I sought rest, fitfully dozing only to be awakened by a banging sound: my cabin door swinging back and forth—rusty hinges <u>rasping</u>—with the gentle sway of the ship.

► What does Charlotte hear outside her cabin? Does she understand what she hears?

Then I heard, "The only one I could get to come, sir, is the Doyle girl. And with *them* looking on, I had to put on a bit of a show about wanting to keep her off."

"Quite all right, Mr. Keetch. If there has to be only one, she's the trump.[8] With her as witness, they'll not dare to move. I'm well satisfied."

"Thank you, sir."

The voices trailed away.

For a while I tried to grasp what I'd heard, but I gave it up as incomprehensible. Then, for what seemed forever, I lay listening as the *Seahawk,* tossed by the ceaseless swell, heaved and groaned like a sleeper beset by evil dreams.

At last I slept—only to have the ship's dreams become my own.

---

8. **trump.** Advantage held in reserve until needed

Words For Everyday Use	**rasp** (rasp) *vt.,* scrape; make a grating sound

Chapter Three

awoke the next morning in my narrow bed—fully clothed—and a <u>stark</u> truth came to me. I was where no proper young lady should be. I needed only to close my eyes again to hear my father use those very words.

But as I lay there, feeling the same tossing motion I'd felt when falling asleep—I took it to be that of a ship moored to the dock—I recollected Mr. Grummage saying that the *Seahawk* was due to leave by the morning's first tide. It was not too late. I would ask to be put ashore, and in some fashion—I hardly cared how—I'd make my way back to the Barrington School. There, with Miss Weed, I would be safe. *She* would make the necessary decisions.

◄ What does Charlotte think she will do when she wakes up?

Having composed my mind I sat up with some energy only to strike my head upon the low ceiling. <u>Chastened</u>, I got myself to the cabin floor. Now I discovered that my legs had become so weak, so rubbery, I all but sank to my knees. Still, my desperation was such that nothing could stop me. Holding on to now one part of the wall, now another, I made my way out of the cabin into the dim, close steerage and up the steps to the waist of the ship, only to receive the shock of my life.

Everywhere I looked great canvas sails of gray, from mainsail to main royal, from flying jib to trysail, were bellied out. Beyond the sails stretched the sky itself, as blue as a baby's bluest eyes, while the greenish sea, crowned with lacy caps of foaming white, rushed by with unrelenting speed. The *Seahawk* had gone to sea. We must have left Liverpool hours before!

◄ What does Charlotte see when she reaches the deck?

As this realization took hold, the *Seahawk,* almost as if wishing to offer final proof, pitched and rolled. Nausea choked me. My head pounded.

Weaker than ever, I turned around in search of support. For a fleeting but horrible second I had the notion that I was alone on board. Then I realized that I was being watched with crude curiosity. Standing on the quarterdeck was a red-faced man whose slight stoop and powerful broad shoulders conspired to give the impression of <u>perpetual</u> suspicion, an

---

Words For Everyday Use

stark (stärk) *adj.*, harsh, bleak

chas • ten (chās´ən) *vt.*, make purer, refine; punish

per • pet • u • al (pər pech´o͞o əl) *adj.*, continuing forever

effect heightened by dark, deep-set eyes partially obscured by craggy eyebrows.

"Sir . . ." I called weakly. "Where are we?"

"We're coasting down the Irish Sea,[1] Miss Doyle," replied the man, his voice raspy.

" . . . I . . . I shouldn't be here," I managed. But the man, seemingly indifferent to my words, only turned and with a slab of a hand reached for a bell set up at the head of the quarterdeck in a kind of gallows. He pulled the clapper three times.

▶ What do the sailors look like to Charlotte?

Even as I tried to keep myself from sinking to the deck, nine men suddenly appeared in the ship's waist, from above as well as below, fore as well as aft. All wore the distinctive sailor's garb of canvas britches and shirts. A few had boots, while some had no shoes at all. One or two wore tar-covered hats, others caps of red cloth. Two had beards. One man had long hair and a ring in his left ear. Their faces were dark from sun and tar.

They were, in all, as sorry a group of men as I had ever seen: glum in expression, defeated in posture, with no character in any eye save <u>sullenness</u>. They were like men recruited from the doormat of Hell.

I did recognize the sailor who had given me the warning the night before. But he paid no attention to me. And when I looked for the man who called himself Zachariah, I finally found him peering out from beneath the forecastle[2] deck, no more concerned with me than the others. They were all looking elsewhere. I shifted to follow their gaze.

The broad-shouldered man had been joined by another. Just to see him made my heart leap joyously with recognition and relief. From his fine coat, from his tall beaver hat, from his glossy black boots, from his clean, chiseled <u>countenance</u>, from the dignified way he carried himself, I knew at once—without having to be told—that this must be Captain Jaggery. And he—I saw it in a glance—was a gentleman, the kind of man I was used to. A man to be trusted. In short, a man to whom I could talk and upon whom I could rely.

▶ What does Charlotte see right away about Captain Jaggery?

But before I composed myself to approach, Captain

---

1. **Irish Sea.** Sea between Ireland and Great Britain
2. **forecastle.** Upper deck of a ship in front of the foremast

Words For Everyday Use

sul • len • ness (sul´ən nis) *n.*, dullness and resentment

coun • te • nance (koun´tə nəns) *n.*, face

Jaggery turned to the man who had rung the bell and I heard him say, "Mr. Hollybrass, we are short one."

◄ Why is the crew one short?

Mr. Hollybrass—I was soon to discover that he was the first mate—looked <u>scornfully</u> at the assembled men below. Then he said, "The second mate did the best he could, sir. No one else could be got to sign articles.[3] Not for anything."

The captain frowned. Then he said, "The others will have to take up the slack. I'll not have any less. Have the men give their names."

Hollybrass nodded <u>curtly</u>, then took a step forward and addressed the assembled crew. "Give your names," he barked.

One by one the sailors shuffled forward a step, lifted their heads, doffed their caps, and spoke their names, but slumped into broken postures again once they returned to the line.

"Dillingham."

"Grimes."

"Morgan."

"Barlow."

"Foley."

"Ewing."

"Fisk."

"Johnson."

"Zachariah."

When they had done, Hollybrass said, "Your crew, Captain Jaggery."

At first the captain said nothing. He merely studied the men with a look of <u>contempt</u>, an attitude that, because I shared it, made me respect him even more. "Who is the second mate?" I heard him ask.

"Mr. Keetch, sir. He's at the wheel."

"Ah, yes," the captain returned, "Mr. Keetch. I might have guessed." He studied the line of sailors, smiled <u>sardonically</u>, and said, "But where, then, is Mr. Cranick?"

◄ Who, according to Captain Jaggery, is missing?

"Sir?" Hollybrass said, clearly puzzled.

"Cranick."

"I don't know the name, sir."

"Now there's an unlooked-for blessing," the captain said,

---

3. **articles.** Contracts

Words For Everyday Use

scorn • ful • ly (skôrn´fəl lē) *adv.*, with contempt or disdain

curt • ly (kurt´lē) *adv.*, bluntly to the point of rudeness

con • tempt (kən tempt´) *n.*, attitude of one who looks down on somebody or something

sar • don • i • cal • ly (sär dän´ik lē) *adv.*, sarcastically, bitterly sneering

his manners nonetheless courtly. All this was said loudly enough for the crew—and me—to hear.

Captain Jaggery now took a step forward. "Well, then," he said in a clear, firm voice, "it's a pleasure to see you all again. I take it kindly that you've signed on with me. Indeed, I suspect we know each other well enough so each understands what's due the other. That makes it easy."

His confident tone was tonic[4] to me. I felt myself gain strength.

▶ Why doesn't Captain Jaggery want to talk to the crew again?

"I have no desire to speak to any of you again," the captain continued. "Mr. Hollybrass here, as first mate, shall be my voice. So too, Mr. Keetch as second mate. Separation makes for an honest crew. An honest crew makes a fair voyage. A fair voyage brings a profit, and profit, my good gentlemen, doth turn the world.

▶ What warning does the captain give the crew?

"But," Jaggery continued, his voice rising with the wind, "I give warning." He leaned forward over the rail much as I'd seen teachers lean toward <u>unruly</u> students. "If you give me less—*one finger less*—than the particulars of the articles you have signed, I shall *take* my due. Make no mistake, I will. You know I mean what I say, don't you? No, we shall have no democracy here. No parliaments. No congressmen. There's but one master on this ship, and that is me." So saying he turned to his first mate. "Mr. Hollybrass."

"Sir?"

"An extra issue of rum as a gesture of good will toward a pleasant, quick passage. Let it be understood that I know the old saying: no ship sails the same sea twice."

"Very good, sir."

"You may dismiss them," the captain said.

"Dismissed," echoed the first mate.

For a moment no one moved. The captain continued to look steadily at the men, then slowly, but with great deliberation, he turned his back upon them.

"Dismissed," Hollybrass said again.

After the crew had gone he murmured some words to Captain Jaggery, the two shook hands, and the first mate went below. Now the captain was alone on the quarterdeck. Glancing upward at the sails from time to time, he began to

---

4. **tonic.** Anything that restores healthy feelings or good spirits

Words For Everyday Use   **un • rul • y** (un rōōl´ē) *adj.,* hard to control

pace back and forth in almost leisurely fashion, hands clasped behind his back, a study in deep thought.

I, meanwhile, still clung to the rail, braced against the heaving ship. But I had new hope. I had *not* been abandoned. My perception of Captain Jaggery made me certain that my world was regained.

Summoning such strength and courage as was left me, I mounted the steps to the quarterdeck. When I reached the top the captain was moving away from me. Grateful for the momentary <u>reprieve</u>, I stood where I was, fighting the nausea I felt, gathering all my womanly arts so as to present myself in the most agreeable fashion, making sure my hair, my best asset, fell just so—despite the breeze—to my lower back.

At last he turned. For a moment his severe eyes rested on me and then . . . he smiled. It was such a *kind,* goodnatured smile that my heart nearly melted. I felt I would—I think I did—shed tears of gratitude.

"Ah," he said with <u>unimpeachable</u> refinement, "Miss Doyle, our young lady passenger." He lifted his tall hat in formal salutation. "Captain Andrew Jaggery at your service." He bowed.

I took a wobbly step in his direction, and despite my weakness tried to curtsy.

"Please, sir," I whispered in my most modest, ladylike way, "my father would not want me here on this ship and in this company. I must go back to Liverpool. To Miss Weed."

Captain Jaggery smiled brilliantly, then laughed—a <u>beguiling</u>, manly laugh. "Return to Liverpool, Miss Doyle?" he said. "Out of the question. Time, as they say, is money. And nowhere is this truer than on board a ship. We are well off and we shall continue on. God willing, we shall touch no land but welcome ports.

"I am sorry you have such rude company. I know you are used to better. It could not be helped. But in a month, no more than two, we shall have you safe in Providence, no worse off but for a little salt in that pretty hair of yours. In the meanwhile, I promise that when you're well—for I can see by your <u>pallor</u> that you have a touch of seasickness—I'll have you in my quarters for tea. We shall be friends, you and I."

◄ *Why does Charlotte have new hope?*

◄ *How does Charlotte feel when the captain smiles at her?*

◄ *What does Charlotte tell the captain she must do? How does he respond?*

◄ *Who will be Charlotte's friend?*

Words For Everyday Use

re • prieve (ri prēv´) *n.,* temporary relief

un • im • peach • a • ble (un´im pē´chə bəl) *adj.,* that which cannot be doubted, questioned, or discredited

be • guil • ing (bē gīl´iŋ) *adj.,* charming or delightful

pal • lor (pal´ər) *n.,* lack of color

"Sir, I shouldn't be here."

"Miss Doyle, you have my word on it. No harm shall
come your way. Besides, it's said a pretty child—a pretty
woman—keeps the crew in a civilized state, and this crew
can do with some of that."

"I feel so ill, sir," I said.

"That's only to be expected, Miss Doyle. In a few days it
will pass. Now, you will excuse me. Duty calls."

Turning, he made his way to the stern where the second
mate stood at the wheel.

Checked by his courteous but *complete* dismissal of my
request, and feeling even weaker than before, I somehow
made my way back to my cabin.

I did manage to crawl into the bed. And once there I must
have fallen into some kind of swoon. In any case I remained
there, too ill, too weak to do anything, certain I'd never rise
again.

Now and again I would feel a rough-skinned but gentle
hand beneath my head. I would open my eyes, and there was
Zachariah's ancient black face close by, murmuring soft,
comforting sounds, spooning warm gruel[5] or tea into my
mouth—I didn't know which—as if I were some baby.
Indeed, I was a baby.

And from time to time the face of Captain Jaggery loomed
large too, a welcome and tender gift of sympathy. Indeed, I
believed it was the sight of him more than anything else that
<u>sustained</u> me. For I suffered real and terrible stomach pains,
and dreadful headaches. Even my dreams were haunted by
ghastly visions. So real were they that once I started up and
found Zachariah's dirk in my hand. I must have plucked it
from beneath my mattress and was <u>brandishing</u> it against
some imagined evil. . . . I heard a sound. I looked across the
cabin. A rat was sitting on my journal, nibbling at its spine.
Horrified, I flung the dirk at it, then buried my head in the
coverlet, burst into tears, and cried myself to sleep again.

This bad time passed. At length I was able to sleep in
peace. How long I slept I am not sure. But then at last I truly
awoke.

► What effect will
Charlotte have on
the crew?

► What is Charlotte
surprised to find
herself doing during
her illness?

---

5. **gruel.** Thin, easily digested porridge

Words For Everyday Use

sus • tain (sə stān´) *vt.*, support, strengthen the spirits
brand • ish (bran´dish) *vt.*, wave, shake, or flourish

Chapter Four

hen I awakened that time—to the sound of four bells[1]—I had no idea whether I had slept one day or seven. I knew only that I was hungry. I sensed my own filthiness too. And I had an almost desperate desire for fresh air.

I lowered myself to the cabin floor and was pleased to find that my legs would—after a fashion—hold. But then, as I moved toward the door, my foot stepped on something. I almost fell. Bending down to investigate I realized I'd stepped on the dirk. When I recalled the circumstances as to why I'd thrown it, I resolved to return the dagger immediately.

So it was with dirk in hand that I left my cabin and went up the ladder and onto the deck, fully expecting to see the same brilliant scene of sky, sails, and sea that had greeted me when I had <u>ventured</u> on deck the first time. It was not to be so. Though the *Seahawk* heaved and rolled, creaked and groaned, her sails hung limply. The sky was different too; low, with a heavy dampness that instantly wet my face, though I felt nothing so distinct as rain. As for the sea, it was almost the same color as the sky, a menacing claylike gray. And yet, it was in constant motion, its surface heaving rhythmically like the chest of some vast, discomforted sleeper.

◄ *What change has taken place since Charlotte was last on deck?*

I looked about. A few of the sailors were working ropes or scouring decks with heavy holystones.[2] Their sullen silence, their dirty clothing, was hardly a reassuring sight. Then I realized that one of them—Dillingham was his name—was staring right at me. He was a bearded, bald, and barrel-chested man, with great knuckled fists and a perpetually sulky frown. Suddenly, I saw that it was not so much me he was looking at but the blade I held in my hand.

◄ *Why is Dillingham staring at Charlotte?*

Turning abruptly, I tried to hide the dirk in the folds of my skirt. When I stole a glance over my shoulder I noted that Dillingham had gone off. All the same the incident

---

1. **four bells.** Bells are used on ship to mark the time.
2. **holystones.** Large, flat stones used for scouring a ship's wooden deck

Words For Everyday Use

ven • ture (ven′chər) *vi.,* do or go at some risk

reminded me I had come on deck to give the knife back to Zachariah.

Concerned mostly that the other sailors not see what I held, I hastily made my way to the galley. Fortunately, Zachariah was there. Standing at the bulkhead,[3] I mumbled, "Good morning."

The old man turned from his pots. "Ah! Miss Doyle," he cried. "I am glad to see you. And most pleased too that you've found your—what sailors call—sea legs."

"Mr. Zachariah, " I said, weak and breathless, but holding out the dirk. "Take this back. I don't want it."

► What does Charlotte intend to do with the dirk?

It was as if he had not heard me. "Would Miss Doyle wish some tea?"

I continued to offer the dirk. "Mr. Zachariah, please . . ."

"Come," he said, "do as they do in big houses. Enter, drink, and eat. When one recovers one's legs, there's still a stomach to contend with. Then, perhaps, I'll talk with Miss Doyle about my gift."

I was not sure what to do. It was the smell of food that decided me. "I am very hungry."

Immediately he reached into a tin chest and brought out what looked like a flat lump of hard dough. "Would Miss Doyle like this?" he asked as if offering a fine delicacy.

My nose wrinkled. "What is it?"

"Hardtack. Sailor's bread. Come, Miss Doyle, sit."

As loathsome as the food appeared, hunger dictated. I stepped forward, settled myself on the stool, and took the hardened cake. Meanwhile, I put the dirk in my dress pocket.

As I ate—not an easy task, for the biscuit was rock hard and close to tasteless—he busied himself in getting tea. "How long have I been ill?" I asked.

► How long was Charlotte ill?

"On toward four days now."

After a moment I said, "I wish to thank you for your kindness during that time."

He turned and beamed. "Zachariah and Miss Doyle—together."

Fearing he was taking liberties, I changed the subject. "Is it possible," I asked, "to go where my trunk is? I need to get some fresh clothes as well as my reading."

"For that," he said, "you will need to apply to Mr. Hollybrass." He offered me the tea.

I took the cup and began to sip at it. After a moment, I said, "Mr. Zachariah, when I finish my tea I intend to leave the dirk."

---

3. **bulkhead.** Upright partition used to separate parts of a ship

The old man studied me. "Miss Doyle"—his hand touched his heart—"believe me. There may be a need."

"What kind of need?" I said, <u>dismayed</u>.

"A ship, Miss Doyle . . . is a nation of its own."

"Mr. Zachariah . . ."

"The nations of the earth, Miss Doyle, they have kings, and emperors . . ."

"And presidents," I added, loyal American that I was.

◀ What is a captain on a ship?

"Yes, and presidents. But when a ship is upon the sea, there's but one who rules. As God is to his people, as king to his nation, as father to his family, so is captain to his crew. Sheriff. Judge and jury. He is all."

"*All?*" I said.

"Aye," he said solemnly, "and hangman too if it comes to that. Now, Miss Doyle, if ever a man was master of his ship, it's our Captain Jaggery. I saw you upon the deck that first day. Did you not mark his words?"

I drew myself up. "Mr. Zachariah," I said, "the captain is a fine man."

◀ What does Charlotte think of Captain Jaggery?

"Do you think so?"

"I know so."

For a moment Zachariah merely gazed at me with a look of curiosity. Then he turned away and busied himself with his pots.

"Mr. Zachariah, why do I need the dirk?"

When he paused in his work, I sensed he was trying to make up his mind. After a moment he turned back to me. "Miss Doyle," he said, "listen." Even as he spoke he stole a quick glance out the door, crept forward, and lowered his voice.

"One year ago, Miss Doyle, on this same ship, *Seahawk,* one poor sailor came under the captain's <u>ire</u>, the captain's judgment, the captain's rage."

"Mr. Zachariah, I don't wish to hear personal—"

"Miss Doyle has asked," he said, cutting me off, "now she *must* listen. That poor jack went by the name of Mr. Cranick."

"Cranick?" I said. "Didn't the captain ask Mr. Hollybrass about him?"

"Ah, you *do* listen."

Words For Everyday Use

dis • mayed (dis mād´) *adj.,* filled with alarm or apprehension

ire (īre) *n.,* anger

"What about him?" I asked, already sorry I had pressed for this explanation.

"Mr. Cranick did not tie a knot to Captain Jaggery's particular pleasure. The captain punished Mr. Cranick. Punished him hard."

"I'm sure this . . . Mr. Cranick deserved it."

Zachariah cocked his head to one side. "Miss Doyle, do you believe in justice?"

"I am an American, Mr. Zachariah."

"Ah! Justice for *all?*"

"For those who deserve it."

"Captain Jaggery said Mr. Cranick's laboring arm was *his* by rights. Miss Doyle, Mr. Cranick has but one arm now. He was that much beaten by Captain Jaggery, who, as he said himself, *took the arm.* I was first surgeon, then carpenter to Mr. Cranick."

Appalled, I jumped off the stool. "I don't believe you!" I exclaimed. "Justice is poorly served when you speak ill of your betters." It was a phrase I had heard my father use many times.

"Whether you believe me or not, Miss Doyle, it is true," he said, moving to block me from the exit.

It was my turn to offer him my back.

"Now, that crew," he continued all the same, "each and every jack of them—once ashore—petitioned the admiralty courts against the captain. It was no use, Miss Doyle. No use. Jaggery had his way. All he needed to say was that Cranick refused a lawful order and he received not one word of <u>censure</u>. It's a sad commonplace. I've yet to see a master charged.

"Ah," Zachariah pressed on, "but the captain must sail again. Sailing is his life. He has his reputation for fast crossings to keep up, speeds that bring ripe profits. But to sail, even Jaggery needs a crew . . ."

"Mr. Zachariah, I must beg you to refrain—"

"But Andrew Jaggery could find not one other jack to sign with the *Seahawk.* They were all warned away."

As soon as he said that my mind went to the Liverpool dock men who fled, the one upon hearing the captain's name, the other upon seeing the *Seahawk.*

But the next moment I turned and said, "But Mr. Zachariah, what about these men?"

▶ What is Charlotte's belief about justice?

▶ According to Zachariah, what did Captain Jaggery do to Cranick?

▶ What did the crew do once ashore? To what results?

▶ What does Charlotte remember when Zachariah tells her all the other sailors were warned away?

Words For Everyday Use

cen • sure (sen´shər) *n.,* strong disapproval

"On this ship?"

"Yes."

"Miss Doyle, I only said *other* men were kept away."

Suddenly I began to understand. "Are these his *former* crew?" I asked.

His eyes were hard upon me now, frightening me.

"On the *Seahawk?*" I demanded.

He nodded. "Only Mr. Hollybrass is new." Then he added, "And Mr. Cranick could not sign."

I stared at him for a moment and by sheer force of will said, "If Captain Jaggery was so cruel, why should they have signed on again?"

Zachariah leaned close to me. *"Revenge,"* he whispered.

"Revenge?" I echoed weakly.

The old man nodded. "Because of all this I gave you that dirk."

Automatically my hand touched it in my pocket.

"They"—he lowered his voice even as he indicated the deck with a movement of his head—"know your father's name. They know the captain works for him. They assume you'll stand . . ."

"Mr. Zachariah," I cut in with the only voice I had—a faint whisper—"I have nothing but respect for the captain."

"Exactly."

For a moment neither of us spoke.

Then Zachariah asked, "Where have you kept this dirk I gave you?"

"Under my mattress."

"Miss Doyle, I *beg* of you—keep it there still."

At that very instant we were startled by a noise. We looked around. It was Mr. Hollybrass, peering at us from behind his shaggy brows like some spy, his frown indicative of his displeasure in seeing us closeted so.

"Miss Doyle," the first mate said. "Compliments of Captain Jaggery. And would you be kind enough to join him in his quarters for tea?"

◀ Who are the sailors who have signed onto the Seahawk? Why have they signed on?

◀ Who comes to get Charlotte? How does he react to seeing Charlotte talking with Zachariah?

Chapter Five

ever had I met with such <u>impertinence</u>! That this Zachariah, my inferior, a cook, should tell such a <u>slanderous</u> tale of violence and cruelty regarding Captain Jaggery to *me*—as though it were a *confidence*—was deeply <u>mortifying</u>. I would not, could not believe it! You can imagine then my relief at being rescued by Mr. Hollybrass.

With head held high and fingers smoothing dress and hair as best I could, I hurriedly followed the first mate from the galley to the captain's cabin—at the far end of the steerage—under the ever-watchful eyes of the crew. More than once I touched the dirk that lay in my pocket. I was resolved to give it to the captain.

Whether or not I should *tell* the captain what I'd just heard was a more delicate question. To confess that I'd even been spoken to in such an offending fashion would have made me feel acutely uncomfortable. But not to speak of it would smack of <u>complicity</u>.

Before I could make up my mind, Mr. Hollybrass had knocked upon the captain's door, and upon hearing an "Enter!" he opened it. I stepped forward.

Every other place I'd seen aboard the *Seahawk* had a rough, crude look, with not the slightest hint of style or culture about them. The captain's cabin was a world apart.

It extended the full width of the *Seahawk*. And I found I could stand up in it with room to spare. The walls were richly paneled and hung with miniatures[1] and pretty pastoral prints[2] of dear England. On the back wall—the stern of the ship—there was a row of windows, below which stood a handsome stuffed sofa. A high bed was built into the port side. A desk with neatly stacked charts and nautical instruments in velvet boxes faced it on the starboard wall. Next to the desk was an iron cabinet that I took to be a safe, not unlike my father's. In one corner I spied a chessboard, pieces at the ready. Finally, a table, with a few chairs about it, had been laid with a silver service for tea.

► *What does Charlotte decide to do?*

► *Why does Charlotte hesitate to tell the captain what she has heard?*

► *In what way does Captain Jaggery's cabin differ from the rest of the ship?*

---

1. **miniatures.** Very small paintings
2. **pastoral prints.** Printed artwork (usually paintings) depicting rural and nature scenes

---

Words For Everyday Use

im • per • ti • nence (im pʉrt´'n əns) *n.*, lack of respect

slan • der • ous (slan´dər əs) *adj.*, damaging to another person's character

mor • ti • fy (môrt´ə fī) *vt.*, cause to feel shame or humiliation

com • plic • i • ty (kəm plis´ə tē) *n.*, state of being an accomplice

Had there been no creak and groan of timbers, no rattle of rigging and chain, no hiss of waves, I might have been excused for forgetting that we were at sea.

To complete this elegant picture, Captain Jaggery sat upon one of a pair of armchairs in fine full dress, an open book on his knee. It was, in fact, the Bible. When I came in he rose to his feet and made an elegant bow.

Could anything be in greater contrast to my meeting with Zachariah? I was charmed.

"Miss Doyle," he said, "how kind of you to visit."

Wishing to present myself in the best possible fashion, I moved forward with one hand out. He took it graciously. Then he turned to the first mate. "Mr. Hollybrass," he said briskly, "that will be all."

Mr. Hollybrass presented a salute and retired.

"Miss Doyle," Captain Jaggery continued with a gracious smile even as he carefully closed and put down his Bible, "would you be good enough to sit." He held the other upholstered seat out for me.

◄ How does Charlotte react to the captain's welcome?

"Thank you," I said, thrilled to be treated in this ladylike fashion.

"You seem surprised," he said, "to find such fine things in my cabin."

I blushed that he should discover me so. "It is very nice," I admitted.

"How gracious of you to appreciate it," he said soothingly. "It's not often I have a person of cultivation—like you—aboard my ship to notice. I fear a crew such as mine has little liking for good taste or, alas, order. It offends them. But then, you and I—people of our class—we understand the better things of life, don't we?"

◄ What do the captain and Charlotte have in common? In what way do they differ from the crew?

Again I blushed, this time with pleasure.

"May I," he said, "offer you some tea?"

I was awash with tea, but was not about to refuse him.

"Some biscuits?" He offered a tin of Scottish thins. I took one and nibbled daintily. Crisp and buttery. Delicious.

"A ship like the *Seahawk*," he went on, "is not designed for comfort, but for commerce, for making money. Still, I do the best I can." He poured a cup of tea for himself.

"I was informed," he said, resuming his seat, "that you had recovered, and was so glad to hear it. May I urge you, Miss Doyle, to promenade[3] in the fresh air as much as possible. You will soon be as healthy—healthier—than you ever were."

---

3. **promenade.** Walk

► Why does the captain regret that the other two families did not come on the ship?

"Thank you, sir."

"It is regrettable that those other two families could not join us. They would have made your voyage that much more pleasant. Mine too."

"Yes, sir."

He smiled. "Do you know, I have a daughter."

"Do you?"

He got up, removed a little picture from a wall, and held it up for me to see. It was the face of a dear little child, her eyes large, her mouth sweet. "Victoria is her name. She's only five. Some day I hope to have her and her mother on board with me. But for the moment the child is too delicate."

"She's very lovely, sir," I said, reaching for the picture. He drew it back as if unable to part with it even for a moment.

"If I may take the liberty of saying so, Miss Doyle, you and she could be charming sisters. I do miss her." His eyes lingered on the picture in a most affecting way. Then he placed it carefully back on the wall, never for a moment taking his eyes from the child's face. He turned about. "Are you comfortable in your cabin?" he asked.

"Oh, yes, sir," I assured him.

"A bit cramped no doubt."

"Only a little."

► What does the captain offer Charlotte?

"Miss Doyle, I offer you the freedom of the ship. As for your meals, you may join me whenever you choose. I don't think you will find the crew to your liking, of course, but there will be no harm in being friendly to them. The truth is, you will do *them* a world of good."

"It's kind of you to say, sir," I replied, appreciating the compliment. He was watching me with an <u>earnestness</u> I found irresistible.

► What does the captain suggest Charlotte should do with the crew?

"Talk to them, Miss Doyle," he urged. "Show them a little softness. Read to them from your moral books. Preach the gospel if you have a mind. Listen to their tales. I promise, they will fill your pretty head with the most fantastical notions."

"I'm sure, sir," I said, thinking back to all Zachariah had told me. The captain's behavior at tea was proof enough—for me—of his true goodness.

"I gather," he continued, "that Mr. Zachariah has already befriended you."

Words For Everyday Use

ear • nest • ness (ʉrʹnist nəs) *n.,* seriousness

I drew myself up. "He's been a bit <u>presumptuous</u>."

"These sailors . . ." the captain said lazily. "They have no natural tenderness. They must be instructed." He studied me a while. "How old are you Miss Doyle?"

"Thirteen, sir."

"And your father, I understand, is an officer of the company that owns this ship."

"Yes, sir."

He smiled. "Then, you see, I have even more reason to make sure your time with us is as comfortable as possible. I shall want a good report from you."

"Oh, sir," I exclaimed enthusiastically, "I'm sure I'll not be <u>stinting</u> in my praise. You seem so—"

"Yes?"

"You remind me of my father," I said, blushing yet again.

◄ *What praise does Charlotte give the captain?*

"High praise, which I hope to deserve!" he cried with such obvious pleasure that I could not help but be gratified. Then he set down his teacup and leaned forward. "Miss Doyle, forgive my rough tongue, but, since we are to be friends—we are already friends, are we not?"

"I would very much like that, sir."

"And you said I remind you of your esteemed father."

"You do, sir."

"Then may I be frank with you?"

"If you wish, sir," I returned, flattered anew.

"A ship, Miss Doyle, I will be the first to admit, is not the most wholesome place for a refined young lady like yourself. And a captain has not the easiest of tasks, considering the nature of the crew he must command. They are godless men, I fear. Sailors often are.

"There will be moments," he continued, "when I will appear harsh to you. Believe me, if I could with kindness encourage the men to achieve their tasks I would do it. Alas, I would gain no respect. They don't understand kindness. Instead, they see it as weakness. Instead, they *demand* a strong hand, a touch of the whip, like dumb beasts who require a little bullying. I must do what is best for the ship, the company—which is to say your father—and for them. I am a <u>punctilious</u> man, Miss Doyle. Without order there is chaos. Chaos on shipboard is sailing without a rudder. As for danger . . ." He gestured toward the iron safe.

◄ *What does the captain warn Charlotte she may see?*

Words For Everyday Use

pre • sump • tu • ous (prē zump´choo̅ əs) *adj.,* too bold or forward

stint • ing (stint´iŋ) *adj.,* sparing

punc • til • i • ous (puŋk til´ē əs) *adj.,* very careful about every detail; exacting

► What does the captain assure Charlotte?

"Do you see that cabinet?"

I nodded.

"A rack of muskets. All loaded. But *locked,* the key secured. You have my word, Miss Doyle, there are *no* other guns aboard but mine."

"I'm very glad, sir," I replied with a shiver.

"And so you and I, Miss Doyle, shall understand one another, shall we not?"

"Oh, yes, sir. I'm sure, sir."

"You do my heart good!" he cried. "And you have permission to come to me if you are troubled in any way, Miss Doyle. If something frightens you, or . . . if perhaps, you become . . . how shall I say . . . <u>apprehensive</u>. If you hear rumors among the men . . . This crew, like all crews, grumbles and complains. You go to school?" he asked suddenly.

I nodded.

► To what does Captain Jaggery compare a crew's relationship to a captain?

► What does the captain ask Charlotte to do for him?

"And though you love it, and love your mistresses, I'm sure even you and your companions have critical things to say."

"I'm afraid so."

"It's much the same here, Miss Doyle. All friends, but . . . a few grumbles too. In fact I shall ask you to help me. You can be my eyes and ears among the men, Miss Doyle. May I depend on you for that?"

"I'll try sir."

"If ever you see something like this . . ." From the Bible he withdrew a paper. On it was a drawing of two circles, one within the other and with what looked like signatures in the space between.

Words For Everyday Use	**ap • pre • hen • sive** (ap rē hen´siv) *adj.,* anxious or fearful about the future, uneasy

I looked at it blankly.

"A round robin," he said. "The men sign it this way so no name shall appear on top, or bottom. How typical of them not to accept responsibility for their own <u>wayward</u> actions. It's a kind of pact."

"I don't understand."

"Miss Doyle, those who sign such a thing—a round robin—mean to make dangerous trouble. For me. And you. If ever you see one about the ship you must tell me immediately. It might save our lives.

"Well," he said briskly, changing his dark tone as he put the paper away, "I believe you and I shall be fast friends."

"Oh, yes sir," I assured him.

He drank the last of his tea. "Now, is there anything I can do for you?"

"My trunk was put away, sir. I should like to remove some clothing from it, and my reading."

"Do you wish the trunk up?" he asked.

"My room is too small, sir. I thought I could go to it."

"I shall have one of the men lead you there."

"Thank you, sir."

"Anything else?"

"Yes, sir."

"What is it."

I drew the dirk from my pocket. He started.

"Where did you get that?" he asked severely.

"I don't know if I should say, sir."

His face had grown stern. "Miss Doyle, was it from one of my crew?"

What flashed through my mind was Zachariah's kindness that first night I came aboard. In truth, I didn't care for the black man; he had been most unpleasantly forward. But the severity that had crept into the captain's eyes as he asked his question gave me pause. I did not wish to bring trouble to Zachariah. No doubt he meant well.

"Miss Doyle," the Captain said firmly, "you *must* tell me."

"Mr. Grummage, sir," I blurted out.

"I don't know the man."

"The gentleman who brought me to the *Seahawk*, sir. A business associate of my father's."

"From Liverpool?"

◄ Why must Charlotte tell Captain Jaggery if she ever sees a round robin?

◄ Why doesn't Charlotte want to tell Captain Jaggery where she got the dirk?

Words For Everyday Use

way • ward (wā´wərd) adj., willful, disobedient

"I think so, sir. A gentleman."

"Quite!" he said and, seeming to relax, he reached for the dirk. I gave it to him. He tested its point. "A true blade," he exclaimed. Then to my surprise—he offered it back.

"If it gives you a sense of security, put it . . . under your mattress."

"I had it there, sir. I don't want it."

"I think you had better."

"Why?" I asked faintly.

"In hopes you never need it," he replied. "Now, I insist."

I returned the dirk to my dress pocket but resolved to fling it into the ocean at the first opportunity.

Captain Jaggery laughed pleasantly, and then asked me questions about family and school that quickly helped me regain a sense of ease and comfort. I was speaking of Miss Weed when five bells struck. The captain stood.

"Forgive me," he said. "I must return to the deck. Let me find someone to go with you to your trunk. Do you know exactly where it was stowed?"

I shook my head. "A Mr. Barlow had charge of it," I explained.

"Come then," he said. "I'll get him to accompany you."

At the open door he paused, and with a <u>flourish</u>, extended his arm. Glowing with pleasure, I took it and the two of us swept out of his cabin.

▶ Why does Captain Jaggery give the blade back to Charlotte?

Words For Everyday Use

flour • ish (flur´ish) *n.,* showy, wavy motion

Chapter Six

EVER mind that my dress—having been worn for four days—was creased and misshapen, my white gloves a sodden gray. Never mind that my fine hair must have been hanging like a horse's tail, in almost complete disarray. With all eyes upon us as we crossed the ship's waist to the bowsprit and figurehead, I felt like a princess being led to her throne.

◄ How does Charlotte look as she crosses the deck with the captain? How does she feel?

Not even the same lowering mist I'd observed when I first came from my cabin could dampen my soaring spirits. Captain Jaggery was a brilliant sun and I, a Juno[1] moon, <u>basked</u> in reflected glory.

"Captain Jaggery, sir," I said, "this ship seems to be moving very slowly."

"You observe correctly," he replied, ever the perfect gentleman. "But if you look up there," he pointed beyond the mainmast, "you'll notice some movement. The cloud cover should be breaking soon and then we'll gain. There, you see," he exclaimed, "the sun is struggling to shine through."

As if by command a thin yellow disk began to appear where he pointed, though it soon faded again behind clotted clouds.

From the forecastle deck we crossed to the quarterdeck and then to the helm. Foley, a lean, bearded man, was at the wheel. Mr. Keetch, as unsmiling as ever, stood by his side. The wheel itself was massive, with hand spikes for easier gripping.

When the captain and I approached, the two men stole fleeting glances in our direction but said nothing.

Captain Jaggery released my arm and gazed up at the sails. At length he said, "Mr. Keetch."

The second mate turned to him. "Yes, sir."

"I believe," the captain said, "we shall soon have a blow."

Mr. Keetch seemed surprised. "Do you think so, sir?"

"I hardly would have said so otherwise, now would I, Mr. Keetch?"

---

1. **Juno.** Queen of the gods in Roman mythology

Words For Everyday Use	**bask** (bask) *vi.,* enjoy a warm or pleasant feeling from being in a certain situation

The man darted a glance at me as if I held the answer. All he said however was, "I suppose not, sir."

"Thank you, Mr. Keetch. Now, I want to take advantage of it. Tighten all braces, and be ready with the jigger gaff."[2]

"Aye, aye, sir."

▶ What does the captain order Mr. Keetch to do?

"And bring the studding sails to hand. We may want them to make up for lost time."

"Aye, aye, sir." After another glance at me, Mr. Keetch marched quickly across the quarterdeck and at the rail bellowed, "All hands! All hands!"

Within moments the entire crew assembled on deck.

"Topgallant and royal yardmen in the tops!" he cried.

The next moment the crew scrambled into the shrouds and standing rigging, high amidst the masts and spars. Even as they ascended Mr. Keetch began to sing out a litany of commands—"Man topgallant mast ropes! Haul taut! Sway and unfid!"—that had men hauling on running lines and tackle until the desired sails were shifted and set. It was a grand show, but if the ship moved any faster for it, I didn't sense a change.

The captain now turned to Foley. "One point south," he said.

"One point south," Foley echoed and shifted the wheel counterclockwise with both hands.

"Steady on," the captain said.

"Steady on," Foley repeated.

Now it was Mr. Hollybrass who approached the helm. The moment he did so Captain Jaggery hailed him.

"Mr. Hollybrass!"

"Sir!"

"As convenient, Mr. Hollybrass, send Mr. Barlow to Miss Doyle. She needs to learn where her trunk was stowed."

"Yes, sir."

"Miss Doyle," the captain said to me, "please be so good as to follow Mr. Hollybrass. I have enjoyed our conversation and look forward to many more."

▶ How does Charlotte react to the captain's farewell? How does Mr. Hollybrass react?

Then and there—beneath the eyes of all the crew—he took up my hand, bowed over it, and touched his lips to my fingers. I fairly glowed with pride. Finally I followed—per-

---

2. **jigger gaff.** Pole supporting a small sail

Words For Everyday Use   **lit • a • ny** (lit´'n ē) *n.*, repetitive listing

haps floated is a better word—after Mr. Hollybrass. Barely concealing a look of <u>disdain</u> for the captain's farewell to me, he made his way across the quarterdeck and stood at the rail overlooking the ship's waist. There he studied the men while they continued to adjust the rigging, now and again barking a command to work one rope or another.

"Mr. Barlow," he called out at last.

"Here, sir!" came a response from on high.

Some sixty feet above I saw the man.

"Get you down!" Mr. Hollybrass cried.

Despite his decrepit appearance, Barlow was as <u>dexterous</u> as a monkey. He clambered across the foreyard upon which he had been perched, reached the mast, then the rigging, and on this narrow thread of rope he seemed to actually run until he dropped upon the deck with little or no sound.

"Aye, aye, sir," he said, no more out of breath than I—or rather less than I, for to see him at such heights moving at such speeds had taken *my* breath away.

"Mr. Barlow," Hollybrass said. "Miss Doyle needs her trunk. I understand you know where it is."

"I put it in top steerage, sir."

"Be so good as to lead her to it."

"Yes, sir." Barlow had not yet looked my way. Now, with a shy nod, and a touch to his forelock, he did so. I understood I was to follow.

The normal entry to the cargo areas is through the hatchway located in the center of the ship's waist. Since that was lashed down for the voyage, Barlow led me another way, to a ladder beneath the mates' mess table—in steerage—just opposite my cabin door.

◄ *Where does Mr. Barlow lead Charlotte?*

After setting aside the candle he'd brought along, he scrambled under the mess table, then pulled open a winged hatch door that was built flush into the floor. Once he had his candle lit, I saw him twist about and drop partway down the hole.

"If you please, miss," he beckoned.

Distasteful though it was, I had little choice in the matter. I crawled on hands and knees, backed into the hole, and climbed down twelve rungs—a distance of about eight or nine feet.

▶ What does Mr. Barlow tell Charlotte about the hold?

"Here, miss," Barlow said at my side, next to the ladder. "You don't want to go down to the hold."

I looked beneath me and saw that the ladder continued into what appeared to be a black pit.

"More cargo," he explained <u>laconically</u>. "Rats and roaches too. And a foul bilge.[3] That's where the brig is."

"Brig?"

"The ship's jail."

"A jail on a ship?"

"Captain Jaggery wouldn't sail without, miss."

I shuddered in disgust.

Barlow held out one of his hard, gnarled hands. Reluctantly I took it and did a little jump to the top cargo deck. Only then did I look about.

It was a great, wood-ribbed cavern I had come to, which—because Barlow's candlelight reached only so far—melted into blackness fore and aft. I recall being struck by the notion that I was—Jonah-like—in the belly of a whale.[4] The air was heavy, with the <u>pervasive</u> stench of rot that made me gag.

▶ To what does Charlotte compare being in top cargo?

"What's that?" I asked, pointing to a cylinder from which pipes ran, and to which handles were attached.

"The pump," he said. "In case we take on sea."

In all directions I saw the kinds of bales, barrels, and boxes I had seen upon the Liverpool docks. The sight was not romantic now. These goods were piled higgledy-piggledy one atop the other, braced and restrained here and there by ropes and wedges, but mostly held in place by their own bulk. The whole reminded me of a great tumble of toy blocks jammed into a box.

"There's more below," Barlow said, observing me look about. "But your trunk's over there." Sure enough, I saw it up along the alleyway created by two stacks of cargo.

"Would you open it, please," I requested.

Barlow undid the hasps and flung open the top. There lay my clothing, wrapped in tissue paper and laid out beautifully. The school maids had done a fine job. A sigh escaped my lips at this glimpse of another world.

---

3. **bilge.** Bottommost interior part of a ship
4. **Jonah-like . . . whale.** Refers to Biblical story in which Jonah is thrown overboard for disobeying God and is swallowed by a big fish

Words For Everyday Use

la • con • ic (la kän´ik) *adj.*, brief in speaking, using few words

per • va • sive (pər vā´siv) *adj.*, spread throughout

"I can't take everything," I said.

"Well, miss," Barlow said, "now that you know where it is, you could fetch things on your own."

"That's true," I said, and, kneeling, began to lift the layers carefully.

After a while Barlow said, "If it pleases, miss, might I have a word?"

"You see I'm very busy Mr. Barlow," I murmured.

For a moment the sailor said nothing, though I was conscious of his nervous presence behind me.

"Miss," he said unexpectedly, "you know I spoke out when you first arrived."

◄ What does Barlow say that relates to his earlier warning?

"I have tried to forget it, Mr. Barlow," I said with some severity.

"You shouldn't, miss. You shouldn't."

His earnest, pleading tone made me pause. "What do you mean?"

"Just now, miss, the captain put us on display. All that hauling and pulling. It was to no account. Mocking us—"

"Mr. Barlow!" I interrupted.

"It's true, miss. He's abusing us. And you. Mark my words. No good will come of it."

I pressed my hands to my ears.

After a moment the man said, "All right, miss. I'll leave you with the candle. You won't go into the hold now, will you?"

"I shall be fine, Mr. Barlow," I declared. "Please leave me."

So _engrossed_ was I in my explorations of my trunk that I ceased paying him any attention. Only vaguely did I hear him retreat and ascend the ladder. But when I was sure he was gone I did turn about. He had set the candle on the floor near where the ladder led further into the hold. Though the flame flickered in a draft, I was satisfied it would burn a while. I turned back to my trunk.

As I knelt there, making the difficult but delicious choice between this petticoat and that—searching too for a book suitable for reading to the crew as the captain had suggested—the sensation crept upon me that there was something else hovering about, a _presence,_ if you will, something I could not define.

At first I tried to ignore the feeling. But no matter how

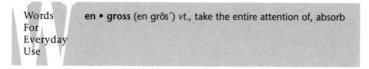

Words For Everyday Use

en • gross (en grōs´) _vt._, take the entire attention of, absorb

▶ What does Charlotte begin to sense as she is sorting through her trunk? What does she see when she looks behind her?

much I tried it could not be denied. Of course it was not exactly quiet down below. No place on a ship is. There were the everlasting creaks and groans. I could hear the sloshing of the bilge water in the hold, and the rustling of all I preferred not to put a name to—such as the rats Barlow had mentioned. But within moments I was absolutely certain— though how I knew I cannot tell—that it was a *person* who was watching me.

As this realization took hold, I froze in terror. Then slowly I lifted my head and stared before me over the lid of the trunk. As far as I could see, no one was there.

My eyes swept to the right. No one. To the left. Again, nothing. There was but one other place to look, *behind.* Just the thought brought a prickle to the back of my neck until, with sudden panic, I whirled <u>impulsively</u> about.

There, jutting up from the hole through which the hold might be reached, was a grinning *head,* its eyes fixed right on me.

I shrieked. The next moment the candle went out and I was plunged into utter darkness.

Words For Everyday Use

im • pul • sive • ly (im pul′siv lē) *adv.,* suddenly, spontaneously

Responding to the Selection

Charlotte has been given several warnings about being on the *Seahawk*. Predict what you think will happen during the voyage.

Investigate, Inquire, and Imagine

Recall: GATHERING FACTS

1a. What is Charlotte's first warning about the *Seahawk?* What does she learn from Mr. Grummage when they arrive at the ship?

2a. According to Zachariah, what do he and Charlotte have in common?

3a. What is Charlotte's opinion of the captain when she first meets him? Of whom does Charlotte say the captain reminds her?

Interpret: FINDING MEANING

1b. Why doesn't Charlotte think she should travel on the *Seahawk?* Why does she board the ship despite these thoughts?

2b. Do you think Charlotte and Zachariah will be friends? Why, or why not?

3b. What do Charlotte and the captain have in common? Why isn't Charlotte completely honest with the captain when they are discussing the dirk?

Analyze: TAKING THINGS APART

4a. Outline the hierarchy of positions on the ship. What relationships exist between the different levels?

Synthesize: BRINGING THINGS TOGETHER

4b. How does the class system on the ship relate to that on land? What might happen if the crew were to overthrow the captain as he fears they will try to do?

Evaluate: MAKING JUDGMENTS

5a. Evaluate the warnings Charlotte hears from Zachariah and from Captain Jaggery about what she may see or what is likely to happen aboard the ship. Which person do you think Charlotte should trust? Which person is she most likely to trust?

Extend: CONNECTING IDEAS

5b. On what characteristics has Charlotte based her judgment of the characters of Zachariah and Captain Jaggery? On what basis do you judge character?

Understanding Literature

Adventure is a genre of literature in which the main character faces many dangerous and exciting experiences. Based on the introduction to *The True Confessions of Charlotte Doyle,* identify some of the adventures Charlotte will face throughout the course of this novel. Make a prediction about how each will happen.

Suspense is a feeling of expectation, anxiousness, or curiosity created by questions raised in the mind of a reader or viewer. Identify three ways in which Avi creates suspense in Chapters 1–6. Then as you read, track other suspenseful elements.

Dialogue is conversation involving two or more people or characters. Examine the dialogue Charlotte hears just before falling asleep at the end of chapter 2. What does Charlotte make of this conversation? What do you think is the significance of this dialogue?

Chapter Seven

was too frightened to cry out again. Instead I remained absolutely still, crouching in pitch blackness while the wash of ship sounds <u>eddied</u> about me, sounds now intensified by the frantic knocking of my heart. Then I recollected that Zachariah's dirk was still with me. With a shaking hand I reached into the pocket where I'd put it, took it out, and removed its wooden sheath which slipped through my clumsy fingers and clattered noisily to the floor.

"Is someone there?" I called, my voice thin, wavering.

No answer.

After what seemed forever I repeated, more boldly than before, "*Is someone there?*"

Still nothing happened. Not the smallest breath of response. Not the slightest stir.

Gradually, my eyes became accustomed to the creaking darkness. I could make out the ladder descending from the deck, a square of dim light above. From that point I could follow the line of the ladder down to where it plunged into the hold below. At that spot, at the edge of the hole, I could see the head more distinctly. Its eyes were glinting wickedly, its lips <u>contorted</u> into a grim, satanic smirk.

Horrified, I nonetheless stared back. And the longer I did so the more it dawned on me that the head had not in fact moved—not at all. The features, I saw, remained unnaturally fixed. Finally, I found the courage to edge aside my fear and lean forward—the merest trifle—to try and make out who—or what—was there.

With the dirk held awkwardly before me I began to crawl forward. The closer I inched the more distorted and grotesque grew the head's features. It appeared to be positively inhuman.

When I drew within two feet of it I stopped and waited. Still the head did not move, did not blink an eye. It seemed as if it were *dead.*

With trembling fingers I reached out and managed to brush the thing, just lightly enough to sense that it was hard—like a skull. At first I cringed, but then puzzlement

◀ *What gives Charlotte some sense of security despite the dark and her sense that somebody is there?*

◀ *What does Charlotte realize about the head she sees?*

Words For Everyday Use

ed • dy (ed´ē) *vt.,* move in a whirlpool-like motion

con • tort (kən tôrt´) *vi.,* twist, distort violently

began to replace fear. I touched the head more forcibly. This time it rolled to one side, as though twisting down upon a shoulder yet all the while glaring hideously at me. I pulled back.

By then I had drawn close enough so that, accustomed to the dark, my eyes could make out the head more or less distinctly. I realized that this humanlike face was a grotesque *carving* cut into some large, brown nut.

Emboldened, I felt for it again, trying to grasp it. That time the head quivered, teetered over the edge of the hold, then dropped. I heard it crash, roll about, then cease to make any sound at all.

Torn between annoyance for what I had done and relief not to be in any danger, I put the dirk back into my pocket— I never did find the sheath—retrieved the candle and started climbing the ladder. Halfway up I remembered my clothing, the reason for my being below in the first instance. For a moment I hung midpoint wondering if I should go back and fetch some of what I needed.

Insisting to myself that there was nothing to worry about, I groped my way back to the trunk, feeling for and taking up what I had previously laid out. Then I turned, half expecting to see the head again—but of course I did not—and rung by rung, squeezing clothing and books under my arm, climbed to the top of the ladder. After closing the hatch's double doors, I crawled out from beneath the table and retreated hastily to my cabin.

There I changed my clothes, and soon felt quite calm again. I was able to reflect on all that had just happened.

The first question was, what exactly had I seen? A grotesque carving, I told myself, though I had to admit I couldn't be sure. Even if it *was* a carving, could a carving reasonably put out a candle? Surely that must have been done by a *human* hand. My thoughts fastened upon Barlow.

On further reflection, however, I was quite convinced that—other than the candle—Barlow had been empty-handed. Yes, I was certain of it. Besides, though I hardly knew the man, he seemed too submissive, too beaten about, to be capable of such a malicious trick. After all, it was he who had warned me twice about possible trouble.

But—if it had *not* been Barlow, there must have been a *sec-*

► *What is it that was watching Charlotte?*

► *What conclusion does Charlotte draw about her experience?*

Words For Everyday Use	**quiv • er** (kwiv´ər) *vi.*, shake, tremble **ma • li • cious** (mə lish´əs) *adj.*, spiteful; intentionally mischievous

ond person, someone to place the head where I'd seen it. Once I put my mind to that possibility, I realized with a start that, yes, I had seen *two* faces.

The first one—I was mortally certain—had been a *human's*, belonging to the person who snuffed out the candle and who then, under cover of dark, set up the carving to deceive and frighten me.

Though I prided myself on my ability to remember sights and sounds, I was unable to make a match at all between *that* face and any man I had seen among the crew. Someone new? That was *impossible*. We were at sea. Visitors did not stop to call![1]

Very well then, I reasoned, the person in the hold had to be someone I'd simply not recognized. After all, my sighting was the quickest of glimpses. But if I could not identify *who* it was then the next question became: *why* had he shown himself?

Why indeed? To frighten me! I had no doubt about that. Well then, to what end? To make me think that what I'd seen was not real? I recalled Barlow's words: perhaps I was being *warned*.

◀ Why had the unfamiliar face shown itself?

But why, I wondered, should anyone want to warn *me*? True, I had been told not to board the ship. And Zachariah's words concerning the crew and their desire to be revenged on Captain Jaggery for his so-called cruelty were unnerving—even if I did not believe them. Then too, I reminded myself of the captain's own warning that the black man was given to exaggeration.

There were too many puzzles. Too many complexities. Unable to <u>fathom</u> the mystery I ended up scolding myself, convinced that I was making something out of nothing.

This then was my conclusion: it was *I* who had not seen properly. The candle—I decided—must have been blown out by a sudden current of air. As for the carving, no doubt it had been there all along. I simply had not noticed it.

Thus I forced myself to believe that I had acted the part of a foolish schoolgirl too apt to make the worst of strange surroundings. And so I found a way to set aside my worries and fears.

---

1. **call.** Pay a visit

Words For Everyday Use

fath • om (fath´əm) *vt.,* get to the bottom of

"There now," I said aloud, "the proof is this: has anything bad *really* happened?" To this I was forced to say: discomfort, well yes; but ill treatment? No, not really.

Still, I wondered if I should inform Captain Jaggery. Had he not just asked me to tell him of *anything* untoward? Had I not agreed?

▶ Why does Charlotte choose not to tell Captain Jaggery about what has happened?

Upon careful reflection, I decided to remain silent. If I were to go to the captain with such a tale he would think me a sorry, troublesome *child*. That was the last thing I desired.

Such thoughts led me to consider my most pleasant talk during tea with him. He had left me in quite a different frame of mind than Zachariah had.

Captain Jaggery and Mr. Zachariah! Such unlike men! And yet, quite suddenly I was struck by the thought that each of them, in his own way, was courting[2] *me*.

▶ What do Captain Jaggery and Zachariah have in common? What does Charlotte resolve?

Courting me! I could not help but smile. Well no, not *courting* in the real sense. But surely courting me for friendship.

What a queer notion! But I must confess, it filled me with <u>smug</u> pleasure. I resolved to stay on the good side of both men. No harm *there*, I told myself. Quite the contrary. It was the safest course. I would be *everybody's* friend, though—need I say?—infinitely more <u>partial</u> to the captain.

With my morning's adventures so resolved, I—for the first time since my arrival on the *Seahawk*—felt good!

But I was *hungry*. After all, I still had not really eaten for several days. Neither Zachariah's hardtack nor the captain's biscuits had been very nourishing. Just the thought made my stomach growl. I decided to return to the cook and request a decent meal.

But before I went, I had one more task to perform. At the moment it seemed trifling enough, though <u>momentous</u> it proved to be. I took up the dirk that had caused me so much anxiety and—since it had no sheath—wrapped it in one of my own handkerchiefs and placed it again in my pocket, determined to fling all into the ocean.

▶ What does Charlotte do with the dirk? Why does she make this decision?

At that fateful moment, however, I paused, recollecting that *both* Captain Jaggery and Zachariah had urged me to keep the weapon. What if each chanced to ask of it again?

---

2. **courting.** Pay attention to in an attempt to get love or something else from another

---

Words For Everyday Use

smug (smug) *adj.*, self-satisfied to an annoying degree

par • tial (pär´shəl) *adj.*, favoring one person or thing more than another

mo • men • tous (mō men´təs) *adj.*, very important

Here I reminded myself that a few moments before—when I'd been frightened—I *had* found a need of it, or at least I thought I'd needed it to defend myself.

Finally, with the notion of pleasing *both* captain and cook, I returned the knife—still wrapped in my handkerchief—to its hiding place under my mattress. As far as I was concerned, it could stay there and be forgotten.

Alas, such would not be the case.

Chapter Eight

aving made up my mind to forget what had happened, I passed the next seven days in comparative tranquility. By the end of the week I grew so firm in my footing that I hardly noticed the pitch and roll of the ship, nor minded the ever-present damp.

During this same time the weather held. No storms came our way. Though days were not always bright and clear, we ran before a steady wind that graced our helm and ruffled our hair. With every sail bent we were making good progress, or so Captain Jaggery assured me. In my ignorance I even stood above the figurehead in hopes of seeing land. Naturally, all I saw was an empty, unchanging, and boundless sea. One day seemed much like another:

▶ Why did Charlotte stand above the figurehead?

At the end of the morning watch, sometime toward six bells, I would wake. Now I had been taught that at the start of each day I should present myself as a proper young gentlewoman to my parents, or, when at school, to the headmistress. On shipboard it was only natural that the captain should be the one I wished to please. But it must be said that preparing to appear on deck was not easy. My day began with a search—usually successful—for fleas. Afterward came a brushing of my hair for a full twenty minutes (I did the same at night). Finally, I parted it carefully, wanting it smoothly drawn—anything to keep it from its natural and to me obnoxious wildness.

▶ What order does Charlotte put to her days?

Then I dressed. Unfortunately my starched clothing had gone everlastingly limp and became increasingly soiled. Hardly a button remained in place. Though I tried not to touch anything, those white gloves of mine had turned the color of slate.

So dirty did I become that I resolved that one of my four dresses would be saved—neat and clean—for my disembarkation in Providence. It was a great comfort to me to know I would not shame my family.

▶ What plan does Charlotte make for her arrival in Rhode Island?

If I wanted to wash things—and I did try—I had to do it myself, something I'd never been required to do before. Moreover, to do washing on ship meant hauling a bucket of

Words For Everyday Use

tran • quil • i • ty (tran kwil´ə tē) n., calmness, serenity

seawater up to the deck. Fortunately, the captain was willing to order the men to lift water for me on demand.

Breakfast was set out in steerage, at the mates' mess. Served by Zachariah, it consisted of badly watered coffee and hard bread with a dab of molasses, though as days passed, the molasses grew foul. Dinner at midday was the same. Supper was boiled salted meats, rice, beans, and again bad coffee. Twice a week we might have duff, the seaman's delight: boiled flour and raisins.

In the evenings I retired to my room to write the particulars of the day in my journal, after which I walked out to gaze at the stars. So many, many stars! And then to bed.

Sundays were remarkable only in that religious observances were briefly held. The captain kindly allowed me to read a biblical passage to the men before he offered reminders of their duty to ship and God. Sundays were also the one day of the week on which the men shaved—if at all—and washed their clothes, sometimes.

◀ What is different about Sunday?

With no chores to perform I spent the bulk of my day in idleness. I could wander at will from galley to forecastle deck, mates' mess to wheel, but, try as I might not to show it, I was sorely bored.

◀ How does Charlotte feel about her time on the ship?

It should be no surprise that the high point of my day was tea with the captain. It was a <u>cherished</u> reminder of the world as I knew it. He always showed interest in what I had to say, in particular my observations of the crew. So flattered was I by his attentions that I took pains to search for things to tell him and then prattled away. Unfortunately tea lasted only from one bell to the next, a mere half an hour. Too soon I had to return to the less <u>congenial</u> world of the crew.

◀ What is the high point of Charlotte's day? Why is this time so special?

I did take care—at first—to keep my distance from them, believing it not proper for me to mingle. My one friendly gesture was to read uplifting selections to them from my books. As the days wore on, however, it was increasingly difficult to refrain from some degree of intimacy. I could not help it. I've always been social by nature. In any case I concluded that I was simply doing what the captain had suggested, in fact, kept urging—that is, keeping a lookout for any act or word that hinted of criticism or hostility.

Though I desired to make it clear that the crew and I were on different levels, I found myself spending more and more

Words For Everyday Use

cher • ish (cher´ish) *vt.*, hold dear, appreciate

con • gen • ial (kən jēn´yəl) *adj.*, having the same tastes; agreeable

▶ Why does
Charlotte spend more
and more time with
the crew?

time in their company. In truth, I had endless questions to ask as to what this was and what was that. They in turn found in me a naive but eager recipient for their answers.

Then there were their yarns. I hardly knew nor cared which were true and which were not. Tales of castaways on Pacific atolls[1] never failed to move me. Solemn accounts of angels and ghosts appearing miraculously in the rigging were, by turns, thrilling and terrifying. I learned the men's language, their ways, their dreams. Above all, I cherished the notion that my contact with the crew improved *them*. As to what it did to me—I hardly guessed.

▶ How does
Charlotte's
relationship with the
crew change?

At first standoffish and suspicious, the crew began to accept me. I actually became something of a "ship's boy," increasingly willing—and able—to run their minor errands.

Of course there were places on the *Seahawk* where I did not venture. Though I returned several times to my trunk, and was not frightened again, I forebore exploring the hold. Barlow's words—and my experience—were sufficient to scare me off.

The other place I shunned was the crew's quarters, the forecastle area before the mast. That I understood to be off-limits.

But as I grew more comfortable, as the crew grew more comfortable with me, I mingled more often with them on deck. In time I even tried my hand and climbed—granted neither very high nor very far—into the rigging.

▶ On whom does
Charlotte focus
"particular
attentions"? Why?

As might be expected I fastened particular attentions upon Zachariah. He had the most time to spend with me and had sought to be kind, of course, from the beginning. Being black, he was the butt of much cruel humor, which aroused my sympathy. At the same time, despite the crew's verbal abuse, he was a great favorite, reputed to be a fine cook. Indeed his good opinion of me gained me—in the crew's world—the license to be liked.

Zachariah was the eldest of the crew, and his life had been <u>naught</u> but sailing. When young, he had shipped as a common sailor, and he swore he'd been able to climb from deck to truck—top of the mainmast—in twenty seconds!

But all in all, as he himself freely told me, he was much

---

1. **atolls.** Ring-shaped coral islands

| Words For Everyday Use | **naught** (nôt) *n.*, nothing |

the worse for his labor, and therefore grateful for his cook's position which paid better than a common tar. For he was aging rapidly, and though he claimed no more than fifty years of age I thought him much older.

He had saved nothing of his wages. His knowledge—as far as I could tell—was limited to ship and sea. He knew not how to read, nor to write more than his mark.[2] He knew little of true Christian religion. Indeed, as he confessed, he was much distressed as to the state of his soul and took comfort (as did others) in my reading aloud from the Bible, which they believed had the power to compel truth. In particular, it was the story of Jonah that had a hold on them.

Since Zachariah never mentioned the dirk, nor again spoke discourteously of the captain, I took it as an indication that he knew I would not <u>condone</u> such talk. This meant that our conversations were increasingly free and easy. It was he, more than anyone else, who encouraged me to engage with the crew.

"Miss Doyle has been kind to me," he said to me one morning, "but if she's to go scampering about she'll need, for modesty and safety's sake, something better than skirts." So saying he presented me with a pair of canvas trousers and blouse, a kind of miniature of what the crew wore—garments he himself had made.

While I thanked him kindly, in fact I took the gift as a warning that I had been forgetting my station. I told him—rather stiffly, I fear—that I thought it not proper for me, a girl—a lady—to wear such apparel. But, so as not to offend too deeply, I took the blouse and trousers to my cabin.

Later on, I admit—I tried the garments on, finding them surprisingly comfortable until, shocked, I remembered myself. Hurriedly, I took them off, resolving not to stoop so low again.

I resolved more. I determined to keep to my quarters and then and there spent two hours composing an essay in my blank book on the subject of proper behavior for young women.

When I emerged for tea with Captain Jaggery, I begged permission to read him some of what I had written. So

◄ Why is Zachariah grateful for his cook's position? What worries might he have?

◄ What gift does Zachariah give Charlotte?

◄ How does Charlotte react to the gift?

---

2. **mark.** Symbol standing for a name

Words For Everyday Use

con • done (kən dōnˊ) *vt.*, forgive or pardon

► Why is Charlotte doubly pleased by Captain Jaggery's praise?

unstinting was he in his praise, that I gained a double pleasure. For in his commendation I was certain I had won my father's approval too—so much were their characters alike.

The captain spent his days in punctilious attention to the ship, pacing off the quarterdeck from wheel to rail, from rail to wheel, ever alert to some disorder to correct. If his eyes were not upon the sails, they were upon the ropes and spars. If not upon those, they rested on the decking.

It was just as he had warned me: the crew was <u>prone</u> to laxness. But—since he had the responsibility of the ship, not they—he was forced, with constant surveillance and commands, to bring discipline to their work.

► What kinds of things does Captain Jaggery find that the crew must do?

Things I never would have thought important he could find at grievous fault. From tarnish upon a rail to limp sails and ragged spars, whether it was rigging to be overhauled or new tar to be applied, blocks, tackle, shrouds, each and all were forever in want of repair. Decks had to be holystoned, caulked, and scrubbed anew, the bow scraped and scraped again, the figurehead repainted. In short, under his keen eye everything was kept in perfect order. For this all hands would be called sometimes more than twice a watch. I heard the calls even at night.

Indeed, so mindful was the captain's sense of responsibility toward the ship ("my father's firm," as he was <u>wont</u> to remind me) that no man on watch was ever allowed to do *nothing*, but was kept at work.

"You are not paid to be idle," the captain often declared, and he, setting an example, was never slack in *his* duty. Even at our teas, he was vigilant—again, so like my father—and patiently examined me as to what I had seen, heard, or even thought—always ready with quick and wise correction.

He was not so patient with the first and second mates, to whom he gave all his orders, depending upon whose watch it was. These men, Mr. Hollybrass and Mr. Keetch, were as different from the captain as from each other.

► In what ways do Mr. Keetch and Mr. Hollybrass differ?

Mr. Keetch when summoned would scuttle quickly to his side, nervous, <u>agitated</u>, that look of fear forever about him, and absorb the captain's barked orders with a cringing servility.

Mr. Hollybrass, the first mate, would approach slowly, seeming to take his own silent soundings about the captain's

---

Words For Everyday Use	**prone** (prōn) *adj.,* inclined to
	wont (wänt) *adj.,* accustomed
	ag • i • tat • ed (aj´i tāt id) *adj.,* perturbed, excited

demands. He might lift his shaggy eyebrows as if to object, but I never heard him actually contradict the captain in words. Indeed the captain would only repeat his commands, and then Mr. Hollybrass would obey.

"Have Mr. Dillingham redo the futtock[3] shrouds," he'd say. Or, "Get Mr. Foley to set the fore gaff topsail proper." Or again, "Have Mr. Morgan set that main clewgarnet to rights."

The men of the crew, hardly finished with one task, would have to set about another, though they did so with dark looks and not-so-silent oaths.

The captain, gentleman that he was, appeared to take no notice. But more than once I watched him call upon Mr. Hollybrass—or less often Mr. Keetch—to punish a man for some slackness or slowness I could not detect. If provoked sufficiently, the captain might resort to a push or a slap with his own open hand. And, much to my surprise, I saw him strike Morgan—a short, stocky, squinty-eyed monkey of a man—with a belaying pin, one of the heavy wood dowels used to secure a rigging rope to the pin rail. In dismay, I averted my eyes. The fellow was tardy about reefing a sail, the captain said, and went on to catalog further likely threats: Confinement in the brig. Salary docking. No meals. Lashings. Duckings in the cold sea or even keelhauling, which, as I learned, meant pulling a man from one side of the ship to the other—under water.

◄ What acts of discipline does Charlotte see? Does she think these acts are warranted?

"Miss Doyle," he might say when we took our daily tea, "you see them for yourself. Are they not the dirtiest, laziest dogs?"

"Yes, sir," I'd reply softly, though I felt increasingly uncomfortable because I could sense resentment growing among the crew.

◄ Why does Charlotte feel increasingly uncomfortable?

"And was ever a Christian more provoked than I?"

"No, sir."

"Now," he would always ask, "what have *you* observed?"

Dutifully, I would report everything I'd seen and heard, the dodges from work, the clenched fists, the muttered oaths of defiance that I had tried hard not to hear.

When I'd done he always said the same. "Before we hove[4] home, Miss Doyle, I shall break them to my will. Each and every one."

One afternoon the wind ceased. And for days after the *Seahawk* was becalmed. It was like nothing I'd ever experienced. Not only did the breeze vanish and the heat rise, but

---

3. **futtock.** Curved timbers that make up the hull of a ship
4. **hove.** Move, proceed

the sea lay like something dead. Air became thick, positively wringing wet, <u>searing</u> to the lungs. Fleas and roaches seemed to crawl out from every timber. The ship, <u>festering</u> in her own <u>malodorous</u> breath, moaned and groaned.

Five times during those days Captain Jaggery ordered the jolly boats[5] lowered. With Mr. Hollybrass in command of one, Mr. Keetch the other, they towed the *Seahawk* in search of wind. It was useless. No wind was to be found.

Then the captain, abruptly accepting the ship's windless fate, set the men to work harder than ever, as though the doldrums[6] had been prearranged in order that he might refit and burnish the *Seahawk* as though new-made. "Sweet are the uses of adversity," he instructed me.

The complaints of the crew grew louder. The oaths became, by perceptible degrees, darker yet.

When I reported all this to the captain he frowned and shook his head. "No one ranks for creative genius like a sailor <u>shirking</u> work."

► *What does Charlotte suggest to Captain Jaggery? How does the captain respond?*

"The crew is tired," I murmured, trying to suggest in a hesitant, vague way that even I could see that the men were fatigued and in need of rest.

"Miss Doyle," he said with a sudden hard laugh, even while urging a second sweet biscuit upon me, "you have my word. They shall wake up when we run into storm."

How right he was. But the storm was—at first—man-made.

---

5. **jolly boats.** Sailing vessel's small boats
6. **doldrums.** Area near the equator notorious for its dead calms or complete lack of wind

Words For Everyday Use	
sear (sir) *vt.*, burn
fes • ter (fes´tər) *vi.*, decay
mal • o • dor • ous (mal ō´dər əs) *adj.*, having a bad odor
shirk (shʉrk) *vt.*, neglect or evade doing work

Chapter Nine

or three more days we drifted upon the glassy sea. The helplessness of it, I could tell, drove Captain Jaggery nearly to distraction. Though the sun grew fiercer, he kept sending the men out in jolly boats to tow the *Seahawk* for two hours at a time in search of wind. He found only more to complain about.

And then it happened.

It was late afternoon, eighteen days into our voyage. The first dog watch. I was on the forecastle deck with Ewing. Ewing was a young, blond Scot—handsome, I thought—with a shocking tattoo of a mermaid upon his arm. That and his Aberdeen[1] sweetheart, about whom he loved to talk, fascinated me. I rather fancied sweetheart and mermaid were one.

At the time he was sitting cross-legged, quite exhausted. That morning the captain had ordered him to spend the day in the highest reaches of the yards, putting new tar on the stays. The sun was brutal. The tar was sticky. Now an old canvas jacket lay in his lap, and with trembling fingers he was attempting to patch it, using needle and awl.[2]

While he labored I read to him from one of my favorite books, *Blind Barbara Ann: A Tale of Loving Poverty.* He was listening intently when his needle snapped in two.

He swore, hastily apologized for cursing in my presence, then cast about for a new needle. When he couldn't find one, he murmured something about having to get another from his box in the forecastle and made to heave himself up.

Knowing how tired he was, I asked, "Can I get it for you?"

"It would be a particular kindness, Miss Doyle," he answered, "my legs being terrible stiff today."

"Where should I look?" I asked.

"Beneath my hammock, in the topmost part of my chest," he said. "In the forecastle."

"Will someone be able to point it out?"

"I should think so," he said.

Without much thought other than that I wished to do the man a kindness, I turned and hurried away.

I had scampered down the forecastle entryway before pausing to think. The forecastle was one of the few areas I had not been in before—the one place on the *Seahawk* that

◄ *What does Charlotte offer to do for Ewing? Where does she have to go?*

◄ *What makes Charlotte pause?*

---

1. **Aberdeen.** From eastern Scotland
2. **awl.** Pointed tool for making holes in leather, wood, etc.

the sailors called their own. Not even Captain Jaggery ventured there. No one had ever said I was *not* to go. But I assumed I would not be welcome.

With this <u>reservation</u> in mind I hurried to the galley in hopes of finding Zachariah. I would ask him to fetch the needle. The galley, however, was deserted.

Since I did not wish to disappoint Ewing, I decided I must go and fetch the needle myself. Timidly, I approached the forecastle door. As I did I heard muted voices from within. Indeed, it was only because they *were* vague and <u>indistinct</u> that I found myself straining to listen. And what I heard was this:

"... I say *I'll* be the one to give the word and none other."

"It had better be soon. Jaggery's pushing us hard."

"How many names do we have?"

"There's seven that's put down their mark. But there's others inclined."

"What about Johnson?"

"It doesn't look right. He's not got the spirit."

"It won't do. He needs to be with us or not. No halfway. And I don't like that girl always spying."

"Her being here isn't anyone's fault. We tried. You remind yourself—we kept those other passengers off."

I heard these words—spoken by at least four voices—but I did not at the moment fully grasp their meaning. Understanding would come later. Instead I was caught up in embarrassment that I should be eavesdropping where I hardly belonged. It was not a very ladylike thing to do. Yet I was—in part—the subject of their conversation.

And the errand was still to be done. Wanting to do what I'd promised, I knocked upon the door.

Sudden silence.

Then, "Who's there!"

"Miss Doyle, please."

Another pause. "What do you want?" came a demand.

"It's for Mr. Ewing," I returned. "He's sent me for a needle."

There was some muttering, swearing, then, "All right. A moment."

I heard rustling, the sound of people moving. Then the door was pushed open. Fisk looked out. He was a very large

▶ *What does Charlotte hear as she approaches the crew's quarters?*

| Words For Everyday Use | **res • er • va • tion** (rez ər vā´shən) *n.*, limiting condition or qualification |
| | **in • dis • tinct** (in di stiŋkt´) *adj.*, not seen or heard clearly |

man, lantern-jawed, his fists clenched more often than not as though perpetually prepared to brawl. "What do you say?" he demanded.

"Mr. Ewing wants a needle from his chest," I said meekly.

He glowered. "Come along then," he said, waving me in.

I stepped forward and looked about. The only light came from the open door, just enough for me to see that the low ceiling was <u>festooned</u> with dirty garments. I was <u>accosted</u> by a heavy stench of sweat and filth. Scraps of cheap pictures— some of a scandalous nature—were nailed here and there to the walls in aimless fashion. Cups, shoes, belaying pins, all lay jumbled in heaps. In the center of the floor was a trunk on which sat a crude checkerboard, itself partly covered with a sheet of paper. Along the walls hammocks were slung, but so low I could not see the faces of those in them. What I did see were the arms and legs of three men. They seemed to be asleep, though I knew that could not be true. I had heard more than one voice.

"Mr. Ewing's chest is there," Fisk said, gesturing to a corner with a thumb. He lumbered back to his hammock, sat in it and, though he said no more, watched me suspiciously.

The small wooden chest was tucked under one of the empty hammocks.

<u>Apprehensively</u>, I knelt, briefly turning to Fisk to make sure that this chest was indeed Ewing's.

He grunted an affirmation.

Then I turned back, drew the small trunk forward, and flipped open the top. The first thing that met my eyes was a *pistol*.

The sight of it was so startling that all I could do was stare. One thought filled my mind: Captain Jaggery had told me— bragged to me—that there were no firearms anywhere on board but in *his* cabinet.

My eyes shifted. I saw a piece of cork into which some needles were stuck. I pulled one out, and hastily shut the chest in hopes that no one else had seen what I had. Then I came to my feet, and turned to leave.

Fisk was looking hard at me. I forced myself to return his gaze, hoping I was not revealing anything of my feelings. Then I started out, but in my haste stumbled into the trunk in the center of the area. The sheet of paper fluttered to the

◀ How many people does Charlotte see?

◀ What does Charlotte see when she opens Ewing's trunk? Why is she surprised?

Words For Everyday Use

fes • toon (fes tōōn´) *vt.*, adorn or hang with items in a loop or curve

ac • cost (ə kôst´) *vt.*, greet in an unwelcome way

ap • pre • hen • sive • ly (ap rē hen´siv lē) *adv.*, fearfully, uneasily

► What does Charlotte see after stumbling into the trunk?

floor. Apologetic, I stooped to gather it and in a glance saw that on the paper two circles had been drawn, one inside the other. And there appeared to be names and marks written *between* the lines.

The instant I saw it I knew what it was. A round robin.

Clumsily, I pushed the paper away, murmured a "Thank you," then fled.

I was trembling when I left the forecastle. To make matters worse, the first person I saw was the second mate, Mr. Keetch, who was passing on his way to the galley. I stopped short, with what was, no doubt, a guilty cast to my face. Fortunately, he paid no attention to me, giving me hardly a look beyond his normal, nervous frown. Then he continued on. But though he was gone I simply stood there not knowing what to think or do. Unconsciously I clasped my hand, jabbing my palm with the needle.

Ever faithful to my sense of duty—even in that moment of crisis—I hurried to Ewing and gave the needle to him.

"Here, miss," he said, scrutinizing my face as he took it, "have you taken ill?"

"No, thank you," I whispered, attempting to avoid his look. "I am fine."

I fled hastily back to my cabin and secured the door behind me. Once alone I climbed atop my bed and flung myself down, then gave myself over entirely to the question of what I should do.

► What does Charlotte assume is happening?

You will understand that there was no doubt in my mind regarding *what* I had seen. There had been a pistol. There had been a *round robin*. With the warnings given to me by Captain Jaggery—and ever-mindful of the possibilities revealed to me by Zachariah—I had little doubt about the meaning of my discoveries. The crew was preparing a <u>rebellion</u>.

Regaining some degree of calmness I thought over who it was that had been in the forecastle. To begin with there was Fisk. He was part of Mr. Keetch's watch, so it was reasonable to assume that the other members of his watch were with him.

► Why is Charlotte confused?

There were, I knew, four men in that watch: Ewing, Morgan, Foley, and of course Fisk himself.

But as I reviewed these names my feelings of puzzlement

Words For Everyday Use

re • bel • lion (ri bel´yən) *n.*, defiance to authority

---

grew. What I had observed did not make sense. Then I grasped it. I had *seen* Fisk. It was he who had opened the forecastle door. And Ewing was on the forecastle *deck*. But when I stepped inside there had been *three* hammocks occupied with men. In short, I had seen a total of five men *off* watch. Assuming the other hammocks indeed held members of the watch, who then was the fifth man? Could it have been Mr. Keetch himself? No. I had seen him just *outside* the forecastle when I emerged. Nor could it have been someone who was *on* duty. The captain would never have tolerated that. Who then was that fifth man?

I began to wonder if I'd not been mistaken about the number, reminding myself that a hammock full of clothing would have looked much the same as one occupied by a man.

But the more I recollected what I'd seen—the weight of the hammocks, the dangling arms and legs—the more convinced I grew that I'd indeed seen *four* men.

Suddenly—like the crack of a wind-whipped sail—I recalled my dim vision when waiting to board the *Seahawk* the night of my arrival: of a man hauling himself up ropes to the ship. Of course! A *stowaway!*[3]

◀ *What does Charlotte suddenly realize? With what does she connect this realization?*

But where could such a man have hidden himself?

No sooner did I ask myself *that* than I remembered the face which had so frightened me in the top cargo when I'd gone for my clothing. It had been a face that I'd *not* recognized. Indeed, it was just that lack of recognition that convinced me I'd imagined it. In *fact*—I now realized—I must have seen the stowaway! No wonder I did not recognize him! He had been hiding in the hold, which explained Barlow's dire words about the place, as well as the grinning carving. The man sought to scare me from the place!

But having arrived at that conclusion I asked myself this: what was I to *do* with my discovery? To ask the question was to have the answer: Captain Jaggery. It was to him I owed my <u>allegiance</u>—by custom—by habit—by law. To him I *must* speak. And the truth was, in addition to everything else, I was now consumed by guilt—and terror—that I had *not* told

◀ *Why must Charlotte tell Captain Jaggery what she has seen?*

---

3. *stowaway.* Person who boards and hides on a ship without paying for passage

Words For Everyday Use

al • le • giance (ə lē´jəns) *n.,* obligation or loyalty to a leader or country

him before of the incident in the top cargo. So it was that by the time I had come full course in my thinking, I knew I mustn't wait a moment longer. I needed to get to Captain Jaggery.

Recollecting the time—three bells of the second dog watch—I knew that the captain would most likely be found by the helm.

Nervously, I emerged from my cabin and went onto the deck in search of him. The first man I saw was Morgan, leaning against the starboard rail. He was a <u>gangly</u>, long-limbed, muscular fellow, with a fierce mustache and long hair. As he was one of Mr. Keetch's watch—not currently on duty—he should have been among those in a forecastle hammock when I'd been there. I say he *should* have been because I had not seen his face. His presence was only a <u>surmise</u>.

But there he was, on deck. Brought to a dead stop I gazed dumbly at him; he in return gazed right at me. Surely, I thought, he was there to observe me.

► What sign does Morgan make?

For that long moment we stood looking at one another. I saw no emotion on his face, but what he did next left me with little doubt as to his real intentions. He lifted a hand, extended a stilettolike[4] forefinger, and drew it across his own neck as if *cutting* it.

A spasm of horror shot through me. He was—in the crudest way—warning me about what might happen to me if I took my discovery to the captain.

For a moment more I remained rooted to the spot. Then I turned to lean upon the portside topgallant rail and stared out over the ocean, trying to recover my breath.

When I had sufficiently steadied my nerves I turned back cautiously. Morgan was gone. But he had achieved his purpose. I was twice as frightened as I'd been when first I stepped upon the *Seahawk*.

Anxiously, I glanced about to see if I was being watched by anyone else. Sure enough, now it was Foley whom I spied atop the forecastle. He was busily splicing[5] a rope. At least that's what he seemed to be doing. The instant I saw him, he looked up and <u>pinioned</u> me with a gaze of <u>blatant</u> scrutiny.

---

4. **stilettolike.** Like a small, narrow dagger or other instrument
5. **splicing.** Join together

Words
For
Everyday
Use

gan • gly (gaŋ´lē) *adj.,* tall, thin, and awkward
sur • mise (sər mīz´) *n.,* guess
pin • ion (pin´yən) *vt.,* confine or shackle
bla • tant (blāt´'nt) *adj.,* glaringly conspicuous or obtrusive

Then, quickly, he shifted his eyes away. He too was spying on me.

Completely unnerved, I retreated to my cabin and bolted the door. The warnings had an effect quite opposite to what was doubtless intended. More terrified than ever, I now felt that the *only* person who could help me was Captain Jaggery. But so fearful was I of going on deck in search of him, I decided to wait in his cabin till he returned, certain that the crew would not dare to pursue me there.

◄ How does Charlotte react to the warning of Morgan and the spying of Foley?

Cautiously I pulled the door open again, poked my head out, and when I saw—to my relief—no one was nearby, I rushed to the captain's door and out of a habit of politeness, knocked.

To my indescribable relief I heard, "Come in."

I flung the door open. Captain Jaggery was looking over some charts. Mr. Hollybrass was at his side.

The captain turned about. "Miss Doyle," he said politely. "Is there something I can do for you?"

"Please, sir"—I was finding it difficult to breathe—"I should like a private word."

He looked at me quizzically. I had not come to him in agitation before. "Is it important?"

"I think so, sir . . ."

"Perhaps it can wait until . . ." No doubt it was the <u>distraught</u> expression on my face; he changed his mind. "Come in and shut the door," he said, his manner becoming alert.

Mr. Hollybrass made a move to go. The captain reached out to restrain him. "Do you have any objections to Mr. Hollybrass being here?" he asked.

◄ Who else is present when Charlotte tells the captain what she has seen?

"I don't know sir."

"Very well. He shall stay. There's no one I trust more. Now then, Miss Doyle, step forward and say what's troubling you."

I nodded, but could only gulp like a fish out of water.

"Miss Doyle, if you have something of importance to tell me, speak it."

I lifted my eyes. The captain was studying me with great intensity. In a flash I recollected a time when my much-loved brother broke a rare vase, and I, out of a high sense of duty told on him despite what I knew would be my father's certain fury.

Words For Everyday Use

dis • traught (di strôt´) *adj.*, extremely troubled

"I was fetching a needle for Mr. Ewing," I got out.

"A needle," he returned, somewhat deflated. Then he asked, "Where did you find it?"

"In the forecastle."

"The forecastle," he echoed, trying to prime my tongue. "Is it your habit to frequent that place, Miss Doyle?"

"Never before, sir."

"What happened when you went there?"

"I saw . . . I saw a pistol."

"Did you!"

I nodded.

"Where exactly?"

I glanced around. Mr. Hollybrass's normally red face had gone to the pallor of wet salt, whereas the captain was suddenly flushed with excitement.

"Must I say, sir?"

"Of course you must, Miss Doyle. *Where did you see the pistol?*"

"In . . . Mr. Ewing's . . . chest, sir."

"Mr. Ewing's chest," the captain repeated, exchanging a glance with the first mate as if to affirm something. Then the captain turned back to me. "Anything else?"

I bit my lip.

"There is more, isn't there?" he said.

"Yes, sir."

"Out with it!"

"I saw a . . ." I could not speak.

"A *what* Miss Doyle?"

"A . . . round robin."

Now it was the captain who gasped. "*A round robin!*" he exclaimed. "Are you quite sure?"

"Just as you showed me, sir. I'm certain of it."

"Describe it."

▶ What does the captain want to know about the round robin?

I did.

"And there were names written in, were there?"

"And marks. Yes, sir."

"How many?"

"I'm not certain. Perhaps five. Six."

"Six!" the captain shouted with a darting glance at Mr. Hollybrass. "A wonder it's not nine! Could you see whose names they were?"

"No, sir."

"I'm not certain I believe you," he snapped.

"It's true!" I cried and to prove my honesty I hurriedly gave him an account of my experiences in the top cargo as well as my conclusion that the ship carried a stowaway. By the time I was done he was <u>seething</u>.

"Why the devil did you not tell me before?" he demanded.

"I didn't trust my own senses, sir."

"After all I have done for . . . !" He failed to finish the sentence. Instead, he growled, "So be it," and said no more before turning from me and pacing away, leaving both Mr. Hollybrass and me to watch.

"Mr. Hollybrass," he said finally.

"Sir . . ."

"Call all hands."

"Sir, what do you intend to do?"

"I intend to crush this <u>mutiny</u> before it starts."

◄ Why is the captain angry at Charlotte?

◄ What does the captain intend to do?

Chapter Ten

► Where is the key
to the gun case
hidden?

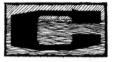aptain Jaggery strode across the room and from the wall removed the portrait of his daughter. Affixed to its back was a key. With this he unlocked the gun safe, and in a moment he and Mr. Hollybrass were by the door, ready. The captain held two muskets and had two pistols tucked into his belt. Mr. Hollybrass was similarly armed.

Terrified by the response my words had caused, I simply stood where I'd been. The captain would have none of that.

"Miss Doyle, you are to come with us."

"But . . . !"

"Do as I tell you!" he shouted. "There's no time for delay!" He flung one of his muskets to Mr. Hollybrass who miraculously caught it, then grabbed me by an arm and pulled me after him.

We ran out along the steerage into the waist of the ship, then quickly mounted to the quarterdeck. Only then did the captain let me go. He now grasped the bell clapper and began to pull wildly, as though announcing a fire, while shouting, "All hands! All hands!"

That done, he held his hand out to Mr. Hollybrass, who returned the extra musket to him.

► How does
Charlotte feel as the
captain calls all
hands to the deck?

► What does
Charlotte realize?

I looked about not knowing what to expect, save that I truly feared for my life.

Then I realized that the ship appeared to be completely unmanned. Not a sailor was to be seen anywhere, aloft or on deck. The sails hung like dead cloth, the wheel was abandoned, the rigging rattled with eerie <u>irrelevance</u>. The *Seahawk* was adrift.

The first person to appear below us was Mr. Keetch. Within seconds of the bell sounding he came bolting from below, took one look at the captain and Mr. Hollybrass armed above him and stopped short, then turned as if expecting to see others. He was alone.

"Mr. Keetch!" the captain cried out to him. "Where do you stand?"

The second mate turned back to the captain, a look of panicky confusion upon his face. But before he could

---

**Words
For
Everyday
Use**   **ir • rel • e • vance** (ir rel´ə vəns) *n.*, uselessness

respond or act on the captain's question the rest of the crew burst from beneath the forecastle deck with wild, blood-curdling yells.

The crew's first appearance was fierce enough, though almost grotesquely comical, the nine of them looking like so many beggars. When I'd seen them on the day we went to sea they seemed unkempt. Now they looked <u>destitute</u>, their clothing torn and dirty, their faces unshaved, their expressions contorted with fear and fury. Of the nine only Zachariah was not armed. The rest were. Some carried pistols. I recall two having swords. Dillingham had an ancient cutlass in hand, Barlow a knife.

◄ How does the crew look when they finally appear?

Hardly had they flown out upon the deck than they perceived the captain standing on the quarterdeck, one musket pointing directly at them, the other leaning against the rail within easy reach. They stopped frozen.

If they had rushed forward, they might have overwhelmed the three of us. But it was now Captain Jaggery—and the muskets—that held them in check.

With a start I realized there was a tenth man standing below us. He was muscular and stocky, with a red kerchief tied around his neck and a sword in his hand. As I looked at him in astonishment I saw that he had but one arm.

◄ What does Charlotte realize about the tenth man?

I recalled Zachariah's tale of the sailor the captain had so severely punished—the man whose arm was so beaten it had to be amputated. Standing before us was Cranick himself! It was his face I had seen in the top cargo! *The stowaway!*

I gasped.

Captain Jaggery stepped swiftly to the rail and spoke.

"Ah, it is Mr. Cranick!" he said boldly, holding his musket aimed directly at the man's burly chest. "I wondered where you'd gone. Not to hell as I'd hoped—but here. May I," he went on with heavy sarcasm, "be the last to welcome you aboard the *Seahawk*."

The man took a shuffled step forward. He was clearly the crew's leader. "Mr. Jaggery," he began—pointedly declining to say "Captain"—"I said we would be revenged upon you, did I not?"

"I heard your usual brag, Mr. Cranick, if that's what you mean," the captain replied, "but I paid no more mind to it then than I do now."

Words For Everyday Use

des • ti • tute (des´tə to͞ot) *adj.*, abandoned, forsakened, poverty-stricken

► What does Cranick declare to the captain?

At that Cranick lifted his one hand and, still managing to hold the sword, savagely pulled a paper from where it had been tucked into his trousers. He held the paper up.

"Mr. Jaggery," he called, his voice ragged, "we've got a round robin here, which declares you unfit to be captain of the *Seahawk*."

There were murmurs of agreement from behind him.

"And what do you intend to do with it, Mr. Cranick?" the captain retorted. "I should think even you, in your mongrel[1] ignorance, would know the days of piracy are long gone. Or do you have that much desire to bring back the practice of hanging in chains, of letting men rot so that crows might peck upon their putrid eyes?"

► According to Cranick, what is the crew seeking?

"No piracy for us, Mr. Jaggery," Cranick replied with a vigorous shake of his head. "Only justice. We could not get it on land. We shall have it at sea."

"Justice, say you! Under whose authority?" the captain demanded.

"All of us! Our authority!" Cranick cried and made a half turn to the men behind him. There were murmurs and nods of approval.

"And what kind of justice do you offer?" the captain asked. "Nothing precisely legal, I presume."

"We demand you stand before us in a trial of your peers," Cranick answered.

"Trial! Peers!" the captain cried mockingly. "I see nothing but <u>ruffians</u> and villains, the scum of the sea!"

"Then we proclaim ourselves your peers," Cranick cried. With that he flung down the paper and took another step forward. "You can have anyone you want defend you," he persisted. "Have that girl, if you like. She seems to be your eyes and ears. Let her be your mouth too."

► What does Captain Jaggery do as Cranick steps forward?

It was at that exact moment that Captain Jaggery fired his musket. The roar was <u>stupendous</u>. The ball struck Cranick square in the chest. With a cry of pain and mortal shock he dropped his sword and stumbled backward into the crowd. They were too stunned to catch him, but instead leaped back so that Cranick fell to the deck with a sickening thud. He

---

1. **mongrel.** Mixed breed

Words For Everyday Use	ruf • fi • an (ruf´ē ən) *n.*, hoodlum, lawless person
	stu • pen • dous (stoo pen´dəs) *adj.*, overwhelming

began to groan and thrash about in dreadful agony, blood pulsing from his chest and mouth in ghastly gushes.

I screamed. Mr. Hollybrass moaned. In horror, the crew retreated further. Captain Jaggery hastily dropped his spent musket, picked up the second, and aimed it into their midst.

"Who shall be next!" he screamed at them.

To a man, they looked up with burning, terrified eyes.

"Let Cranick lie there!" the captain continued to shout. "Anyone who moves forward shall receive the same!"

The crew began to edge further away.

"Leave your guns and swords," the captain shouted. "Quickly now! I'll fire upon the first who doesn't."

Pistols, swords, and knives dropped in a clatter.

"Mr. Hollybrass! Collect them!"

The first mate scurried down the steps and, while glancing upward, began to gather the weapons. It was clear he feared the captain more than the crew.

"Their round robin too!" the captain called to him.

Too shocked to speak, I could only watch and feel enormous pain.

Cranick had stopped moving. The only sign of life in him were the small pink bubbles of blood that frothed upon his lips.

It was then that I saw Zachariah slip from the frozen tableau and move toward the fallen man. He held his hands before him, waist high, palms up, as if to prove he carried no weapon. He kept his eyes on the captain.

◄ Who stepped forward despite the captain's orders?

"Let him be, Mr. Zachariah," the captain barked. "He's a stowaway. He has no claim to any care."

The old man paused. "As a man," he said in a voice wonderfully calm midst the chaos, "he claims our mercy."

The captain lifted his musket. "No," he said firmly.

◄ Why according to the captain does Cranick deserve no care? Why according to Zachariah does he deserve mercy?

Zachariah looked at him, then at Cranick. I may have imagined it but I believe he may even have looked at me. In any case he continued on with slow, deliberate steps toward the fallen man.

I watched, terrified but fascinated, certain that the angry captain would shoot. I saw his finger on the trigger tighten, but then . . . he relaxed.

Zachariah knelt by Cranick and put his hand to the man's wrist. He let it fall. "Mr. Cranick is no more," he announced.

The stillness that followed these words was broken only by the soft, sudden flutter of a sail, the tinkling toll of a chain.

"Get him over," the captain said finally.

No one moved.

► Why does Zachariah again disobey the captain's orders?

"Mr. Zachariah," the captain repeated with impatience. "Get him over."

Once again Zachariah held out his open hands. "Begging the captain's pardon," he said. "Even a poor sinner such as he should have his Christian service."[2]

"Mr. Hollybrass," the captain barked.

The first mate, having unloaded the crew's pistols, had returned to the quarterdeck. "Sir?" he said.

"I want that dog's carcass thrown over."

"Cannot Mr. Zachariah say a few words—"

"Mr. Hollybrass, do as you're ordered!"

The man looked from the captain to the crew. "Aye,[3] aye, sir," he said softly. Then slowly, as if a great weight had been cast upon him, he descended to the deck. Taking hold of the fallen man by his one arm, he began to drag him toward the rail. In his wake he left a trail of blood.

"Mr. Zachariah!" the captain thundered. "Open the gate."

Zachariah gazed at the captain. Slowly he shook his head.

For a moment the two merely looked at one another. Then the captain turned to me.

"Miss Doyle, open the gate."

I stared at him in shocked disbelief.

"Miss Doyle!" he now screamed in a <u>livid</u> rage.

"Sir . . ." I stammered.

"Open the gate!"

"I . . . can't . . ."

Abruptly, the captain himself marched down the steps, pistols in hand. When he approached the railing he tucked one gun under his arm and quickly unlatched the gate so that it stood gaping above the sea.

"Mr. Hollybrass," he snapped.

Mr. Hollybrass, sweat running down his hot, red face, pulled the body close but then he paused and offered a look of appeal to Captain Jaggery.

The captain spat at Cranick's body. "Over!" he insisted.

The first mate pushed the body through the gate opening. There was a splash. My stomach turned. I saw some of the sailors wince.

---

2. **Christian service.** Religious service for a funeral
3. **Aye.** Yes

Words For Everyday Use

liv • id (liv´id) *adj.*, extremely angry

The captain spoke again. "Mr. Cranick was not a part of this ship, " he said. "His coming and going have nothing to do with us. They shall not even be entered in the log.

"Beyond all that you should know you are a very poor set of curs.[4] It took only this girl"—he nodded up to me—"to unmask you."

Sullen eyes turned toward me. Ashamed, I looked away, trying to stifle my tears.

"As for the rest," the captain continued, "I ask only that one of you—your second in command if you have one—come forward and take his punishment. Then the voyage shall go on as before. Who shall it be?"

When no one spoke, the captain turned to me. "Miss Doyle, as our lady, I'll give you the privilege. Which one of these men shall you choose?"

I gazed at him in horrified astonishment.

"Yes, you! Since it was you who uncovered this <u>despicable</u> plot, I give you the honor of ending it. Whom shall you pick to set an example?"

I could only shake my head.

"Come, come. Not so shy. You must have some favorite."

"Please, sir," I whispered. I gazed down on the crew, looking now like so many broken animals. "I don't want . . . "

"If you are too soft, I shall choose."

"Captain Jaggery . . . " I attempted to plead.

He <u>contemplated</u> the men. Then he said, "Mr. Zachariah, step forward."

◄ Why is Cranick's passing unimportant?

◄ What does the captain ask Charlotte to do?

◄ Whom does the captain choose to punish?

---

4. **curs.** Dogs

Words For Everyday Use	**des • pi • ca • ble** (des´pi kə bəl) *adj.,* deserving to be despised, not worthy of respect
	con • tem • plate (kän´təm plāt) *vt.,* look at intently

Chapter Eleven

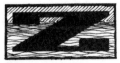achariah did not so much step forward as those about him shrank away. He stood there as alone as if he'd been <u>marooned</u> upon a Pacific isle. Though he did not lift his eyes he seemed nonetheless to sense his abandonment. Small, wrinkled man that he was, he appeared to have grown smaller.

"Mr. Zachariah," the captain said. "Do you have anything to say?"

Zachariah remained silent.

▶ Why does the captain say Zachariah had better speak for himself?

"You had best speak for yourself," the captain taunted. "I doubt your friends will say a word in your defense. They are all cowards." He paused as if waiting for someone to challenge him. When no one spoke, he nodded and said, "So much for your shipmates, Mr. Zachariah. So much for your round robin. Now, sir, I ask you again, have you anything to say on your own behalf?"

At first Zachariah stared dead ahead; then he shifted his gaze slightly. I was certain he was looking right at me now.

I tried to turn away but couldn't. Instead, I stood gazing at him, eyes flooded with tears. Zachariah began to speak. "I . . . I have . . . been a sailor for more than forty years," he said slowly. "There . . . have been hard captains and easy ones. But you, sir, have . . . have been the worst.

▶ What does Zachariah say about Captain Jaggery?

"No, I'll not regret rising against you," he continued in his halting way. "I can only wish I'd acted sooner. I forgive the girl. You used her. She did not know better. I forgive my mates too. They know where Captain Jaggery takes command . . . no . . . god signs on."

"A pretty speech," the captain said scornfully. "And as much a confession as anything I have ever heard. You may all note it in case anyone bothers to ask questions, though I shouldn't think anyone will care." He looked contemptuously over the rest of the crew. "*Is* there any jack among you that will second this black man's slanders?"

No one spoke.

"Come now!" he baited them. "Who will be bold enough to say that Captain Andrew Jaggery is the worst master he's

---

Words For Everyday Use

ma • roon (mə rō̄on´) *vt.*, stranded in a desolate place ever served. Speak up! I'll double the pay of the man who says yea!"

Though the glitter of hatred in their eyes was <u>palpable</u> enough, no one dared give voice to it. The captain had them that much <u>cowed</u>.

"Very well," he said. "Mr. Hollybrass, string Mr. Zachariah up."

The first mate hesitated.

"Mr. Hollybrass!"

"Aye, aye, sir," the man mumbled. With a kind of shuffle he approached Zachariah, but then stood before the old man as if nerving himself. Finally he reached out. Zachariah stepped back but it was of no avail. The first mate caught him by the arm and led him back up the steps.

As I looked on, aware only that something terrible was about to happen, Mr. Hollybrass set Zachariah against the outer rail and stripped him of his jacket. The skin of the old man's chest hung loose and wrinkled like a ragged burlap bag.

Mr. Hollybrass turned Zachariah so that he faced into the shrouds, then climbed up into these shrouds and with a piece of rope bound his hands, pulling him so that the old man was all but hanging from his wrists, just supporting himself on the tips of his bare toes.

Zachariah uttered no sound.

I turned to look at Captain Jaggery. Only then did I see that he had a whip in his hands, its four strands twitching like the tail of an angry cat. Where he got it I don't know.

Feeling ill, I made to leave the deck.

"Miss Doyle!" the captain cried out. "You will remain."

I stopped dead.

"You are needed as witness," he informed me.

Now the captain held the whip out to his first mate. "Mr. Hollybrass," he said, "he's to have fifty lashes."

Again Hollybrass hesitated, eyebrows arched in question. "Captain," he said, "fifty lashes seem—"

"Fifty," the captain insisted. "Start!"

Hollybrass grasped the whip. As he took his time squaring away behind Zachariah, I could see his hand flex nervously, his temples pulse.

"Quickly!" the captain demanded.

◀ How does the crew feel about Captain Jaggery?

◀ What does the captain order Mr. Hollybrass to do to Zachariah? How does Mr. Hollybrass approach his task?

◀ Why does Captain Jaggery insist that Charlotte stay on deck?

◀ What does Mr. Hollybrass think of the captain's orders?

Words For Everyday Use	**pal • pa • ble** (pal´pǝ bǝl) *adj.*, tangible, perceived by the senses **cow** (kou) *vt.*, intimidate, make submissive

Hollybrass lifted his arm and cocked it. Once more he paused, took a deep breath, until, with what appeared to be the merest flick of his wrist, the whip shot forward; its tails hissed through the air and spat against Zachariah's back. The moment they touched the old man's skin four red welts appeared.

I felt I would faint.

"With *strength*, Mr. Hollybrass," the captain urged. "With *strength!*"

Hollybrass cocked his arm. Again the wrist twisted.

The whip struck. Zachariah's body gave a jerk. Four new red welt lines crossed the first.

"Captain Jaggery!" I cried out suddenly, as much surprised as anyone that I was doing so.

The captain, startled, turned to look at me.

"Please, sir," I pleaded. "You mustn't."

For a moment the captain said nothing. His face had become very white. "Why *mustn't* I?" he asked.

"It's . . . it's not . . . fair," I <u>stammered</u>.

"*Fair?*" he echoed, his voice thick with <u>derision</u>. "Fair? These men meant to murder me and no doubt you, Miss Doyle, and you talk of *fair?* If it's fairness you want, I could quote you chapter and line of the admiralty codes that say I'd serve justice best by shooting the cur."

"Please, sir," I said, tears running down my cheeks. "I shouldn't have told you. I didn't know. I'm sure Mr. Zachariah meant no harm. I'm sure he didn't."

"No harm, Miss Doyle?" The captain held up the round robin. "Surely they teach you better logic than that in school."

"But I had no idea that . . ."

"Of course you had an idea!" the captain snapped, his voice rising so all could hear. "You came to me in shock and terror to inform me about what you'd seen. How right you were to do so. And right is what we do here. Proper order will be maintained."

He swung about. "Mr. Hollybrass, you have given but two lashes. If you can do no better you'd best stand aside for someone who has the <u>gumption</u>."

Sighing, but summoning up his strength, Hollybrass

▶ What reason does Charlotte give Captain Jaggery to try to make him stop? How does she feel about informing him of the crew's plan?

Words For Everyday Use

stam • mer (stam´ər) *vi.*, speak with pauses

de • ri • sion (di rizh´ən) *n.*, contempt or ridicule

gump • tion (gump´shən) *n.*, courage and initiative

struck once more. Zachariah was no longer standing on his toes. He was simply hanging.

Again the whip lashed. That time the old man moaned.

I could bear it no longer. In a surge of tears and agonized guilt, I hurled myself at Hollybrass, who, hardly expecting an attack, twisted, then tumbled to the deck. I fell with him.

In the scramble I managed to snatch hold of the whip handle and leap to my feet. I was trying to throw it overboard.

◀ What does Charlotte try to do with the whip?

But Captain Jaggery was too quick. With a snarl he grabbed hold of me. Frantic, I slipped out of his grasp and stood facing him, panting, weeping, gripping the whip handle hard. "You mustn't," I kept saying, "You mustn't!"

"Give me that!" the captain cried, advancing upon me again, his face blazing. "Give it!"

"You mustn't," I kept repeating, "You mustn't!"

He took another step toward me. I'd wedged myself against the outward rail. In a gesture of defense I pulled up my arm, and so doing flicked the whip through the air, inflicting a cut across the captain's face.

◀ What does Charlotte do by mistake?

For an instant a red welt marked him from his left cheek to his right ear. Blood began to ooze.

I stood utterly astonished by what I'd done.

The captain remained motionless too, his face transfigured by surprise and pain. Slowly he lifted a hand to his cheek, touched it delicately, then examined his fingertips. When he saw they were bloody he swore a savage oath, jumped forward and tore the whip from my hand, whirled about and began beating Zachariah with such fury as I had never seen. Finally, spent, he flung the whip down and marched from the deck.

Mr. Hollybrass, his face ashen, swallowed hard and murmured, "All hands resume your stations." Groaning, he bent to gather up the guns and other weapons and followed after the captain.

For a moment no one did or said anything. Perhaps they had not heard the first mate. It was Fisk who broke the spell. "Cut him down!" I heard him cry.

◀ What does the crew do when told to return to their stations?

Ewing hurried forward and climbed into the shrouds. In moments Zachariah's scarred and bloodied body dropped to the deck.

Keetch knelt over the fallen man while the others, standing in a close circle, looked down in terrible silence. I could see nothing of what was happening. Instead I waited alone, trembling, trying to absorb all that I had seen and done.

But as I watched from outside their circle I felt myself grow sicker and sicker until, clutching my stomach I turned and vomited into the sea.

Shaken, weak with tears, I looked back to the sailors. They had picked Zachariah up and were carrying him toward the forecastle.

I had been left alone.

▶ *How is Charlotte left?*

Chapter Twelve

 obbing in absolute misery, I threw myself onto my bed. I wept for Zachariah, for Cranick, even for Captain Jaggery. But most of all I wept for myself. There was no way to avoid the truth that all the horror I'd witnessed had been brought about by me.

◀ Why is Charlotte weeping for herself?

As the ghastly scenes repeated themselves in my mind, I realized too that there was no way of denying what the captain had done. Captain Jaggery, my friend, my guardian—my father's employee—had been unspeakably cruel. Not only had he killed Cranick—who was, I knew, threatening him— he had clearly meant to kill Zachariah for no reason other than that he was helpless! He singled him out *because* he was the oldest and weakest. Or was it because he was black? Or was it, I asked myself suddenly, because he was *my* friend?

◀ Why might Captain Jaggery have singled out Zachariah?

Just the thought made me shiver <u>convulsively</u>. Tears of regret and guilt redoubled.

My weeping lasted for the better part of an hour. Aside from reliving the fearsome events, I was trying desperately to decide what to *do*. As I grasped the situation, the crew would have nothing but loathing for me who had so betrayed them. And they were right. After their kindliness and acceptance I *had* betrayed them.

◀ Why might both the crew and the captain have turned against Charlotte?

And Captain Jaggery? Without intending to hadn't I done *him* a great wrong when I'd cut his face—<u>albeit</u> unintentionally—with the whip? Could he, would he, forgive me?

Beyond all else I had been educated to the belief that when I was wrong—and how often had my patient father found me at fault—it was *my* responsibility—mine alone—to admit *my* fault and make amends.

Gradually then, I came to believe that no matter how distasteful, I must beg the captain's forgiveness. And the sooner I did so, the better.

With this in mind I rose up, brushed my hair, washed my face, smoothed my dress, rubbed my shoes. Then, as ready as I could ever hope to be under the circumstances, I went to his cabin door and knocked timidly.

Words For Everyday Use

con • vul • sive • ly (kən vul′siv lē) *adv.,* shake involuntarily
al • be • it (ôl bē′it) *conj.,* even though

There was no answer. Again I knocked, perhaps a little more boldly.

This time I heard, "Who is it?"

"Charlotte Doyle, sir."

▶ How does this greeting differ from the greeting Charlotte has come to expect from Captain Jaggery?

My words were met by an <u>ominous</u> silence. But after a while he said, "What do you want?"

"Please, sir. I beg you let me speak with you."

When silence was again the response, I nearly accepted defeat and went away. But at last I heard steps within. Then came the word "Enter."

I opened the door and looked in. Captain Jaggery was standing with his back to me. I remained at the threshold waiting for him to invite me to proceed further. He neither moved nor spoke.

"Sir?" I tried.

"What?"

"I . . . I did not mean . . ."

"You did not mean *what?*"

"I did not mean to . . . interfere," I managed to say, now meekly advancing toward him. "I was so frightened . . . I didn't know . . . I had no intention . . ." When the captain maintained his silence I faltered. But gathering up my strength again, I stammered, "And when I had the whip . . ."

Suddenly I realized he was about to turn. My words died on my lips.

▶ Why does Charlotte shudder? What has she done?

He did turn. And I saw him. The welt I'd made across his face was a red open wound. But it was his eyes that made me shudder. They expressed nothing so much as <u>implacable</u> hatred. And it was all directed at me.

"Sir . . ." I tried, "I did not mean . . ."

"Do you know what you have done?" he said, his voice a hiss.

"Sir . . ."

"*Do you know!*" he now roared.

My tears began to flow anew. "I didn't mean to, sir," I pleaded. "I didn't. Believe me."

"You insulted me before my crew as no man should ever be insulted."

"But . . ."

"Insulted by a sniffling, self-centered, ugly, contemptible girl," he spat out, "who deserves a horsewhipping!"

| Words For Everyday Use | om • i • nous (ăm´ə nəs) *adj.*, threatening |
| | im • pla • ca • ble (im plā´kə bəl) *adj.*, cannot be appeased, relentless |

I sank to my knees, hands in prayerlike <u>supplication</u>.

"Let *them* take care of you," he snarled. "In any way they want. I withdraw my protection. Do you understand? I want nothing to do with you. *Nothing!*"

"Sir . . ."

"And don't you dare presume to come to my cabin again," he shouted. "*Ever!*"

I began to weep uncontrollably.

"Get out!" he raged. "Get out!" He made a move toward me.

In great fright I jumped up—tearing the hem of my dress—and fled back to my cabin. But if the truth be known—and I swore when I began to set down this tale that I would tell only the truth—even at that moment all my thoughts were of finding some way to <u>appease</u> the captain and regain his favor. If I could have found a way to gain his forgiveness—no matter what it took—I would have seized the opportunity.

This time I did not cry. I was too numb, too much in a state of shock. Instead, I simply stood immobile—rather like the moment when I'd first cast eyes upon the *Seahawk*—trying confusedly to think out what I could do.

I tried, *desperately,* to imagine what my father, even what my mother or Miss Weed, might want me to do, but I could find no answer.

In search of a solution I finally stepped in dread out of the cabin and made my way to the deck. I told myself that what I wanted, needed, was fresh air. In fact, I was motivated by a need to know how the crew would receive me.

The ship was still adrift. No wind had caught our sails. The decks once more appeared deserted. My first thought was that the crew had fled! All I heard was the soft flutter of canvas, the clinking of chain, the heaving of boat timbers. It was as if the engines of the world itself had ground to a halt.

But when I looked to the quarterdeck I did see the crew. Heads bowed, they were standing together quietly. Then I heard the deep voice of Fisk, though exactly what he was saying I could not at first make out.

Hollybrass, I saw, was standing somewhat apart from the men, his dark eyes watching intently. There was a pistol in his hand but in no way was he interfering with them.

◀ What does the captain say before throwing Charlotte out?

◀ What would Charlotte give anything to do?

◀ How does Charlotte try to find a solution to her problem?

◀ Is Hollybrass participating in the crew's activity?

► What does
Charlotte realize
about the hammock
she sees?

Timidly, I climbed the steps to the quarterdeck for a better look. Now I realized that the crew was clustered around something—it looked to be a sack—that lay upon the deck. On closer examination I realized it was a canvas hammock such as the men slept in. This one was twisted around itself and had an odd, bulky shape.

No one took notice of me as I stood by the forward rail. Gradually I perceived that Fisk was saying a prayer. In a flash I understood: the hammock was wrapped about a body. And that body had to be Zachariah's. He had died of the beating. I had come upon his funeral. The men were about to commit his body to the sea.

Fisk's prayer was not a long one, but he delivered it slowly, and what I heard of it was laced with bitterness, a calling on God to avenge them as they, poor sailors, could not avenge themselves.

When Fisk had done, Ewing, Mr. Keetch, Grimes, and Johnson bent over and picked the hammock up. Hardly straining at the weight they bore, they advanced to the starboard railing, and then, emitting a kind of grunt in unison, they heaved their burden over. Seconds later there was a splash followed by murmurs of "amen . . . amen."

I shuddered.

Fisk said a final short prayer. At last they all turned about—and saw me.

I was unable to move. They were staring at me with what I could only take as loathing.

"I . . . I am sorry," was the best I could stammer. No one replied. The words drifted into the air and died.

"I didn't realize . . ." I started to say, but could not finish. Tears were streaming from my eyes. I bowed my head and began to sob.

Then I heard, "Miss Doyle . . ."

I continued to cry.

"Miss Doyle," came the words again.

► What does Fisk tell
Charlotte to do?

I forced myself to look up. It was Fisk, his countenance more fierce than usual. "Go to the captain," he said brusquely. "He is your friend."

"He's not!" I got out between my sniffling. "I want nothing to do with him! I hate him!"

Fisk lifted a fist, but let it drop with weariness.

Words For Everyday Use	e • mit (ē mit´) vt., send out, give off

"And I want to help *you*," I offered. "To show how sorry I am."

They merely stared.

"Please . . ." I looked from him to the others. I saw no softening.

Brokenhearted, I groped my way down to my cabin, pausing only to look upon the captain's closed door.

Once alone I again gave way to hot tears. Not only did I feel completely isolated, but something worse: I was certain that all the terrible events of the day—the death of two men!—had been caused by *me*. Though I could find a reason for Cranick's death, I could hardly blame anyone but myself for the murder of Zachariah! It was I—despite clear warnings—who had refused to see Captain Jaggery as the villainous man he was, I who had fired his terrible wrath by reporting to him Ewing's pistol, the round robin, and the stowaway.

◄ Why does Charlotte believe she is responsible for the deaths of two men?

Yet my new found knowledge brought me no help with my need to *do* something.

I was still in my bed—it might have been an hour when I heard the ship's bell begin to clang. Then came a cry from Mr. Hollybrass. "All hands! All hands!"

I sat up and listened. My first thought was that perhaps a wind had risen, that this was a call to trim the ship. Yet I heard none of the welcome sounds—the breaking waves, the hum of wind in the sails—that would have come with a weather change.

◄ Why does Charlotte think the bell might have been rung?

Then I thought that some new fearfulness was upon us. Alarmed—but unable to keep myself from curiosity—I slipped from my bed and cautiously opened my door.

Once again I heard the bell clanging, and the cry, "All hands! All hands!"

Increasingly apprehensive, I stole into the steerage, then poked my head out so I could see the deck. The crew stood in the waist of the ship, looking up.

I crept forward.

Captain Jaggery was clutching the quarterdeck rail so tightly his knuckles were white. The welt across his face had turned crimson. It caused me pain just to see it.

Mr. Hollybrass was by his side.

". . . meant what I said," I heard the captain say.

"Through your own folly you've lost Zachariah," he continued. "Not that he did much work. Not that any of you do. Mr. Fisk will assume Zachariah's duties in the galley. As for Mr. Keetch, since he seems to prefer serving you rather than me . . . I place him in the forecastle where he will be more comfortable. The position of second mate, thus vacated, I

◄ What new positions have been assigned?

give to Mr. Johnson. He, at least, had the dog's wit not to sign your round robin. Mr. Johnson's position on his watch . . . you *all* will be responsible for that. I don't care how you do it, but each watch shall be filled with a full complement[1] of four plus mate."

These words—the last of which I did not understand—were met at first by stony silence.

It was a moment or two later that Morgan stepped forward. "Request permission to speak, sir." I think I had never before heard his voice.

The captain turned slightly, <u>glowered</u> at the man, but nodded.

▶ *Why can't the captain require the men to work more than one watch? Why does Captain Jaggery say he can under the circumstances?*

"Captain Jaggery, sir," Morgan called out. "Nowhere is it written that a captain can require a man to work more than one watch. Only in an emergency."

The captain gazed at Morgan for a moment. Then he said, "Very well Mr. Morgan, then I do say it: *this is an emergency.* If these orders cause inconvenience, blame it on your darling Mr. Cranick. Or the impertinence of Mr. Zachariah. And if you still have so much pity on these fools, you can work the extra shift yourself."

So saying, he turned to Mr. Hollybrass. "Set the second watch to scrape the bow until a wind comes up. Dismiss the rest," he barked.

Mr. Hollybrass turned to the crew, and repeated the captain's commands.

Without a word, the men backed off, some shuffling to the bow to work, the others ducking below into the forecastle. All that remained on deck was the stain of Cranick's blood.

Uncertainly, I made my way to the galley. Fisk was already there, his great bulk filling the small space as Zachariah never had. I stood just beyond the entryway hoping he would notice me. When he didn't I whispered, "Mr. Fisk . . ."

He turned but offered nothing more than a hostile glare.

"What did the captain mean?" I asked, my voice small.

Fisk continued to stare bleakly at me.

"Tell me," I pleaded. "I have to know."

"The crew was short to begin with," he said. "Now he's

---

1. **complement.** Full crew

Words For Everyday Use	**glow • er** (glou´ər) *vt.*, scowl angrily

insulted me. Advanced Johnson. Dumped Keetch. All in all it leaves us shorter than before. The captain intends to work us till we drop."

"Can I . . . can I help in any way?"

"*You?*" Fisk said with <u>incredulous</u> scorn. He turned away.

"Mr. Fisk, you must believe me. I want to help."

"You are the lady passenger, Miss Doyle. The informer."

My tears began to fall again. "I had no idea . . ."

Now angry, he swung about. "I find Miss Doyle mistaken. You *did* have an idea. You had it from Zachariah. I know you did. He told us he tried to convince you. 'Oh, Miss Doyle believes in honor,' he'd say. 'She's the very soul of justice!'" Fisk spat on the floor. "Honor! What you mean to say, Miss Doyle, is that you didn't choose to heed his words because Zachariah was an old black who lacked the captain's graces!"

I bowed my head.

"Can you cook?" he growled. "Reef sails? Turn the wheel? I think not, miss. So you'd do best keeping the place you have. When you reach Providence you can walk off free and, I warrant, you'll think no more on us."

"That's not true!"

"Go to the captain, Miss Doyle. He's your darling master."

"Mr. Fisk," I begged, my voice as small as my pride, "the captain will have nothing to do with me."

"No, he'll not forgive you so soon. Beware your friend, Miss Doyle, beware him!"

"I didn't mean—"

He cut me off abruptly. "Gentlefolk like you never *mean*, Miss Doyle. But what you *do* . . ."

I could not bear it anymore. I retreated to my cabin. Once again I gave myself up to guilt and remorse.

That night I remained in my cabin. I couldn't eat. Now and again I slept, but never for long. There were times I fell on my knees to pray for forgiveness. But it was from the crew as much as God that I sought pardon. If only I could make <u>restitution</u>, if only I could convince the men that I accepted my responsibility.

Close to dawn an idea began to form, at first only an echo of something Fisk had said. But the mere thought of it was <u>appalling</u> and I kept pushing it away. Yet again and again it flooded back, overwhelming all other notions.

◄ *What does the captain intend to do? What does Charlotte offer?*

◄ *Why does Fisk claim that Charlotte did have an idea of what she was doing?*

◄ *Whose pardon does Charlotte now seek?*

Words For Everyday Use	**in • cred • u • lous** (in krej´oo ləs) *adj.*, skeptical, unable to believe **res • ti • tu • tion** (res tə too´shən) *n.*, giving back to rightful owner; reimbursement	**ap • pall • ing** (ə pôl´iŋ) *adj.*, horrifying, causing dismay

At last I heaved myself off the bed, and from under it brought out the canvas seaman's garments Zachariah had made for me. Some roaches skittered away. I held the wrinkled clothing up and looked at its crude shape, its mean design. The feel of the crude cloth made me falter.

I closed my eyes. My heart was beating painfully as if I were in some great danger. No, I could not. It was too awful. Yet I told myself I *must* accept my responsibility so as to prove to those men that it had been my head that was wrong, not my heart. Slowly, fearfully, I made myself take off my shoes, my stockings, my apron, at last my dress and linen.

▶ Why does Charlotte choose to use Zachariah's gift? What does she intend to do?

With fumbling, nervous hands I put on the seaman's clothing. The trousers and shirt felt stiff, heavy, like some skin not my own. My bare toes curled upon the wooden floor.

I stood some while to question my heart. Zachariah's words to Fisk, that I was the "very soul of justice" echoed within me.

I stepped out of my cabin and crept through the steerage. It was dawn. To the distant east, I could see the thinnest edge of sun. All else remained dark. I moved to the galley, praying I would meet no one before I reached it. For once my prayers were answered. I was not noticed. And Fisk was working at the stove.

I paused at the doorway. "Mr. Fisk," I whispered.

He straightened up, turned, saw me. I had, at least, the satisfaction of his surprise.

"I've come," I managed to say, "to be one of the crew."

Responding to the Selection

Imagine you are one of the crew. How would you react to Charlotte's offer? What reasons would you give for accepting or rejecting her plan?

Investigate, Inquire, and Imagine

Recall: GATHERING FACTS

1a. How did the crew treat Charlotte at first? What role does she take on as she becomes more comfortable with them? What gift does Zachariah give her that demonstrates the crew's changing feelings toward her?

2a. When Charlotte visits the crew's quarters, what two things does she see that alarm her? What puzzles her?

3a. How does Captain Jaggery stop the uprising? What does Charlotte do accidentally to Captain Jaggery?

Interpret: FINDING MEANING

1b. Why do the feelings of the crew toward Charlotte change? Why does Charlotte begin to develop friendships with the crew that she never would have developed on land?

2b. Have Charlotte's feelings toward the crew changed again when she tells Captain Jaggery about what she has seen? Explain.

3b. What does Charlotte think of Captain Jaggery's actions? How does she feel about her decision to tell Captain Jaggery what she saw?

Analyze: TAKING THINGS APART

4a. Identify examples of Charlotte's changing opinion of Captain Jaggery. Compare and contrast these feelings to her changing feelings toward the crew. How do her actions related to the mutiny affect her relationships with both the captain and the crew?

Synthesize: BRINGING THINGS TOGETHER

4b. Predict what will happen to Charlotte now that both the captain and the crew have shunned her.

Evaluate: MAKING JUDGMENTS

5a. Assess whether Charlotte made the right decision to tell Captain Jaggery what she saw. What led her to make this decision? What are the implications of her decision?

Extend: CONNECTING IDEAS

5b. What would you do if you were asked to inform on your friends to an authority? What factors would you consider in making your decision?

Understanding Literature

Foreshadowing is the act of hinting at events that will happen later in a poem, story, or play. Find two examples of foreshadowing in chapters 7–12.

A **description** portrays a character, an object, or a scene. Descriptions make use of sensory details—words and phrases that describe how things look, sound, smell, taste, or feel. What details are used to describe the crew as they are about to mutiny?

A **conflict** is a struggle between two people or things in a literary work. Describe the conflict related to Charlotte's changing relationships with both captain and crew.

PART TWO

Chapter Thirteen

or a second time I stood in the fore-castle. the room was as dark and mean as when I'd first seen it. Now, however, I stood as a petitioner in sailor's garb. A glum Fisk was at my side. It hadn't been easy to convince him I was in earnest about becoming one of the crew. Even when he <u>begrudged</u> a willingness to believe in my sincerity he warned that agreement from the rest of the men would be improbable. He insisted I lay the matter before them immediately.

So it was that three men from Mr. Hollybrass's watch, Grimes, Dillingham, and Foley, were the next to hear my plea. As Fisk had foretold, they were contemplating me and my proposal with very little evidence of favor.

"I do mean it," I said, finding boldness with repetition, "I want to be the replacement for Mr. Johnson."

► *How do the first three men react to Charlotte's offer?*

"You're a girl," Dillingham spat out contemptuously.

"A *pretty* girl," Foley put in. It was not meant as a compliment. "Takes more than canvas britches to hide that."

"And a gentlewoman," was Grimes's addition, as though that was the final evidence of my essential uselessness.

► *What does Charlotte want to prove?*

"I want to show that I stand with you," I pleaded. "That I made a mistake."

"A mistake?" Foley snapped. "Two able-bodied men have died!"

"Besides," Dillingham agreed, "you'll bring more trouble than good."

"You can teach me," I offered.

"God's fist," Grimes cried. "She thinks this a school!"

"And the captain," Foley asked. "What'll he say?"

"He wants nothing to do with me," I replied.

"That's what he *says*. But you were his darling girl, Miss Doyle. We takes you in and he'll want you back again. Where will that put us?"

So it went, round and round. While the men made objections, while I struggled to answer them, Fisk said nothing.

► *What happens as the men make more objections?*

Though I tried to keep my head up, my eyes steady, it was not easy. They looked at me as if I were some loathsome

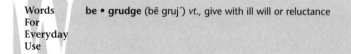

Words
For
Everyday
Use

be • grudge (bē gruj´) *vt.*, give with ill will or reluctance

thing. At the same time, the more objections they made, the more determined I was to prove myself.

"See here, Miss Doyle," Dillingham concluded, "it's no simple matter. Understand, you sign on to the articles, so to speak, and you *are* on. No <u>bolting</u> to safe harbors at the first blow or when an ill word is flung your way. You're a hand or you're not a hand, and it won't go easy, that's all that can ever be promised."

◀ What warning does Dillingham give?

"I know," I said.

"Hold out *your* hands," he demanded.

Fisk nudged me. I held them out, palms up.

Foley peered over them. "Like bloody cream," he said with disgust. "Touch mine!" he insisted and extended his. Gingerly, I touched one of them. His skin was like rough leather.

"That's the hands you'd get, miss. Like an animal. Is that what you want?"

"I don't care," I said <u>stoutly</u>.

Finally it was Dillingham who said, "And are you willing to take your place in the rigging too? Fair weather or foul?"

◀ What question makes Charlotte pause?

That made me pause.

Fisk caught the hesitation. "Answer," he prompted.

"Yes," I said boldly.

They exchanged glances. Then Foley asked, "What do the others think?"

Fisk shook his head and sighed. "No doubt they'll speak the same."

Suddenly Grimes said, "Here's what I say: let her climb to the royal yard. If she does it and comes down whole, and *still* is willing to serve, then I say let her sign and be bloody damned like the rest of us."

◀ What test does Grimes suggest?

"And do whatever she's called on to do!"

"No less!"

With no more than grunts the men seemed to agree among themselves. They turned toward me.

"*Now* what does Miss Doyle say?" Grimes demanded.

I swallowed hard, but all the same I gave yet another "Yes."

Foley came to his feet. "All right then. I'll go caucus[1] the others." Out he went.

---

1. **caucus.** Get together for a private meeting

| Words For Everyday Use | **bolt** (bôlt) *vi.*, start suddenly and run away |
| | **stout • ly** (stout´lē) *adv.*, bravely |

Fisk and I retreated to the galley while I waited for word. During that time he questioned me regarding my determination.

"Miss Doyle," he pressed, "you have agreed to climb to the top of the royal yard. Do you know that's the highest sail on the main mast? One hundred and thirty feet up. You can reach it only two ways. You can shimmy up the mast itself. Or you can climb the shrouds, using the ratlines for your ladder."

► How far does Charlotte have to climb? What options does she have?

I nodded as if I fully grasped what he was saying. The truth was I didn't even wish to listen. I just wanted to get past the test.

"And Miss Doyle," he went on, "If you slip and fall you'll be lucky to drop into the sea and drown quickly. No mortal could pluck you out fast enough to save you. Do you understand that?"

I swallowed hard but nodded. "Yes."

► What two fates can Charlotte fear if she falls?

"Because if you're *not* lucky you'll crash to the deck. Fall that way and you'll either maim or kill yourself by breaking your neck. Still certain?"

"Yes," I repeated, though somewhat more softly.

"I'll give you this," he said with a look that seemed a mix of admiration and contempt, "Zachariah was right. You're as steady a girl as ever I've met."

Foley soon returned. "We're agreed," he announced. "Not a one stands in favor of your signing on, Miss Doyle. Not with what you are. We're all agreed to that. But if you climb as high as the royal yard and make it down whole, and if you still want to sign on, you can come as equal. You'll get no more from us, Miss Doyle, but no less either."

► How does the crew feel about Charlotte signing on with them? What agreement do they make?

Fisk looked at me for my answer.

"I understand," I said.

"All right then," Foley said. "The captain's still in his cabin and not likely to come out till five bells. You can do it now."

"*Now?*" I quailed.

"Now before never."

So it was that the four men escorted me onto the deck. There I found that the rest of the crew had already gathered.

Having fully committed myself, I was overwhelmed by my <u>audacity</u>. The masts had always seemed tall, of course,

---

Words For Everyday Use

au • dac • i • ty (ô das´ə tē) *n.*, shameless boldness

---

but never so tall as they did at that moment. When I reached the deck and looked up my courage all but crumbled. My stomach turned. My legs grew weak.

Not that it mattered. Fisk escorted me to the mast as though I were being led to die at the stake. He seemed as grim as I.

◄ How does Charlotte feel as Fisk escorts her to the mast?

To grasp fully what I'd undertaken to do, know again that the height of the mainmast towered one hundred and thirty feet from the deck. This mast was, in fact, three great rounded lengths of wood, trees, in truth, affixed one to the end of the other. Further, it supported four levels of sails, each of which bore a different name. In order, bottom to top, these were called the main yard, topsail, topgallant, and finally royal yard.

My task was to climb to the top of the royal yard. And come down. In one piece. If I succeeded I'd gain the opportunity of making the climb fifty times a day.

◄ What will happen if Charlotte succeeds?

As if reading my terrified thoughts Fisk inquired gravely, "How will you go, Miss Doyle? Up the mast or on the ratlines?"

Once again I looked up. I could not possibly climb the mast directly. The stays and shrouds with their ratlines would serve me better.

"Ratlines," I replied softly.

"Then up you go."

I will confess it, at that moment my nerves failed. I found myself unable to move. With thudding heart I looked frantically around. The members of the crew, arranged in a crescent, were standing like death's own jury.

It was Barlow who called out, "A blessing goes with you, Miss Doyle."

To which Ewing added, "And this advice, Miss Doyle. Keep your eyes steady on the ropes. Don't you look down. Or up."

◄ What do Barlow and Ewing say to Charlotte? How do their comments make her feel?

For the first time I sensed that some of them at least wanted me to succeed. The realization gave me courage.

With halting steps and shallow breath, I approached the rail only to pause when I reached it. I could hear a small inner voice crying, "Don't! Don't!"

But it was also then that I heard Dillingham snicker, "She'll not have the stomach."

◄ What sound makes Charlotte begin?

Words For Everyday Use

grave • ly (grāv′lē) *adv.*, seriously

I reached up, grasped the lowest deadeye,[2] and hauled myself atop the rail. That much I had done before. Now, I maneuvered to the outside so that I would be leaning *into* the rigging and could even rest on it.

Once again I looked at the crew, *down* at them, I should say. They were staring up with blank expressions.

Recollecting Ewing's advice, I shifted my eyes and focused them on the ropes before me. Then, reaching as high as I could into one of the middle shrouds, and grabbing a ratline, I began to climb.

The ratlines were set about sixteen inches one above the other, so that the steps I had to take were wide for me. I needed to pull as much with arms as climb with legs. But line by line I did go up, as if ascending an enormous ladder.

▶ What mistake has Charlotte made?

After I had risen some seventeen feet I realized I'd made a great mistake. The rigging stood in sets, each going to a different level of the mast. I could have taken one that stretched directly to the top. Instead, I had chosen a line which went only to the first trestletree, to the top of the lower mast.

For a moment I considered backing down and starting afresh. I stole a quick glance below. The crew's faces were turned up toward me. I understood that they would take the smallest movement down as retreat. I had to continue.

And so I did.

Now I was climbing inside the lank gray-white sails, ascending, as it were, into a bank of dead clouds.

▶ What thought makes Charlotte's hands grow damp?

Beyond the sails lay the sea, slate-gray and ever rolling. Though the water looked calm, I could feel the slow pitch and roll it caused in the ship. I realized suddenly how much harder this climb would be if the wind were blowing and we were well underway. The mere thought made the palms of my hands grow damp.

Up I continued till I reached the main yard. Here I snatched another glance at the sea, and was startled to see how much bigger it had grown. Indeed, the more I saw of it the *more* there was. In contrast, the *Seahawk* struck me as having suddenly grown smaller. The more I saw of *her,* the *less* she was!

I glanced aloft. To climb higher I now had to edge myself out upon the trestletree and then once again move up the next set of ratlines as I'd done before. But at twice the height!

Wrapping one arm around the mast—even up here it was too big to reach around completely—I grasped one of the

---

2. **deadeye.** Round, flat block of wood on a ship, used to hold shrouds and stays in place

stays and edged out. At the same moment the ship dipped, the world seemed to twist and tilt down. My stomach lurched. My heart pounded. My head swam. In spite of myself I closed my eyes. I all but slipped, saving myself only by a sudden grasp of a line before the ship yawed[3] the opposite way. I felt sicker yet. With ever waning strength I clung on for dearest life. Now the full folly of what I was attempting burst upon me with <u>grotesque</u> reality. It had been not only stupid, but suicidal. I would never come down alive!

◄ Why does Charlotte suddenly realize the folly of her decision?

And yet I had to climb. This was my restitution.

When the ship was steady again, I grasped the furthest rigging, first with one hand, then the other, and dragged myself higher. I was heading for the topsail, fifteen feet further up.

Pressing myself as close as possible into the rigging, I continued to strain upward, squeezing the ropes so tightly my hands cramped. I even tried curling my toes about the ratlines.

At last I reached the topsail spar, but discovered it was impossible to rest there. The only place to pause was three *times* higher than the distance I'd just come, at the trestletree just below the topgallant spar.

By now every muscle in my body ached. My head felt light, my heart an anvil.[4] My hands were on fire, the soles of my feet raw. Time and again I was forced to halt, pressing my face against the rigging with eyes closed. Then, in spite of what I'd been warned not to do, I opened them and peered down. The *Seahawk* was like a wooden toy. The sea looked greater still.

◄ What does Charlotte do despite the warning given?

I made myself glance up. Oh, so far to go! How I forced myself to move I am not sure. But the thought of backing down now was just as frightening. Knowing only that I could not stay still, I crept upward, ratline by ratline, taking what seemed to be forever with each rise until I finally reached the level just below the topgallant spar.

A seasoned sailor would have needed two minutes to reach this point. I had needed thirty!

◄ How long would a seasoned sailor take to do this climb? How long has Charlotte taken?

Though I felt the constant roll of the ship, I had to rest

---

3. **yawed.** Swung back and forth across its course, as a ship on high waves
4. **anvil.** Iron block on which metal is hammered

Words For Everyday Use

gro • tesque (grō tesk´) *adj.,* fantastic, bizarre

there. What seemed like little movement on deck became, up high, wild swings and turns through <u>treacherous</u> air.

I gagged, forced my stomach down, drew breath, and looked out. Though I didn't think it possible, the ocean appeared to have grown greater yet. And when I looked down, the upturned faces of the crew appeared like so many tiny bugs.

There were twenty-five or so more feet to climb. Once again I grasped the rigging and hauled myself up.

This final climb was torture. With every upward pull the swaying of the ship seemed to increase. Even when not moving myself, I was flying through the air in wild, wide <u>gyrations</u>. The horizon kept shifting, tilting, dropping. I was increasingly dizzy, nauseous, terrified, certain that with every next moment I would slip and fall to death. I paused again and again, my eyes on the rigging inches from my face, gasping and praying as I had never prayed before. My one hope was that, nearer to heaven now, I could make my desperation heard!

Inch by inch I continued up. Half an inch! Quarter inches! But then at last with trembling fingers, I touched the spar of the royal yard. I had reached the top.

Once there I <u>endeavored</u> to rest again. But there the metronome[5] motion of the mast was at its most extreme, the *Seahawk* turning, tossing, swaying as if trying to shake me off—like a dog throwing droplets of water from its back. And when I looked beyond I saw a sea that was infinity itself, ready, eager to swallow me whole.

I had to get back down.

As hard as it was to climb up, it was, to my horror, harder returning. On the ascent I could see where I was going. Edging down I had to grope blindly with my feet. Sometimes I tried to look. But when I did the sight of the void below was so sickening, I was forced to close my eyes.

Each groping step downward was a nightmare. Most times my foot found only air. Then, as if to mock my terror, a small breeze at last sprang up. Sails began to fill and snap, puffing in and out, at times smothering me.

► *Why does the climb become more difficult as Charlotte reaches the top?*

► *Why was going down even harder than climbing up?*

---

5. **metronome.** Device that beats time at a regular rate

Words For Everyday Use	
	treach • er • ous (trech´ər əs) *adj.,* untrustworthy or insecure
	gy • ra • tion (jī rā´shən) *n.,* circular or spiral motion
	en • deav • or (en dev´ər) *vi.,* strive, make a solid attempt

The tossing of the ship grew—if that were possible—more extreme.

Down I crept, past the topgallant where I paused briefly on the trestletree, then down along the longest stretch, toward the mainyard. It was there I fell.

I was searching with my left foot for the next ratline. When I found a hold and started to put my weight upon it, my foot, slipping on the slick tar surface, shot forward. The suddenness of it made me lose my grip. I tumbled backward, but in such a way that my legs became entangled in the lines. There I hung, *head downward.*

◄ What happens as Charlotte approaches the mainline?

I screamed, tried to grab something. But I couldn't. I clutched madly at nothing, till my hand brushed against a dangling rope. I grabbed for it, missed, and grabbed again. Using all my strength, I levered myself up and, wrapping my arms into the lines, made a <u>veritable</u> knot of myself, mast, and rigging. Oh, how I wept! my entire body shaking and trembling as though it would break apart.

When my breathing became somewhat normal, I managed to untangle first one arm, then my legs. I was free.

I continued down. By the time I reached the mainyard I was numb and whimpering again, tears <u>coursing</u> from my eyes.

I moved to the shrouds I'd climbed, and edged myself past the lowest of the sails.

As I emerged from under it, the crew gave out a great "Huzzah!"

◄ What does the crew do as Charlotte is almost finished? How does she feel to hear them?

Oh, how my heart swelled with exaltation!

Finally, when I'd reached close to the very end, Barlow stepped forward, beaming, his arms uplifted. "Jump!" he called. "Jump!"

But now, determined to do it all myself, I shook my head. Indeed, in the end I dropped down on my own two India-rubber legs—and tumbled to the deck.

No sooner did I land than the crew gave me another "Huzzah!" With joyous heart I staggered to my feet. Only then did I see Captain Jaggery push through the knot of men and come to stand before me.

| Words For Everyday Use | **ver • i • ta • ble** (ver´i tə bəl) *adj.,* actual |
| | **course** (kôrs) *vi.,* move swiftly |

Chapter Fourteen

here I stood. Behind me the semicircle of the crew seemed to <u>recoil</u> from the man and from Mr. Hollybrass, who appeared not far behind.

"Miss Doyle," the captain said with barely suppressed fury. "What is the meaning of this?"

I stood mute. How could I explain to *him?* Besides, there were no words left within me. I had gone through too many transformations of mood and spirit within the last twenty-four hours.

When I remained silent he demanded, "Why are you dressed in this scandalous fashion? Answer me!" The angrier he became, the darker grew the color of the welt on his face. "Who gave you permission to climb into the rigging?"

I backed up a step and said, "I . . . I have joined the crew."

Unable to comprehend my words Captain Jaggery remained staring fixedly at me. Then gradually he did understand. His face flushed red. His fists clenched.

"Miss Doyle," he said between gritted teeth, "you will go to your cabin, remove these obscene garments and put on your proper dress. You are causing a disruption. I will not allow it."

But when I continued to stand there—unmoving, making no response—he suddenly shouted, "Did you not hear me? Get to your cabin!"

"I won't," I blurted out. "I'm no longer a passenger. I'm with them." So saying, I stepped back until I sensed the men around me.

The captain glared at the crew. "And you," he sneered. "I suppose you'd have her?"

The response of the men was silence.

The captain seemed unsure what to do.

"Mr. Hollybrass!" he barked finally.

"Waiting your orders, sir."

The captain flushed again. He shifted his attention back to me. "Your father, Miss Doyle," he declared, " . . . he would not allow this."

"I think I know my father—an officer in the company

> ▶ Why does Charlotte feel unable to explain to the captain?

> ▶ What does Charlotte say she has done?

> ▶ Does the crew accept Charlotte as one of them?

Words For Everyday Use	re • coil (rē koil´) *vi.,* draw back; retreat in surprise, fear, or disgust

who owns this ship, and your employer—better than you," I said. "He *would* approve of my reasons."

The captain's uncertainty grew. At last he replied, "Very well, Miss Doyle, if you do not assume your proper attire this instant, if you insist upon playing these games, you shall not be given the opportunity to change your mind. If crew you are, crew you shall remain. I promise, I shall drive you as I choose."

"I don't care what you do!" I threw back at him.

The captain turned to the first mate. "Mr. Hollybrass, remove Miss Doyle's belongings from her cabin. Let her take her place in the forecastle with the crew. Put her down as *Mister* Doyle and list *Miss* Doyle in the log as lost. From this point on I expect to see that *he* works with the rest." With that, he disappeared into the steerage.

No sooner had he done so than the crew—though not Mr. Hollybrass—let out another <u>raucous</u> cheer!

In just such a fashion did I become a full-fledged crewmember of the *Seahawk*. Whatever <u>grievous</u> errors I had made before—in thwarting the mutiny led by Cranick and in causing the resulting cruelty toward Zachariah—the sailors appeared to accept my change of heart and position without reservation. They saw my desire to become a crew member not only as atonement, but as a stinging rebuff to Captain Jaggery. Once I had showed myself willing to do what they did—by climbing the rigging—once they saw me stand up to Jaggery, an intense apprenticeship commenced. And for it the crewmen became my teachers. They helped me, worked with me, guided me past the mortal dangers that lurked in every task. In this they were far more patient with all my repeated errors than those teachers at the Barrington School for Better Girls when there was nothing to learn but penmanship, spelling, and the ancient authors of morality.

You may believe me too when I say that I shirked no work. Even if I'd wanted to, it was clear from the start that shirking would not be allowed. I pounded oakum into the deck. I scraped the hull. I stood watch as dawn blessed the sea and as the moon cut the midnight sky. I tossed the line to measure the depths of the sea. I took my turn at the wheel. I swabbed the deck and tarred the rigging, spliced ropes and tied knots. My mess was shared with the crew. And I went aloft.

◄ *What does Charlotte say her father would approve?*

◄ *What warning does the captain issue? What does he order Mr. Hollybrass to do?*

◄ *Why has the crew's opinion of Charlotte changed?*

◄ *What kinds of tasks does Charlotte do as part of the crew?*

Words For Everyday Use

rau • cous (rô′kəs) *adj.*, loud and rowdy
griev • ous (grēv′əs) *adj.*, atrocious, very serious

Indeed, that first journey to the top of the mainmast was but the prelude to many daily climbs. Of course, after that first there were always others who went along with me. High above the sea, my crewmates taught me to work with one hand—the other *must* hold on—to dangle over spars, to reef sails, to edge along the walk ropes. So I came to work every sail, at every hour of the day.

As for the captain, he was as good as his word. No, *better* than his word. He continued to drive his crew without mercy, and since I was now a part of it, he drove them, and me in particular, *harder* than before. But try as he might he could find no cause for complaint. I would not let him.

▶ What changes does Charlotte undergo?

My knowledge of physical labor had been all but <u>nil</u>, of course; hardly a wonder then that from the moment I joined the crew I was in pain. I ached as if my body had been racked. My skin turned pink, then red, then brown. The flesh upon my hands broke first into oozing, running sores, then <u>metamorphosed</u> into a new rough hide—all as promised. And when my watch was done I flung myself into my hammock and slept the sleep of righteousness—though never more than four hours and more often less.

A word must be said about where and how I slept. It will be remembered that the captain denied me my cabin, insisting that I take my place in the forecastle with the men. No doubt he thought to humiliate me and force me to return to my former place.

▶ What adjustment does the crew make for Charlotte?

The men caucused that first day, and in a meeting that concluded with a sacred oath, bade me take my place along with them, swearing to give me the utmost privacy they could provide. They would be my brothers. I was no longer to be called Miss Doyle, but Charlotte.

I was given a hammock placed in a corner. Around this a piece of torn sail was tacked up as a kind of curtain. The space was private for me, and kept that way.

True, I heard—and learned—their rough language. I confess too that in my newfound freedom I brandished a few bold terms of my own—to the amusement of the men at first. But after a while, it became rather second nature to me, and to them. I say this not to brag, but to suggest the complete absorption I felt in my new life. I came to feel a sense of exhilaration in it such as I had never felt before.

| Words For Everyday Use | **nil** (nil) *n.*, nothing |
| | **met • a • mor • phose** (met ə môr´fōz) *vt.*, transform |

Thus it was that after a fortnight, I found myself atop the foremast, hugging the topgallant spar, my bare brown feet nimbly balancing on the foot ropes. It was seven bells of the second dog watch, just before dusk. The wind was out of the northwest. Our sails were <u>taut</u>. Our studding sails were set.

Below, the ship's bow—as though pulled by her winged figurehead—plunged repeatedly, stirring froth and foam. This rocking movement seemed effortless to me now, as if, like the ship's namesake, we were flying. Not far off our starboard bow, dolphins chased the waves, flyers themselves.

My hair, uncombed for days, blew free in the salty air. My face, dark with weather, was creased with smile. I was squinting westward into the swollen face of a blood-red sun, which cast a shimmering golden road upon the sea; from where I perched it seemed we were sailing on that road in a dream. And there I was, joyous, new-made, liberated from a prison I'd thought was my proper place!

◄ From what has Charlotte been freed?

The only shadow on my happiness was Captain Jaggery. He came on deck infrequently, and when he did he was enveloped in the murkiest gloom.

Rarely did he speak to anyone but the mates—Mr. Hollybrass and *Mister* Johnson now—and only then to give orders or rebukes.

Naturally, the captain was the principal subject of endless scuttlebutt[1] in the forecastle during off-watch times.

Ewing claimed there was tension between the captain and the first mate, because Mr. Hollybrass didn't approve of Jaggery's ways.

◄ What difference of opinion do Ewing and Keetch have about Hollybrass?

"Don't you believe it," said Keetch, who, if anything, had grown more tense since his demotion. "Hollybrass is glove to Jaggery's hand."

Fisk insisted Jaggery's keeping below so much was only a case of his wanting to hide the welt on his face, of hiding himself in shame.

It was Grimes who swore he was pressing us to make a crossing in good time and so prove he'd done no wrong.

But it was Foley who said that *I* was the cause of the captain's every move.

"What do you mean?" I demanded.

---

1. **scuttlebutt.** Rumor or gossip

Words For Everyday Use   **taut** (tôt) *adj.,* stretched tight

"I've seen him," Foley insisted. "Studied him. He doesn't come out unless it's your watch. One eye keeps the ship in trim. But the other—"

"What?" I said, sensing already that he was right.

"He's always watching you," Foley said, looking around at the others for confirmation. "And there's nothing but hatred in his eye."

The others nodded in agreement.

"But why?" I asked.

▶ Why is the captain waiting for Charlotte to make a mistake?

"He's waiting, wanting you to make a mistake," Morgan put in, taking a deep pull on his pipe, then filling the forecastle with its <u>acrid</u> smoke.

"What kind of mistake?" I asked.

"Something he can use against you. Something to set him right. Look here, Charlotte, you boxed him in."

"I did?"

"It was that first moment you joined us. You mentioned your father, didn't you? said he'd approve of what you've done."

"He would. He believes in justice."

"Be that as it may, Jaggery didn't know what to do. He gave way. Not a thing he likes, you know. So now I say he's waiting for a mistake on your part to set himself back up."

"I don't intend to make a mistake," I stated proudly.

Fisk spat upon the floor. "Neither does he."

It came to pass as Morgan promised.

▶ What is a sail really like?

To a person on land the sight of a ship's sails, bleached by sun, stretched by wind, is the very image of airy lightness. In fact, a sail is made of very heavy canvas. When one gets tangled on a spar it must be pulled loose quickly or it can tear or burst, and in so doing, pull down rigging, spars, even a mast. A sail out of control can flick like a wild whip and send a full-grown sailor into a senseless spin. It often happens.

▶ What dangers does a sailor trying to repair a tangled jib face?

Now the flying jib is set at the furthest point of the bowsprit—at the very tip of it. When you consider that the bow of a speeding ship on a high sea forever rises and falls, you will perceive that a broken jib can dip into the sea itself. Such is the water's force and the driving of the ship, that the bowsprit itself can be caused to snap. Thus the sailor who seeks to repair a tangled jib must contend not only with a

Words
For
Everyday
Use

ac • rid (ak´rid) *adj.*, sharp, bitter, stinging, or irritating in taste or smell

heavy, <u>flailing</u> sail, but the powerful, rushing sea only a few feet—sometimes closer—below him.

One afternoon—two days after our forecastle talk and during my watch—the flying jib became entangled in just the way I have described. As soon as he saw it, Captain Jaggery cried, "*Mister* Doyle! Fix the bowsprit!" In his haste to call on me, he spoke directly, not through one of his mates.

Before I could respond, Grimes leaped forward, calling, "I'll do it, sir!" Grimes was one of the bearded ones, quick to flare, quick to forget.

"The call was for Mr. Doyle," returned the Captain. "Does he refuse?"

"No, sir," I said and hurried to the knighthead from which the bowsprit thrust forward.

Grimes hurried along with me, offering hasty instructions in my ear, as well as urging a splicing knife upon me.

I took it and put it in a pocket.

"Charlotte, do you see that line out there?" he asked, pointing to the twisted line at the far end of the bowsprit that had snarled the jib.

I nodded.

"Don't monkey with the sail itself. All you need do is cut the rope. The sail will free itself and we've got others. Mind, you'll need to cut sharp, then swing down under the bowsprit in one quick jump, or the sail will toss you in. Understand?"

◀ What warning does Grimes offer?

Again I nodded.

"Time yourself proper. If the ship plunges, the sea will up and grab you."

So cocky had I become that I leaped to the head rail with little thought or worry, then set my foot upon the bowsprit itself. I saw that I needed to walk out along this bowsprit some twenty feet—not too difficult a task, I thought, because the back rope was something I could cling to.

◀ Why isn't Charlotte worried about this task?

As I had by now learned to do, I started off by keeping my eyes on the bowsprit and my bare feet, inching step by step along it. The hiss of the water rushing below was pronounced, the bowsprit itself wet and slippery with foam. No matter. What took me by surprise was the bowsprit's wild bobbing.

Halfway along I glanced back. For the first time since I'd

| Words For Everyday Use | **flail • ing** (flāl´iŋ) *adj.*, move in a striking or beating motion |

▶ Why is Charlotte startled?

boarded the ship, I saw the figurehead clearly, the pale white seahawk with wings thrust back against the bow, its head extended forward, beak open wide in a scream. As the bow dipped, this open beak dropped and dropped again into the sea, coming up each time with foam streaming like a rabid dog. So startled was I by the frightful vision that for a moment I froze until a sudden plunge of the ship almost tumbled me seaward.

I reached the crucial point soon enough, but only by curling my toes tight upon the bowsprit, and holding fast onto the back rope line with one hand was I able to free the other to take Grimes's splicing knife from my pocket.

I leaned forward and began to cut. The tightness of the tangled line helped. The knife cut freely. Too much so. The last remaining strands snapped with a crack, the sail boomed out, flicking away at my cutting hand—and the knife went flying into the sea. Even as I lunged for it the bowsprit plunged. I slipped and started to fall. By merest chance I made a successful grab at the bowsprit itself, which left me hanging, feet dangling, only a few feet above the rushing sea.

▶ What happens after Charlotte frees the sail? How does she figure to save herself?

As the *Seahawk* plunged and plunged again, I was dunked to my waist, to my chest. I tried to swing myself up to hook my feet over, but I could not. The sea kept snatching at me, trying to pull me down while I dangled there kicking wildly, uselessly. Twice my head went under. Blinded, I swallowed water, choked. Then I saw that only by timing my leg swings to the upward thrust of the ship could I save myself.

The ship heaved skyward. With all my might I swung my legs up and wrapped them about the bowsprit, but again the *Seahawk* plunged. Into the tearing sea I went, clutching the spar. Then up. This time I used the momentum to swing over, so I was now atop the bowsprit, straddling it, then lying on it.

▶ What happens to help Charlotte?

Someone must have called to the man at the helm. The ship shifted course. Found easier water. Slowed. Ceased to plunge so.

Gasping for breath, spitting seawater, I was able to pull myself along the bowsprit and finally, by stepping on the wooden bird's furious head, climbed over the rail. Grimes was there to help me onto the deck and give me an enthusiastic hug of approval.

▶ How does the crew react to Charlotte's action? How does the captain react?

The captain, of course, watched me stony-faced.

"Mister Doyle," he barked. "Come here!"

Though greatly shaken, I had no time to be frightened. I had done the task and knew I'd done it. I hurried to the quarterdeck.

"When I ask you to do a job," the captain said, "it's you I ask, and not another. You've caused us to change course, to lose time!" And before I could respond, he struck me across the face with the back of his hand, then turned and walked away.

My reaction was quick. "Coward!" I screamed at him. "Fraud!"

He spun about, and began to stride back toward me, his scarred face contorted in rage.

But I, in a rage myself, wouldn't give way. "I can't wait till Providence!" I shouted at him. "I'll go right to the courts! You won't be captain long! You'll be seen by everyone as the cruel <u>despot</u> you are!" And I spat upon the deck by his boots.

◄ What does Charlotte threaten to do when they reach Providence?

My words made him turn as pale as a ghost—a ghost with murder in his eye. But then, abruptly, he gained control of himself and, as he'd done on previous occasions, whirled about and left the deck.

I turned away, feeling triumphant. Much of the crew had seen it all. But there were no more hurrahs.

The moment passed. Nothing more was said, save by Grimes, who insisted that I take lessons in the handling of a knife, carrying it, using it, even throwing it. On my first watch off he had me practice on the deck for three hours.

◄ What does Grimes insist Charlotte must learn?

Two more days passed without incident. In that time, however, the sky turned a perpetual gray. The air thickened with moisture. Winds rose and fell in what I thought was a peculiar pattern. Toward the end of the second day when Barlow and I were scraping down the capstan, I saw a branch on the waves. A red bird was perched on the branch.

"Look!" I cried with delight, pointing to the bird. "Does that mean we're close to land?"

Barlow hauled himself up to take a look. He shook his head. "That bird's from the Caribbean. One thousand miles off. I've seen them there. Blood bird, they call them."

◄ What does Charlotte hope the bird means? What does the sight of the blood bird mean to the experienced sailors?

"What's it doing here?"

After a moment he said, "Storm driven."

I looked at him in surprise. "What kind of storm would blow a bird that far?" I asked, wide-eyed.

"Hurricane."

"What's a hurricane?"

"The worst storm of all."

Words
For
Everyday
Use

des • pot (des′pət) *n.*, anyone in charge who acts like a tyrant

► Why doesn't
Captain Jaggery
want to avoid the
hurricane?

"Can't we sail around?"

Barlow again glanced at the helm, the sails and then at the sky above. He frowned. "I heard Mr. Hollybrass and Jaggery arguing about it. To my understanding," he said, "I don't think the captain wants to avoid it."

"Why not?"

"It's what Grimes has been saying. The captain's trying to move fast. If he sets us right at the hurricane's edge, it'll blow us home like a pound of shot in a two-pound cannon."

"What if he doesn't get it right?"

"Two pounds of shot in a one-pound cannon."[2]

---

2. **pound of shot . . . one-pound cannon.** The first example means the storm will move the ship quickly toward its destination. The second example means the storm will overpower and destroy the ship.

Chapter Fifteen

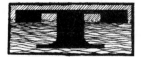

wo bells into the morning of our forty-fifth day, the storm struck.

"All hands! All hands!"

Even as the cry came, the *Seahawk* pitched and yawed violently. Whether I got out of my hammock on my own, or was tossed by the <u>wrenching</u> motion of the ship, to this day I do not know. But I woke to find myself sprawling on the floor, the curtain torn <u>asunder</u>, the forecastle in wildest confusion. Above my head the lantern swung grotesquely, the men's possessions skittered about like billiard balls, trunks rolled helter-skelter. The watch was scrambling up.

As the ship plunged, and plunged again, the cry, "All hands! All hands!" came repeatedly, more urgent than I'd ever heard it.

"Hurricane!" I heard as well.

There was a frantic dash out of the forecastle and to the deck. I followed too, trying to pull on my jacket as I ran against the violent pitching of the ship.

Though long past dawn, the sky was still dark. A heavy rain, flung wildly by wind that screamed and moaned like an army in mortal agony, beat upon the deck in rhythms only a mad drummer could concoct. The sea hurled towering wall upon towering wall of foaming fury over us. One such tossed me like some drop of dew across the deck where I—fortunately—crashed against a wall. As I lay stunned and bruised, gasping for breath, I caught sight of Mr. Hollybrass and Captain Jaggery in the midst of a furious dispute.

". . . no profit to be found at the bottom of the sea!" I heard the first mate cry above the storm.

"Mr. Hollybrass, we sail through!" the captain returned, breaking away to shout, "All hands aloft! All hands aloft!"

I could hardly believe my ears. To go up into the rigging in this! But when I looked skyward I could see the reason why. Under the brutal force of the wind, many of the sails had pulled free from their running ropes and were now tearing and snapping out of control, pulling themselves into wild whips.

◄ How does Charlotte awaken on the morning of the forty-fifth day?

◄ What argument does Charlotte overhear between Mr. Hollybrass and Captain Jaggery?

Words For Everyday Use

wrench • ing (rench´iŋ) *adj.*, suddenly pulling or twisting
a • sun • der (ə sunʹdər) *adv.*, apart or into pieces

"All hands aloft! All hands aloft!" came the cry again. It was pleading, desperate.

I could see the men—bent far over to buck wind and rain—struggling toward the shrouds. I pulled myself to my feet, only to be knocked down by still another wave. Again I staggered up, grasping a rope, managing to hold on with the strength of my two hands. Now I was able to stand—but just barely. Slowly I made my way toward the forward mast. When I reached it—it seemed to take forever—Captain Jaggery was already there, trying frantically to lash down ropes and rigging.

"What shall I do?" I shouted to his back. Shouting was the only way I could make myself heard.

► What does the captain tell Charlotte to do? Where does she get a knife?

"Cut away the foreyard before it pulls the mast down!" he yelled back. I'm not certain he realized it was me. "Do you have a knife?" he called.

"No!"

Even as he reached into a back pocket, he turned. When he saw it was me, he hesitated.

"A knife!" I cried.

He handed one to me.

"Where?" I called.

"Didn't you hear me?" he cried, gesticulating wildly. "Cut that sail away!"

I looked up. I could not see far into the sheets of rain. The *Seahawk*'s wild pitching had set the mast to shaking as if it had the palsy.[1] Only the foreyard was visible, and the sail was blowing from it almost into the shape of a balloon. Suddenly the sail collapsed into itself, then filled again. It would burst soon or fly off with the mast.

"Up, damn you! Up! Hurry!" Captain Jaggery screamed.

I reached into the rigging but stopped, realizing I couldn't climb and hold the knife. With the blade between my teeth I again grasped the rigging, and using both hands I began to climb.

Though I was in fact climbing into the air, I felt as though I were swimming against a rising river tide. But more than rain or waves it was the screaming wind that tore at me. I could hardly make out where I was going. To make matters worse my wet and heavy hair, like a horse's tail, kept whipping across my face. I might have been blindfolded.

► Why does Charlotte cut off her hair?

Desperate, I wrapped my legs and one arm about the ropes. With my one free arm I pulled my hair around, grasped it with the hand entwined in the ropes, and pulled it taut. I took the knife and hacked. With a shake of my head

---

1. **palsy.** Paralysis often accompanied by involuntary tremors or twitches

my thirteen year's growth of hair fell away. Feeling much lighter, I bit down onto the blade again and once more began to climb.

Every upward inch was a struggle, as though I were forcing myself between the fingers of God's angry fist. And it was not just the elements that attacked.

Below me—when I dared to look—the deck blurred into a confusing mass of water, foam, decking, and now and again a struggling man. I was certain the *Seahawk* would flounder, that we were doomed to drown. I told myself not to look, to concentrate on what I had to do.

Up I went. The rain hissed. Thunder boomed. Lightning cracked. Human cries came too, shouts that rose up through the maelstrom,[2] words I couldn't catch. But what they betokened was terror.

As I crept further up the mast the sail billowed out and away from me. The next moment the wind shifted and the great canvas collapsed, smashing its full wet weight against me, as though with a conscious mind to knock me from the rigging. Desperately, I clung to the ropes with legs and arms. Then out the sail snapped. The <u>ensuing</u> vacuum all but sucked me off. God knows how, but I held on and continued up.

I heard, threaded through the wailing wind, a ghastly, shrieking sound, then a tremendous splintering of wood. Could it, I wondered, be *my* mast? Was I about to be hurled into the waves? I dared not stop and think. But the mast held.

Hand over hand, foot after foot, I struggled upward. I was certain we were all about to die, whether above the waves or beneath them, it hardly seemed to matter. All I wanted was to reach that sail, as if by doing so I could rise above the chaos. To cut that sail free was my only purpose. I would not, could not, think of anything else. Sometimes I paused just to hang on, to gasp for breath, to remind myself I lived. But then, once again, I continued up. It felt like hours. It probably took minutes. At last I reached my goal.

◄ *On what is Charlotte focused?*

The foreyard is one of the biggest sails, one of a sailing ship's true engines. But even though it worked hard for the

---

2. **maelstrom.** Large violent whirlpool

Words For Everyday Use   en • su • ing (en soō´iŋ) *adj.,* following, resultant

ship under normal circumstances, in this storm it strained *against* her as if trying to uproot the mast from the deck. Despite the roaring wind that beat about me, I could hear the creaking of the mast, could see it bend like a great bow. What I needed to do—had to do—was cut that sail free and release the terrible strain upon the mast.

Fearful of wasting any time I simply straddled the spar to which the sail's top edge was lashed and backed out toward its end, hacking away at each piece of rope as I came upon it. Fortunately, the lines were so taut, and the blade so sharp, I hardly had to cut. The moment I touched a rope with the knife's edge, strands flew apart as if exploding.

With each rope I cut the sail blew out more freely, flapping in such frenzy it began to shred into tiny strands that I could no longer distinguish from the streaking rain.

► What decision does Charlotte have to make?

Bit by bit I moved along, cutting as I went, until I reached the spar's furthest end. There I had to make another decision: should I cut the lines that held the spar itself? What would happen if I did so? If I did not? I looked about in the vain hope that another of the crew might be near. To my surprise I did see the shadowy form of someone above, but who he was I couldn't tell. In any case, he was climbing further up the mast than I!

I decided not to cut more lines. Someone else could do so if that's what needed to be done. My job was to cut away the rest of the sail, which meant going back the way I'd come and proceeding out along the spar toward the opposite end.

► Why must Charlotte get back to the mast quickly? Why is it difficult for her to do so?

The spar, however—with its lopsided weight, and me at one end—was swinging and lurching about so wildly I feared it might break free and drop with me on it. I had to get back to the mast. But the foot ropes were gone; in my wild hacking I'd cut them free too. I would have to drag myself along. With the knife again clamped between my teeth, arms tightly locked around the spar, I flung myself down and tried to slide forward. But at the next lurch of the spar, my legs slipped away. The knife fell from my mouth. In a small part of a second I was now dangling, legs down, facing *away* from the mast, about to drop into the wildest scene imaginable.

I had no choice. I now had to <u>clamber</u>—hand over hand and *backward*—toward the mast. But as much as I tried for speed I could move only in tiny <u>increments</u>. The wind and

---

Words
For
Everyday
Use

clam • ber (klam´bər) *vi.,* climb clumsily and with great effort

in • cre • ment (in´krə mənt) *n.,* amount of an increase

rain—as well as the tossing motion of the ship—kept <u>imped-ing</u> me. I was dangling in the hurricane winds, twisting.

Over my shoulder I could see that the mast was not far out of reach. But then my arms began to cramp.

"Help!" I screamed. "Help me!" One hand lost its grip.

Four feet from the mast I tried to swing myself back in the vain hope of grasping the mast with my legs. The attempt only weakened my hold more. I was certain I was going to drop.

"Help!" I screamed into the wind.

Suddenly, a figure appeared on the spar. "Charlotte!" I heard. "Take my hand!" And indeed, a hand was thrust toward my face. I reached for it frantically, grabbed it, clung to it, as it clung to me, its fingers encircling my wrist in an iron grip. For a moment I was hanging by that one hand. Then I was yanked upward onto the spar so I could get my legs around it and locked. Gasping for breath, I glanced up at the figure who was now scrambling away. It was Zachariah.

◄ Who helps Charlotte?

For one brief moment I was certain I had died and he was an angel. But I hardly had time for thought. For just above me, I heard a great wrenching explosion. I looked up to see that the foreyard had ripped away. As the sail spun off in the wind I caught a glimpse of its gray mass twisting and turn-ing into <u>oblivion</u> like a tormented soul cast down to Hell.

I spun back around. The man I thought to be Zachariah had vanished. But even as I gazed in wonder, the *Seahawk*, free from the sail's pull and weight, heeled[3] violently. To my horror I saw the ocean rush up toward me. *We were capsizing.*[4] But then suddenly, the ship shivered and righted herself.

◄ What does Charlotte fear is happening?

Gasping for breath I clawed my way forward until I reached the mast, which I hugged as though it were life itself. Without the knife there was nothing more I could do aloft. In any case the sail I had been sent to free was gone. I began to descend, slipping more than I climbed.

I jumped the last few feet onto the deck. I don't know if the storm had somewhat <u>abated</u> or I'd just grown used to it. There were still strong winds and the rain beat upon us as before. But the fury of the hurricane somehow softened. I

---

3. **heeled.** Leaned or pulled to one side
4. *capsizing.* Tipping over

Words For Everyday Use

im • pede (im pēd´) *vt.*, hinder, obstruct, or delay
ob • liv • i • on (ə bliv´ē ən) *n.*, condition of being forgotten
a • bate (ə bāt´) *vi.*, lessen, diminish

looked about. Spars, some entangled with sails, lay in heaps. Railings were splintered. Dangling ropes flapped about. Then I saw some of the men on the quarterdeck working frantically with axes. I hurried to join them.

Only then did I realize the mainmast was gone. All that remained was a jagged stump. I thought of the shriek I'd heard.

Looking toward the stern, I saw Fisk slumped over the wheel. His great arms were spread wide, his hands clutching the wheel spokes. He could not have stayed upright had he not been <u>lashed</u> into place.

I joined the men.

Beneath the continual if now somewhat slackened downpour we all pulled at the great mound of downed spars and sails. Those that were dragging overboard, we cut loose and let go. Those we could move we flung into the waist.

▶ What sight relieves Charlotte?

And then, quite suddenly—as if Heaven itself had triumphed over darkness—the rain ceased. The sea <u>subsided</u> into a roilling calm. Even the sun began to shine. And when I looked up I saw—to my astonishment—a blue sky.

"It's over!" I said breathlessly.

▶ What must she have been dismayed to hear?

Mr. Johnson shook his head. "Nothing like!" he warned. "It's the eye of the storm. There'll only be a pause. And it'll be back in twenty minutes going the other way. But, God willing, if we can clear the deck we may be able to ride it out!"

I looked up at our remaining mast. Only the topgallant was left. The other sails had been cut loose.

▶ Who is found under the pile of sails? What has happened to him?

Working frantically we reached the bottom of the pile. It was Foley who pulled away the last torn sail. There, beneath it, lay Mr. Hollybrass, face down. A knife was stuck in his back, plunged so deeply only the scrimshaw handle could be seen. I recognized the design of a star. This was the dirk Zachariah had given me.

The sight of the dead Mr. Hollybrass—for it was certain that such was the case—left us all dumbfounded. But after all we'd been through in the storm it's hardly to be wondered that we made no response. We were too drained. Too numb.

"What is it?" came a voice. We turned to see Captain Jaggery. He was looking much like the rest of us, wild and disheveled.

Words For Everyday Use

lash (lash) *vt.*, tie or fasten with a rope

sub • side (səb sīd´) *vi.*, become less active or intense

We stepped aside. No one said a word. He came forward. For a moment he too did nothing but stare at the body. Then he knelt and touched the man's face, the back of his neck.

For a moment he hesitated, then pulled Mr. Hollybrass's arm from where it lay twisted under his body. The dead man clutched something in his hand. The captain managed to pry the fingers open, and plucked away what Mr. Hollybrass had been holding. He held it up.

◄ What did the captain find in Hollybrass's hand?

It was my handkerchief.

The captain now used that handkerchief to grasp the handle of the knife and pull it from the dead man's back. He stood up. He was looking directly at me.

At last he turned toward the sky. It was darkening again. And the sea had begun to heave in growing swells. "We shall have fifteen more minutes before the storm returns," he announced. "I want this body removed and placed in the steerage. In the available time the rest of you clear the deck. Mr. Johnson's watch shall man the pumps first. Two from Mr. Hollybrass's watch will hold the wheel and the rest can stay in the forecastle. I will call the rotation. Now, quickly!"

The captain's orders were carried out in silence. Dillingham and Grimes took Mr. Hollybrass's body below. The rest of us roamed the decks alone or in pairs, flinging broken bits of mast, sail, and spar into the sea, or trying to tie down what was possible to save by lashing it on deck.

I followed along, doing what I could, my mind a jumble. Not a word was spoken regarding Mr. Hollybrass or his death. As extraordinary as the event was, there was no time, no mind to consider it.

◄ Why isn't Hollybrass's death discussed?

As predicted, the storm struck within the quarter hour and with as much fury as before. But the *Seahawk,* with one mast and but a single sail hung, was more fit to ride it out.

I rushed to the top cargo, where the pumps were. They were simple suction pumps, each capable of being worked by as few as two. But four we were, Grimes, Keetch, Mr. Johnson, and myself, who heaved the handles in the cold, wet, and lurching darkness, as though our lives depended upon it—which they did.

Again the *Seahawk* became a mere toy to the elements. Wind shrieked and howled; more than once water poured over us from above, or the ship heeled to the gunwales,[5] bringing hearts to mouths. For the merest second we would balance on the brink of capsizing while we pumped with greater will than ever. It was as if that rhythmic action was

---

5. **gunwales.** Upper edge of the side of a boat

the true beating of our own hearts—as if, were we to stop for more than a moment, the heart of the ship might cease all beating too.

To work meant to live. And work we did for upwards of three hours. Then we were released.

I was sent to the forecastle to rest along with Morgan, Barlow, and Fisk. Morgan searched for his tobacco pouch, but most personal belongings were flung about and broken, and those still whole were soaking wet. He swore in frustration.

"Be glad you're breathing air, lad," Fisk said wearily.

Chilled to the bone, exhausted, I tumbled into a hammock and tried to sleep. But I'd hardly closed my eyes before I was called out again. Now I was to stand to the wheel. The captain was there—to his credit he remained at the helm throughout the storm—calling upon us to attempt this adjustment, or that, anything to keep our stern toward the wind.

Barlow, my partner, did most of the work. Great strength was wanted just to hold the wheel steady. Whatever strength I had was fast <u>ebbing</u>.

I was frozen, miserable. It did not matter. From duty at the wheel I returned to the pumps. From the pumps to the forecastle. Thence again to the wheel. Round and again, perhaps three times in all. I lost count.

▶ What does Charlotte remember as she is about to fall asleep?

At last—some seventeen hours after we'd first been called out—the storm abated. I was allowed to return to my hammock where, spent and shivering, I closed my eyes. On the edge of sleep I suddenly recalled the visitation of Zachariah and the demise of Mr. Hollybrass. This thought of the dead served to remind me that I was still alive. And that consolation eased my body and calmed my mind. Within seconds I slept the sleep of the dead who wait—with perfect <u>equanimity</u>—upon the final judgment.

Words For Everyday Use

ebb (eb) *vi.,* weaken or lessen

e • qua • nim • i • ty (ek wə nim´ə tē) *n.,* composure, evenness of mind

Chapter Sixteen

t was fourteen hours before I woke. If I'd known that much time had passed I'd have realized something was <u>amiss</u>. No matter what the circumstances, it's irregular for any member of a crew to be allowed to sleep so long.

◄ How long did Charlotte sleep? Why is this strange?

For the moment, however, I remained in my hammock, <u>blithely</u> assuming it was simply not yet time for my normal watch. The canvas curtain had been restrung and was drawn closed . . . but that was the type of kindness Barlow or Ewing would have done. The familiar sounds of the running ship comforted me. And the truth is, despite the fact that my shirt and trousers were still damp, my body one great ache, I was enjoying my rest, thanking God and Zachariah I was alive.

Suddenly I sat up. *But Zachariah died!* I had seen him beaten to death, committed to the sea.

◄ What memory puzzles Charlotte?

Was it his *ghost* then who had saved me? I remembered thinking of an angel. Had I hallucinated the moment? Made a story of it for myself? It was like the kind of forecastle yarn I'd heard the sailors tell so often. I had not believed them. Not then. And yet—what was I to think other than that a miracle *had* transpired? That—I told myself—was absurd. *But I had not imagined it.* I remembered the man's iron grip. Someone *had* helped me. Someone other than Zachariah. It had to be. But who?

I reached from my hammock and drew back the canvas curtain. I was alone. Puzzled, I got up quickly and ran from the forecastle onto the deck.

What I saw was as perfect a sky as any deepwater sailor could wish. The sun was warm, the breeze, out of the west, strong and even. And the deck was in good order, as if the storm had been but a dream. Even the foremast and bowsprit were fully rigged, their sails taut. Only the jagged stump of the mainmast—on the quarterdeck—stood testimony to the last twenty-four hours.

How much the men had accomplished while I slept! I felt forgotten.

There was Barlow. There was Morgan. Foley. It was *my* watch to be on duty. But why hadn't I been called? Then I

Words For Everyday Use

a • miss (ə mis´) *adv.*, in a wrong way
blithe • ly (blīth´lē) *adv.*, cheerfully, in a carefree way

realized that *both* watches were on deck. When I saw Ewing and Keetch working near at hand I went to them.

"Ewing," I called. "Keetch."

► How does the crew's greetings to Charlotte differ from their normal greetings?

Both men turned about. Instead of giving me his regular, casual greeting, "Morning to you, lass!" Ewing stopped his work and <u>gaped</u> at me with a frown that signaled. . . I knew not what. It gave me sudden pause. I glanced at Keetch, whose pinched face bore his familiar rabbit look of fear. But like Ewing, he said nothing.

"Why wasn't I called?" I asked.

"Called?" Ewing echoed dumbly.

"My watch."

They offered no explanation.

"Answer me!"

Ewing sighed. "Charlotte, we were told not to."

"Told? Who told you?"

"It's not for us to say, miss . . ." Keetch whispered.

"You're not to call me miss!" I cried out in exasperation. "Are you going to tell me or not?"

Ewing looked at me reluctantly. "It's . . . Hollybrass. His . . . murder."

I had put that completely out of my mind.

"What's that to do with not calling me?" I demanded, drawing closer.

Ewing sprang up and backed away—as if frightened. I turned to Keetch but he seemed suddenly absorbed in his work.

"Something else has happened, hasn't it?" I said, more and more apprehensive. "What is it?"

"It's the captain, miss . . ." Keetch began.

"*Charlotte!*" I broke in angrily.

Keetch drew a hand across his mouth as if to stop it.

"*What has happened!*" I persisted. "Are you going to tell me or not? Is it some secret?"

► Of what has the captain accused Charlotte?

Ewing licked his lips. Keetch seemed to be avoiding my eyes. But it was he who said, "The captain told us, when we was committing Hollybrass to the sea, that"—now his darting eyes flicked toward me, then away—"it was you . . . that . . . murdered him."

My breath all but failed. "*Me?*" I managed to get out.

"Aye, you."

Words For Everyday Use	**gape** (gāp) *vi.*, stare with open mouth

"Who could believe such a thing?" I exclaimed. "How? Why?"

"To avenge Zachariah's death," Ewing whispered.

I stood there, open-mouthed. "But Zachariah . . ." I began, not even sure what I was about to say.

The former second mate looked around at me, his eyes narrowed. "What about Zachariah?" he asked, standing up.

"He's dead," I said <u>lamely</u>.

"He's all of that," Ewing agreed.

Keetch began to move away quickly. Ewing started to follow. I grabbed his arm.

"Ewing," I said. "Do you think I did it?"

He shook his arm free. "Captain says that dirk was yours."

"Ewing . . . I left that dirk in my old cabin."

"That's what captain said you'd say."

I took in his meaning. "You believe him, don't you?"

He studied his hand.

"And the others?" I wanted to know.

"You'll have to ask them."

Deeply shaken, I started for the galley in search of Fisk but changed my mind. It was Captain Jaggery I had to see.

I turned and headed for his cabin. But before I had taken five steps I was confronted by the captain himself coming to the quarterdeck. I stopped in surprise. The man before me was not the same Captain Andrew Jaggery I'd seen on the quarterdeck the first day we sailed. True, he still wore his fine clothes, but the jacket was soiled and showed any number of rips. A cuff was frayed, a button gone. Small points perhaps, but not for a man of his <u>fastidiousness</u>. And the whip mark, though no longer so pronounced, had become a thin white line—like a persistent, painful memory.

"Miss Doyle," the captain proclaimed for all to hear, "I charge you in the willful murder of Mr. Hollybrass."

I turned to appeal to the crew—only recently my comrades—who stood looking on.

"I did not do it," I said.

"Have no fear *Miss* Doyle. You shall have a jury of your peers. And a speedy trial."

"It's a lie," I said.

"Mr. Barlow," the captain called, never for a moment turning his cold eyes from me.

◄ *What motivation does the captain claim Charlotte has?*

◄ *What evidence is there against Charlotte?*

◄ *What does the captain say when he sees Charlotte?*

Words For Everyday Use	**lame • ly** (lām ´lē) *adv.,* weakly **fas • tid • i • ous • ness** (fas tid´ē əs nəs) *n.,* daintiness; state of being overrefined

▶ *Where does the captain order Charlotte taken?*

Barlow shuffled forward.

"Take the prisoner to the brig," the captain said, offering up a key that Barlow took. "Miss Doyle, your trial for murder will commence at the first bell of the first dog watch today."

"Come along, miss," Barlow whispered.

I shrank back.

"Easy, Charlotte," he went on, "I'll not do you harm."

His words reassured me somewhat. But no other words of comfort came.

The central hatch cover was slid back. Barlow beckoned me to it and under the eyes of all he followed me down the ladder.

We passed by the top cargo—where Barlow lit a lantern—then groped our way into the hold, the bottom of the ship. I had avoided even thinking of the place since the incident of the false head. As far as I could see—which was not very far—it was like some long-forgotten, tunneled dwelling faced with great wood timbers and rough planking grown <u>corrupt</u> with green slime. The area was crammed with barrels and cases, among which only a narrow passageway of planking had been left. Barlow led me forward as the blackened bilge lapped below. The stench was loathsome.

A few feet ahead I saw the brig, not so much a room as a cage of iron bars with a gate for a door. I could make out a stool for sitting. A pan for slops. Nothing more. Had Cranick, poor man, been its last inhabitant?

Barlow unlocked the rusty padlock on the gate. It took a yanking to free it.

"You'll want to go in," he said.

I hesitated. "You'll leave the light, won't you?" I asked.

Barlow shook his head. "If it tumbled we'd have a fire."

"But it will be completely dark."

He shrugged.

I stepped inside. Barlow closed the gate and locked it. For a moment I just stood helplessly, watching him move away. Suddenly frightened, I called, "Barlow!"

▶ *Does Barlow think Charlotte is guilty?*

He paused to peer back over a shoulder.

"Do you think I killed Mr. Hollybrass?"

He considered for a moment. "I don't know, Charlotte," he said wearily.

Words For Everyday Use	**cor • rupt** (kə rupt´) *adj.,* contaminated, rotten

"You must think *someone* did," I cried, wanting to hold him there as much as I wanted answers.

"I don't know as I allow myself to think," he offered and made hastily for the ladder.

Utterly discouraged, I remained standing in the dark. All about me I heard the hollow groans of the ship, the cargo creaking, water dripping and sloshing, rustling, a sudden squeaking of rats.

Nearly sick with fright I felt about for the stool. I sank down upon it, reminding myself I wouldn't have to stay there for long. Captain Jaggery had promised a trial for that very day. But what kind of trial? Zachariah's words filled my head, that a captain is sheriff, judge, jury . . . and hangman too.

Shivering, I bent over and hugged myself to my knees. Without the crew on my side I would be hard put to prove my innocence. I knew that. Yet they seemed to have turned against me. Of all misfortunes that was the most hurtful to bear.

I shifted the stool so I could lean back against the rear bars of the brig, then closed my eyes against the dark. I ran my fingers through my hair but the gesture only reminded me I'd hacked it short. For a brief moment I caught a distant vision of myself as I had been before the *Seahawk,* before this tumultuous voyage. Was it days or years that had passed since?

I was <u>speculating</u> thus when I heard a different kind of noise. At first I ignored it. But when it came again, a slow, hesitant sound, almost like a human step, I opened my eyes wide and stared into the dark. Was this too my imagination?

The sound drew closer. My heart began to pound. "Who's there!" I called out.

◄ *Who visits Charlotte in the brig?*

After a moment I heard, "Charlotte? Is that you?"

I leaped to my feet.

"Who is it?" I cried.

By way of answer the shuffling drew closer, then suddenly stopped. Now I was certain I heard labored breathing. A spark burst forth. Then a tiny light. Before me loomed the ancient head of Zachariah.

Words
For
Everyday
Use

spec • u • late (spek′yo͞o lāt) *vi.,* consider various aspects of a subject

Chapter Seventeen

is face appeared to be floating in air. Terrified, I could only stare into his hollow and unseeing eyes, for so they seemed in the flickering light.

"Is that you Charlotte?" came a voice. His voice.

"What are you?" I managed to ask.

The head drew closer. "Don't you know me?" the voice said.

I stammered, "Are you . . . *real?*"

"Charlotte, don't you *see* me?" came the voice, more insistent than before. Now the light—it was a small candle—was held up and I could see more of him. The very image of Zachariah—but sadly altered too. In life he had never appeared strong or large. In death he'd become shriveled, gray-bearded.

▶ What does Zachariah want?

"What do you want?" I demanded, shrinking back into the furthest corner of the brig.

"To help you," the voice said.

"But you died," I whispered. "I saw your funeral. They wrapped you in your hammock and dropped you into the sea."

A soft laugh. His laugh. "Close to death surely, Charlotte, but not altogether dead. Come, touch me. See for yourself."

Cautiously, I moved forward, reached out, and touched his hand. Real flesh. And warmth. "And the hammock?" I wondered in astonishment.

▶ What explanation does Zachariah offer for what Charlotte supposed was his funeral?

He laughed again. "A full hammock to be sure, but empty of me. It's an old sailor's trick. No doubt if I'd remained in Jaggery's hands I would have died."

"Have you been in the hold all along?"

"Ever since."

I could only stare.

"Keetch brings me food and water every day," he continued. "The food's not as good as I would have prepared, but enough to keep me alive. Look here, Charlotte, if poor Cranick could hide, why not Zachariah? It was Keetch's notion."

▶ Who thought to hide Zachariah?

"Why wasn't I told?"

"It was decided not to tell you."

▶ Why didn't the crew share the secret with Charlotte?

"Why?"

"You forget, Charlotte—you informed upon us."

"That was then, Zachariah," I said, my face burning.

"True enough. And I have been told about you, young soul of justice. There's much to be admired. I salute you."

"I wanted to fill your place."

He smiled. "Didn't I once say how much we were alike? A prophecy! But you're not regretting I'm alive, are you?"

"No, of course not. But if I hadn't caught sight of you during the storm would I ever have seen you?"

"I cannot say."

"The captain might have discovered you then. Why did you come up?"

"What would be the point of staying here and perishing when I could have been of help?"

"You saved me from falling."

"One shipmate helps another."

"But what about Captain Jaggery?" I asked. "Does he know you're here?"

"Now, Charlotte, do you think if he believed me alive he'd allow me here for even a *moment*? Do you?"

"I suppose not," I admitted.

"There you are. That's all the proof I need that he doesn't know. The hope is this," he went on. "When the *Seahawk* reaches Providence—not very long from now, I understand—you shall see, Jaggery will keep the crew on board, not wanting them to talk to anyone. But I'll be able to get off. And when I do I'll go to the authorities to expose him for what he is. Now what do you think?"

◄ *What is Zachariah's plan?*

Even as I grasped the plan I felt a pang of embarrassment that compelled me to turn away.

"What's the matter?"

The pain in my heart made it impossible for me to speak.

"Tell me," he coaxed.

"Zachariah . . ."

"What?"

"You're . . . a black man."

"That I am. But this state of Rhode Island where we're going, it has no more slaves." He suddenly checked himself. "Or am I wrong?"

◄ *Why doesn't Charlotte think Zachariah's plan will work?*

"A black man, Zachariah, a common sailor, testifying against a white officer . . ." I didn't have the heart to finish.

"Ah, but Charlotte, didn't you once tell me it was your father who's part of the company that owns the *Seahawk*?

Words For Everyday Use

proph • e • cy (präf´ə sē) *n.,* prediction
per • ish (per´ish) *vi.,* die

You did. The plan is to go to him. You'll give me a good character, won't you? And if he's like you, there's nothing to fear."

A tremor of unease passed through me. I wasn't sure what to say. I stole a glance at him. "What about Cranick?" I asked. "Did he die? Truly?"

"More's the pity," he said with a shake of his head and a lapse into silence. Then he looked up. "Now then," he said, "I have talked too much of myself. I saw Barlow bring you here, and lock you in. Did you mock Jaggery again?"

I was taken aback. "Didn't anyone tell you?"

"Tell me what?"

"Zachariah . . . Mr. Hollybrass was murdered."

"Murdered!" he cried. "When?"

"During the storm."

"I wasn't told."

"Why not?"

"I cannot imagine." He grew thoughtful, and even glanced toward the ladder. Then, abruptly, he turned back to me and said, "But what's that to do with you?"

"Zachariah, it's the reason I'm here. The captain has accused me."

"*You?*" Again he seemed surprised.

I nodded.

"But surely, Charlotte, you did nothing of the kind." He looked around. "Or did you?"

"No."

"Then there's no more to be said."

I shook my head. "Zachariah," I went on, "the crew seems to side with Jaggery, to think it *was* me."

"I cannot believe that," he exclaimed.

"Zachariah, it's true."

▶ Why is Zachariah perplexed?

He gazed at me in <u>perplexity</u>. "Now it is my turn to ask— why?"

"The murder was done with the dirk you gave me."

"What proof is that? Someone must have taken it from your things in the forecastle."

"Zachariah, when I moved to the forecastle I left it in my cabin."

"Then of course you have nothing to do with it."

"They don't believe I left it there."

Words For Everyday Use	**per • plex • i • ty** (pər pleks´ə tē) *n.,* bewilderment; confusion

"Charlotte, you are not given to lies," he said.

"When you first saw me, Zachariah, did you think that I would ever go before the mast?"

"No . . ."

"Or climb into the rigging during a storm?"

"Not at all."

"Well then? Why shouldn't I have murdered Mr. Hollybrass as well? I'm sure that's the way they're thinking."

◄ What arguments does Charlotte think can be made against her?

My words silenced him for a few moments. His face clouded. But instead of commenting, he stood up. "I have a store of food and water here. I'll get some." Securing the candle to a plank, he moved into the darkness.

I watched him go, puzzled and troubled by his reaction to what I'd said. While he had appeared genuinely surprised, it seemed impossible that he hadn't been told. And indeed, as he vanished into the gloom, a ghastly notion began to fill my head.

◄ Why is Charlotte troubled by Zachariah's reaction? What thought enters her mind?

Perhaps it was *Zachariah* who had killed Mr. Hollybrass!

No doubt he would have killed the captain, given the chance. As for the first mate . . . Had Zachariah done it to strike fear into Captain Jaggery? The very idea was loathsome to me. And yet . . . My racing mind began to construct an entire <u>conspiracy</u>.

The crew, knowing Zachariah was alive, might have guessed—*perhaps knew for a certainty*—that he had done the crime, but would not acknowledge it. Now, with the captain accusing me, they were being asked to choose between me and Zachariah, their old comrade. A decision on their part to defend him would be understandable, and would go far to explain why they'd abandoned me.

◄ What evidence does Charlotte find to support her idea?

But before I could puzzle out my thoughts, Zachariah returned with a jug of water and a hardtack loaf. Mealy as the bread was, I was glad to have it.

"Do you wish to be free of there?" he asked, nodding toward my cage.

"It's locked."

"A sailor knows his ship," he said slyly. Reaching toward the back of the brig, he pulled two bars out from what I now realized were rotten sockets.

"Come along," he said, "but be ready to bolt in if anyone comes."

Words For Everyday Use	con • spir • a • cy (kən spir´ə sē) *n.*, plot; secret unlawful plan

I did so, and we sat side by side, our backs against a barrel in the flickering candlelight.

"Zachariah," I said, "the captain has said he'd bring me to trial. Do you think he means it?"

"That's his right."

▶ According to Zachariah, what will happen?

"And if he does hold a trial, what will happen?"

"He'll be judge and jury and find you guilty."

"And then . . . ?" I asked. When Zachariah didn't answer I said, "Tell me."

"I cannot believe he'd go so far . . ."

"As to hang me?"

His silence was answer enough. For a while we both remained silent. "Zachariah," I said, "I need to know: did anyone else besides me see you during the storm?"

"I exchanged words."

"With whom?"

"Does it make a difference?"

"Maybe."

▶ Why does Charlotte want to know who saw Zachariah?

He considered. "Fisk," he said after a moment. "And Keetch."

"Then it's likely the entire crew knew you came up."

"It's possible," he said with a sudden frown.

Had he read my mind? "Zachariah," I said softly. "it's bound to be one of your mates who killed Hollybrass."

"Charlotte," he said with a sigh, "that's true. Every one of them might have a good reason. But, look here, once we discover who it is we can decide what to do."

I kept glancing sidelong at him, trying to read *his* mind, more and more convinced that it was he who was the murderer. Still, I lacked the courage to ask.

"Tell me all you know," he said.

I related what little I could, from the discovery of Mr. Hollybrass's body to Captain Jaggery's accusation.

My words made him even more thoughtful. "Charlotte," he said finally. "That dirk. Did you tell anyone else you had it?"

▶ Who else knew that Charlotte had the dirk?

I cast my mind back. "Shortly after you gave the blade to me," I recalled, "I wanted to give it back. Remember? Zachariah, when you refused to take it, I offered it to the captain."

He turned around sharply. "But why?"

"I was afraid of it. And you."

"Still?"

"No. But then I was."

"Did you tell him where you got it?"

I shook my head.

"It's not like him to let the matter go at that. He must have demanded an answer."

"He did."

"And?"

"I made one up."

"Did he believe it?"

"I thought so."

"What followed?"

"He said I should keep it. Place it under my mattress."

"And . . . did you?"

"Yes."

"Did anyone else know you had it?"

I thought hard. "Dillingham!"

"What about him?"

"When I was going to give it back to you, I was holding it in my hand. Dillingham saw it. I know he did."

"And if he told others," Zachariah mused out loud, "then there's not a soul aboard who could not know of it."

The moment he said it I knew he was right. And I remembered something else. *Zachariah also told me to put it under my mattress.* I glanced around and caught him stealing a sidelong look at me.

◀ What does Charlotte remember that Zachariah had told her?

"Zachariah, *I* didn't kill Hollybrass. I was aloft when it happened. And when I went aloft, it was the captain who gave me a knife to use. I didn't even have one."

"What happened to that one he gave you?"

"I lost it."

He grunted. Neither yes nor no.

Once more I could taste my accusation of him on my tongue. Even as I thought it the candle gutted and went out. The darkness seemed to swallow my ability to talk.

But Zachariah talked, a sudden and surprising <u>torrent</u>, dark tales about each member of the crew. Every jack of them, he claimed, had run afoul of the law at some time or other. Not mere snitch thieves or cutpurses[1] either; some were true felons.

More compelling than what he said was what he did *not* say. The more Zachariah talked the more convinced I was that his rambling chatter was meant to keep us from the cru-

◀ What effect does Zachariah's rambling have on Charlotte?

---

1. **cutpurses.** People who cut purse straps so as to steal it; thieves

Words
For
Everyday
Use

tor • rent (tôr´ənt) *n.*, flood or rush

cial question—who killed Mr. Hollybrass? And the more that question was avoided, the more certain I was that it was he.

But how could I accuse him? The captain would have to know that he was alive, and that knowledge would mean Zachariah's certain death! Also, it would mean the end of the crew's plan—which required Zachariah—for bringing Captain Jaggery to justice.

No wonder I couldn't ask him the question. I did not want to know!

A noise startled me. I felt Zachariah's hand on my arm. A warning.

A shaft of light dropped into the darkness. I could see that the cargo hatch on deck had been pulled open. In moments we heard someone on the ladder.

I scurried back into the brig. Zachariah hastened to close the bars. Then he retrieved his water jug and disappeared from my side. I did not know where.

I looked toward the ladder and saw Captain Jaggery descending slowly. He carried a lantern and had a pistol tucked into his belt.

When he reached the foot of the ladder he paused and looked about, as if making an inspection of the hold. Finally he approached the brig. There he lifted the lantern and scrutinized me as if I were some *thing*. It was a look filled with a hatred such as I had never seen before—or since—its clear, precise intensity given greater force by his state of personal disorder, his unkempt hair, his dirty face, the trembling muscle along his jaw.

▶ *Why isn't a trial required? Why will the captain hold one anyway?*

At last he said, "Miss Doyle, to have murdered a ship-mate—an officer—is a capital offense. The penalty for such an act is death by hanging. Let me assure you, a trial is not required, the evidence being altogether clear. I have the right to sentence you without trial. But I insist that you have your 'fairness.' It shall not be me who judges you. I'm not such a fool as that. No, the judgment will be made by those whom you have taken as your equals, your shipmates."

So saying he undid the padlock on the brig and pulled the gate open.

"So be it, Miss Doyle. Your trial commences."

Responding to the Selection

Charlotte is to be judged by a jury of her peers, the other members of the crew. If you were one of the crew, would you deem Charlotte guilty or not guilty? Explain your response.

Investigate, Inquire, and Imagine

Recall: GATHERING FACTS

1a. What does Charlotte have to do to earn her place on the crew?

2a. For what does Captain Jaggery blame Charlotte after she frees the flying jib? How does he punish her?

3a. What argument does Charlotte overhear before they sail into the hurricane? What evidence is there against Charlotte when Mr. Hollybrass is found dead?

Interpret: FINDING MEANING

1b. Does the crew want Charlotte to succeed at her test? Explain.

2b. Why does Captain Jaggery insist that Charlotte perform this task? Why doesn't the crew support Charlotte's outburst against Captain Jaggery?

3b. Why does the crew believe Charlotte is guilty? Why is the captain intent on having Charlotte charged with this murder?

Analyze: TAKING THINGS APART

4a. Charlotte undergoes many changes after becoming a member of the crew. Outline the changes in her appearance, actions, and ideas.

Synthesize: BRINGING THINGS TOGETHER

4b. How do you think Charlotte's family would react if they could see her life on the ship? How do you think Charlotte will adapt to life on land?

Evaluate: MAKING JUDGMENTS

5a. When Captain Jaggery says that Mr. Doyle would not approve of Charlotte's actions, Charlotte replies that her father would approve of her reasons. Do you agree that Charlotte's reasons are justified? Explain your response.

Extend: CONNECTING IDEAS

5b. Do you think that the ends can justify the means or are certain actions always unacceptable? Use examples from your own experience or current events to illustrate your point.

Understanding Literature

A **motive** is a reason for acting in a certain way. What is Charlotte's motive for becoming part of the crew? What beliefs of Charlotte's are embodied by this action?

Mood, or **atmosphere,** is the emotion created in the reader by a piece of writing. A writer creates a mood though the use of concrete details. Examine the scene during the hurricane. Identify six concrete details used by Avi and the mood these details create.

A **simile** is a comparison using *like* or *as*. What simile is used at the end of chapter 14 regarding Captain Jaggery's decision to sail into the hurricane? What is the meaning of this comparison?

Chapter Eighteen

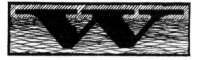hen I emerged on deck from the dark hold, the very perfection of the day—bright sun, dazzling blue sky, clouds both full and white—made me shade my eyes. And though the *Seahawk* pitched and rolled gently upon the softest of seas, I felt as though my legs would give way under me. For when I was able to look about I saw that the captain had arranged a kind of courtroom.

In the ship's waist, on the starboard side, he had assembled the crew in two rows, some sitting on the deck, the rest standing behind the front rank. Before them—atop the central cargo hatch—a chair had been placed. The captain hurried me past the crew—none of whom would look me in the eye—and instructed me to sit in the chair, saying it would serve as the prisoner's dock.

◄ *How does the crew react when Charlotte passes them?*

Now he took his place in one of his fine cabin chairs. It had been set up high behind the quarterdeck rail, a rail that he pounded sharply with the butt of his pistol.

"I proclaim this court to be in session in strict accordance with the law," he said. "Considering the overwhelming evidence against the accused, it needn't be held at all. But as I have told Miss Doyle, she will enjoy the benefit of my generosity."

So saying he now took up his Bible, and though he had just seated himself, rose abruptly and brought it down to the crew. It was Fisk he approached first.

"Place your hand upon this," he demanded.

Fisk did as he was ordered, but, clearly unnerved, touched the book as one might a hot plate.

"Do you, Mr. Fisk," the captain <u>intoned</u>, "swear to tell the truth, the whole truth, and nothing but the truth, so help you God?"

Fisk hesitated. He glanced quickly at me.

"Do you?" Captain Jaggery pressed.

"Yes," Fisk replied finally in a hollow whisper.

Satisfied, the captain went on to the next man, then the next, until he had sworn in the entire crew.

From the solemnity that showed upon their faces, from

Words For Everyday Use

in • tone (in tōn´) *vt.*, utter or recite

► How do the crew feel about taking an oath on the Bible?

► What does Charlotte promise to do that she knows she will not do?

► What offer to save herself does the captain offer Charlotte?

► What statements does Captain Jaggery record?

their nervous fidgets and downcast eyes, it was clear to me that the men were mightily unsettled by the oath they had been made to take. They could not take the Bible lightly.

But I was certain each of them believed—as I did—that the murder was done by Zachariah, whom they themselves had conspired to hide in the hold. It was to *him* they would remain steadfast, not me. They would tell the truth, but in such a way as to protect Zachariah. How could I disagree?

Once Captain Jaggery had sworn in the crew, he approached me. I too laid my hand on his Bible. I too promised to tell the truth even as I knew I would not speak it completely.

The swearing done the captain returned to his chair and again banged his pistol on the rail. "Will the accused stand," he said.

I stood.

"Before this court," he continued, "I, Andrew Jaggery, by my rightful authority as master of the *Seahawk*, charge you, Charlotte Doyle, with the unnatural murder of Samuel Hollybrass, late of Portsmouth, England, first mate on the *Seahawk*. Miss Doyle, how plead you?"

"Captain Jaggery . . ." I tried to protest.

"How *plead* you Miss Doyle?" he repeated sternly.

"I did not do it."

"Then you plead innocent."

"Yes, innocent."

"Miss Doyle," he asked, with what I could have sworn was a slight smile about his lips, "do you desire to withdraw your claim to being a member of this crew? That is to say, do you wish to hide behind your father's name, and thus avoid judgment by these men?"

I turned slightly so as to consider the crew. They were gazing at me intently but offered nothing to help. Though I sensed a trap in the question, I was loath to abandon my trust in the men just when I most needed them.

"Miss Doyle, do you wish to be judged by these men or not?"

"I trust them," I said finally.

"Do you wish to charge someone else with the act of murder?"

"No," I said.

"Let it thus be understood," Jaggery declared, "that the accused insists she be judged by *this* court, and further, charges no one else with this crime." So saying, he pulled a log book onto his lap, and with pen in hand, wrote down my words.

When done, he looked up. "Miss Doyle, do you agree that someone murdered Mr. Hollybrass?"

"Yes."

"Someone on the *Seahawk?*"

"It has to be."

"Exactly. Someone on this ship. And at the moment you are the only one accused."

"*You* have accused me."

"But given the opportunity, Miss Doyle, you accused no one else." It was clear this was a major point with him. All I could reply was, "Yes."

The captain made a note in his book, then shifted his attention to the crew. "Is there any man here who is willing to defend this prisoner?"

◄ Does anyone defend Charlotte?

I turned to the men whom I'd begun to call friends. Ewing. Barlow. Fisk. Not one of them would look at me.

"No one?" the captain asked <u>mockingly</u>.

No one.

"Very well," the captain went on. "Miss Doyle, you will have to defend yourself."

"They are frightened of you," I said. "They won't speak because—"

"Miss Doyle," he interrupted, "is it not my right, my responsibility, as master of this ship, to determine who used the knife and for what reasons?"

"Yes, but—"

Again he cut in. "Have I asked for anything but the truth?"

"No . . ."

"And a murder *was* committed by someone on this ship. That is not open to question. But have you so much as hinted it was someone else?"

"No, but—"

"Miss Doyle, although none of these men wishes to defend you they have all sworn to speak the truth. Can you ask for anything more than that?"

Again I said nothing.

"Very well. We shall begin."

He leaned back in his chair, log book still in his lap, pen in hand, pistol at the ready. "We have agreed that Mr.

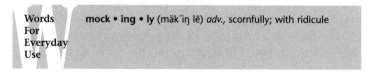

Words For Everyday Use

mock • ing • ly (mäk´iŋ lē) *adv.*, scornfully; with ridicule

► What two things does the captain establish about the murder weapon?

Hollybrass was murdered. Is there anyone here who believes he was killed by other than this weapon?"

He held up the dirk. No one spoke.

The captain continued. "Let us now determine its ownership. Miss Doyle," he asked, "do you recognize this knife?"

"Captain Jaggery, I left it . . ."

"Miss Doyle," he said again. "Do you recognize this knife?"

"Captain Jaggery . . ."

"Was this the blade that killed Mr. Hollybrass?" he repeated.

"Yes."

"Very well then," he said. "I shall ask once more. *Do you recognize this knife?*"

"I do," I said reluctantly.

"Tell us about it."

"Zachariah gave it to me."

"Mr. Zachariah?" he said, pretending to be surprised.

"Yes. And I showed it to you a few days into the voyage."

"But when you showed it to me," he quickly put in, "and I asked who gave it to you, what did you say?"

I said nothing.

► What lie does the captain discover Charlotte made?

"You told me that a certain Mr. Grummage of Liverpool gave it to you. Am I correct?"

"Captain Jaggery . . ."

"Answer the question. Yes or no?"

"Yes."

"Are you saying now that you lied? Yes or no?"

"Yes," I said, appealing to the crew, "but only because I didn't wish to bring harm upon Zachariah."

"Whatever your excuses, Miss Doyle, you admit you *lied* to me."

"Yes," I was forced to say. "And you said I should keep the knife."

"Indeed I told you that. And you did keep it, didn't you?"

"Yes," I said sullenly, sensing he was getting the best of me.

He turned to the crew. "Did any of you see this girl with this knife in hand at any time?"

The men shifted uneasily.

"Come now, gentlemen!" the captain barked. "This is a court of law. All of you are required to speak the truth. You swore upon the Bible to do so. I'll ask again, did any of you see this girl with this knife?"

The crew appeared to be looking every way but at the captain. Then I noticed Dillingham rub the back of his neck.

The captain saw it too. "Mr. Dillingham," he called out sharply. "Do you have something to say? Step forward, sir."

Dillingham came forward awkwardly.

"What have you to say?"

"I saw her with the knife, sir."

"When?"

"Shortly after we set sail."

"Thank you, Mr. Dillingham. I applaud your <u>forthrightness</u>. Now then, did anyone else see her with the knife. Mr. Ewing?"

Ewing said as much as Dillingham. When pressed, so did Foley. So did Mr. Johnson.

The captain was now leaning over the rail, clearly enjoying himself. "Did anyone *not* see her with the knife?" he said dryly.

No one spoke.

"I wish," he said, "to state how *unnatural* it is for a girl to carry a knife."

◄ What point does the captain make about Charlotte having a knife? What is Charlotte's rebuttal?

"You have no reason to say unnatural," I objected. "You even gave me one!"

"Did I?"

"Yes. During the storm."

"Why did I?"

"To cut away the rigging."

"To be sure, that was an emergency. By what reason did you have a knife when there was no emergency?"

"To defend myself."

◄ What reason does Charlotte give for having the knife?

"Defend yourself? Against whom? Against what?"

Fearful of his traps, I was not sure what to say.

"Against what?" he pressed. "Did anyone threaten you? Any of these men?"

"No, not them."

"Who then? Come, speak up."

"You."

"How so?"

"You struck me."

"Miss Doyle, I do strike members of the crew. It is a common enough practice." He turned to the men. "Have any of you ever known a captain who has not, from time to time, struck a member of the crew? Come now, speak up if you have!"

Words
For
Everyday
Use

forth • right • ness (fôrth´rīt nəs) *n.,* directness

▶ How does the
captain respond to
this reason?

No one spoke.

The captain turned back to me. "But do they turn upon me with a knife? Is that what you are suggesting, Miss Doyle? That members of a crew have the right to <u>assault</u> their captain with a weapon?"

He had confused me again.

"Besides," he added, "You had that knife on the *first* day of this voyage. Did you think I would strike you then?"

"No. I believed you were a gentleman."

"So, Miss Doyle, you had the knife *before* you met me, did you not?"

"Yes," I admitted.

The captain smiled with obvious satisfaction. "The knife, then, is clearly yours. And you were seen with it. You admit to all this."

He turned to the crew. "Have any one of you seen a knife in her hand other than during the first few days of this voyage? Step forward if you have."

It was Grimes who did so.

"Ah, Mr. Grimes. You have something to say."

"Begging your pardon, sir, I saw her."

"In what circumstances?"

"I was teaching her to use a knife."

▶ What other time
was Charlotte seen
with a knife?

"*Teaching* her to use a knife?" the captain repeated <u>portentously</u>.

"Yes, sir."

"When?"

"Before the storm."

"And did she learn?"

"Yes, sir."

"Was she good at it?"

"Aye. Uncommon good."

"Mr. Grimes, I ask you, did you ever hear of another girl who desired to learn the use of a knife?"

Grimes hesitated.

"Answer."

"No, sir."

"Do you not think it's unnatural?"

"Sir, I don't know as if . . ."

"Agree or disagree?"

**Words
For
Everyday
Use**

as • sault (ə sôlt´) *vt.,* attack

por • ten • tous • ly (pôr ten´təs lē) *adv.,* pompously; with awe or amazement

He bobbed his head apologetically. "Agree."

"Unnatural again!" the captain proclaimed. "Mr. Hollybrass was murdered during the hurricane. Did anyone see this girl on the deck during the storm?" He looked to the crew. "Anyone?"

There were a few murmurs of "Yes."

"Mr. Barlow, I think you say yes. What was Miss Doyle doing?"

◀ What was Charlotte doing on deck during the hurricane?

"She was with the crew, sir. Doing her part like we all was. And good work too."

"Doing her part like we all was," the captain echoed in a mocking tone. "Mr. Barlow, you are not young. In all your years have you ever seen, ever heard of a *girl* who took up crew's work?"

"No sir, I never did."

"So, then, is it not unusual?"

"I suppose."

"You suppose. Might you say, *unnatural?*"

"That's not fair!" I cried out. "Unusual and unnatural are not the same!"

"Miss Doyle, have you an objection?"

"There was nothing unnatural in what I did!" I insisted.

"Miss Doyle, let me then put the question to you. Have *you* ever heard of a girl joining a crew?"

I felt caught.

"*Have* you?"

"No."

"So even *you* admit to that."

"Yes, but—"

The captain turned to the crew. "Is there anyone here who has ever heard of a girl doing what this Miss Doyle has done?"

No one spoke.

"So what we have here is a girl who admits she owns the weapon that murdered Mr. Hollybrass. A girl who lied about where she got it. A girl who was taught to use a blade, and learned to use it, as Mr. Grimes would have it, 'uncommon' well. A girl who, all agree, is *unnatural* in every way she acts. Gentlemen, do we not, as natural men, need to take heed? Is it not our duty, our *obligation,* to protect the natural order of the world?"

◀ What does the captain say is unnatural about Charlotte?

Once more he turned to me. "Miss Doyle," he said, "Mr. Zachariah was a friend of yours."

"The best of friends."

"What happened to him?"

◀ What relationship does the captain establish?

"He was <u>flogged</u>," I murmured.

"And?"

For the last time I appealed mutely to the crew. They were all looking steadily at me now.

"I asked you a question, Miss Doyle. What happened to Mr. Zachariah?"

" . . . he died," I said softly. "Flogged to death."

"Who flogged him?"

"You did, <u>unmercifully</u>."

"Any one else?"

"Mr. Hollybrass."

▶ What is the captain getting at?

"Mr. Hollybrass. Why was Mr. Zachariah being flogged?"

"There was no reason."

"No reason? Did he not take part in a mutiny?"

"He had every right to . . ."

"A right to mutiny?"

"Yes."

"You yourself, Miss Doyle—in great fear, if I remember—informed me that a mutiny was about to occur. Mr. Zachariah was one of the participants. Yet you think it *unfair* to flog him?"

"You wanted to kill him."

"So you were angry at me?"

I looked into his glinting eyes. "Yes," I declared, "deservedly so."

"And at Mr. Hollybrass?"

After a moment I again said, "Yes."

"Mr. Zachariah was a particular friend of yours, was he not, Miss Doyle?"

"Yes."

"A black man."

"He was my friend!"

"So you resented his being given the punishment he deserved."

"It was not deserved."

"Is murder an unnatural act, Miss Doyle?"

"Yes."

▶ What other things does the captain find "unnatural"?

"Is the way you dress unnatural?"

"Not for the work I do . . ."

"What work is that?"

"As member of the crew."

Words For Everyday Use

flog (fläg) *vt.,* beat with a whip

un • mer • ci • ful • ly (un mʉr´si fəl lē) *adv.,* relentlessly

"Is being a crew member not unnatural for a girl?"

"Unusual," I insisted. "Not unnatural."

"Your hair?"

"I could not work with it long!"

"Work?"

"I am one of this crew."

"Unnatural," he said.

"Unusual," said I.

"So we have in you, Miss Doyle," the captain pressed on, "an unnatural girl, dressing in unnatural ways, doing unnatural things, owning the very knife that killed Mr. Hollybrass. And Mr. Hollybrass was the man you disliked for flogging your particular black friend—"

"You make it seem all wrong when it isn't!" I cried out.

He turned to the crew. "Does anyone wish to make a statement on this girl's behalf?"

No one spoke.

"Miss Doyle," he said, "Do you wish to say anything?"

"My father—"

"Miss Doyle," the captain cried out, "when we began I offered you the opportunity of claiming the protection of your father. You refused it then!"

Miserable, I could only bow my head.

He turned to the crew. "Does anyone wish to make a statement on this girl's behalf?"

No one spoke.

"Miss Doyle," he said. "Do you wish to say anything?"

Miserable, I could only shake my head.

"Very well. I must declare a verdict."

He stood. "As master of the *Seahawk*, it is my judgment that this unnatural girl, this Charlotte Doyle, is guilty of the crime of murdering Samuel Hollybrass."

◄ *What verdict does the captain deliver? What is Charlotte's sentence?*

For a final time he turned to the crew. "Is there anyone who wishes to speak against this verdict?"

No one spoke.

"Miss Doyle," he said to me, "have you anything to say on your behalf now?"

"I did not do it!"

"Miss Doyle, the facts have spoken otherwise. I wish to inform you that the penalty for such a crime is to be hanged by the neck from the yardarm. Within twenty-four hours you shall be hanged until you are dead."

So saying, he brought down his pistol hard upon the rail. The trial was over.

Chapter Nineteen

ithout another word Captain Jaggery led me back to the hold and locked me in the brig. I turned from him, but I believe he stood there, considering me for a while by the gloomy light of his lamp. Then he left. I heard his retreating footfalls and the creak of the ladder, saw the light gradually fade away until the hold grew completely dark again. At last I slumped onto the stool. And though it was dark I closed my eyes.

Startled by a sound I looked up. Zachariah, a candle in his hand, was standing before me.

Silently, he circled the brig and pulled out the bars. I crept from my cage and we sat down close together, backs once more against a barrel, the little candle before us. I told him all that had happened. He remained silent, nodding now and again.

By the time I was done I was weeping <u>copiously</u>. Zachariah let me sob. He waited for my last sniffle, then asked, "How much time does he give you?"

"Twenty-four hours," I murmured.

"Charlotte," he said softly, "he'll not see it through."

"He does what he says he'll do," I said bitterly. "You said as much yourself. And he has the whole crew agreeing with his judgment. He was that careful. Punctilious," I spat out, remembering the word the captain had used to describe himself.

"I don't know the word."

"Everything in order."

"Aye, that's him." Zachariah rubbed the stubble around his chin. "And did no one stand up for you?" he asked.

"No one."

He shook his head. "It's that I don't understand."

I looked up. "Don't you?" For the first time I felt my anger turn toward him. "Why?"

"Had they not become your friends?"

"I have no friends."

"You must not say that, Charlotte. Didn't I tell you right from the beginning: you and me—together."

▶ *What doesn't Zachariah understand?*

Words For Everyday Use

co • pi • ous • ly (kō´pē əs lē) *adv.,* abundantly

I shook my head at the memory.

"What's this?" he said, trying to laugh my response away. "Not friends?"

"Zachariah," I burst out, "I am going to be hanged!" He made a gesture of dismissal. "You won't."

"How can you be so sure!"

"I won't let him."

"You? You'd have to show yourself. What of your plan to go to the authorities?"

"I'll give it up."

"After all that's happened?"

"Yes."

"I don't believe you!"

"Charlotte, why should you say that?"

When I kept silent he said, "Come now, Charlotte, something else is <u>preying</u> upon your thoughts. Something bitter. You must have it out."

"Don't tell me what I *must* and must not do!" I cried. "That's for Jaggery."

"Forgive me. This old black man humbly requests you tell him what's beset your mind."

"Zachariah," I blurted out, "you haven't told me the truth."

He turned to look hard at me. "You must explain yourself."

I retreated to the brig.

He pulled himself closer, pressing his face to the bars. "Charlotte!" he insisted. "Now I am truly begging. Tell me what you mean."

"Zachariah," I said, tearful again, "I *know* who killed Mr. Hollybrass."

"Then why don't you speak it out so I can hear?" he said sharply.

"I'm waiting for him to say it himself," I threw back.

He sighed. "There's an old seaman's saying, Miss Doyle: the Devil will tie any knot, save the hangman's noose. That Jack does for himself. Your silence is foolish. I beg of you, who do you think it is?"

I pressed my lips tight.

"Miss Doyle," he said, "if you want to save your life you will tell me. I am trying to help you, but I cannot manage it

◄ *What would Zachariah do to save Charlotte?*

Words
For
Everyday
Use

prey (prā) *vi.,* weigh heavily

without your thoughts. You have some choices, Miss Doyle. Shall I make them clear? Do you prefer to dangle from a yardarm by your neck? Or do you wish to walk free? What *do* you want, Miss Doyle?"

"To live."

He sighed. "Then speak."

"Mr. Zachariah," I said with increasing weariness, "I already told you, I want the man to come forward himself."

"Most unlikely."

"Apparently," I said with even greater bitterness.

Something in my voice must have alerted him. He <u>scrutinized</u> me shrewdly. "Miss Doyle, why are you calling me *Mister* Zachariah?"

"For the same reason you are calling me Miss Doyle."

He cocked his head to one side. I could feel his gaze upon me. For a moment I had the courage to return it, but quickly glanced away.

He said, "Charlotte . . . you have grown suspicious of me. Am I correct?"

I nodded.

"Look at me."

I did.

He sighed again. "Is it truly possible you think *I* murdered Mr. Hollybrass?"

After a moment I admitted, "Yes."

"And why?"

"Zachariah," I cried out, "you were there on deck. You had every reason to want him dead. And since I'd told you, you knew where I'd left the dirk. I suppose you would have preferred to kill the captain, but thought the first mate would do. And no one would know, would they? Least of all Jaggery.

"I'm certain it's what the rest of the crew believes," I rushed on. "And that's why they wouldn't speak for me! It's to protect you, Zachariah, just as they've done all along. I can hardly blame them!"

I sank onto the floor, sobbing.

For quite a time Zachariah didn't speak. And the longer he remained silent the more certain I was that I'd uttered the truth.

"Charlotte," he said at last, "if you believed all that, why did you not say so before?"

► What is unusual about the conversation between Charlotte and Zachariah? What is the reason for this difference?

► What does Zachariah correctly assume?

Words For Everyday Use

scru • ti • nize (skro͞ot'ʼn īz) *vt.,* examine closely

"Because you're the only one—you told me so yourself, and I believe you—the only one who can get off the *Seahawk* when we reach Providence and go to the authorities about Captain Jaggery!"

"And *that's* why you said nothing?"

"Yes."

"It does you honor," he said very quietly.

"I don't care about honor," I declared. "I'd much rather live! But the least you could do is be honest with me."

He hesitated, then said, "Charlotte, you do not have it correct."

"I don't suppose I know everything . . ."

"Charlotte," he said with the utmost solemnity, "I did not kill Mr. Hollybrass."

I eyed him suspiciously.

"Charlotte," he continued, "we shall either live by believing one another, or, by not believing, die."

"I want to believe you," I told him. "I do." I sank back down on the stool. For a long while neither of us spoke. There seemed nothing to say. Then, in despair, I said, "Zachariah, sometimes I think Jaggery has worked all this out so you and I should blame one another. But you said he doesn't know you are alive."

He started. "Repeat what you said."

"What?"

"The last thing."

"About his not knowing you're alive?"

"Yes." He moved from the brig then and sat down, his mood completely changed. After a while he murmured, "Charlotte!"

"What?"

"When I was on the deck during the storm—Jaggery saw me."

His words sank in slowly. "Zachariah, are you telling me that the captain knows you are *alive* and has done *nothing?*"

"Yes."

"When did he see you?" I demanded.

"As I say, during the storm. I was on deck, trying to reach the mainmast."

"Before or after you helped me?"

He thought a moment. "Before. Yes, I was bent into the wind, doubled over, when I heard voices arguing. I couldn't make them out at first, then I saw Captain Jaggery and Mr. Hollybrass. It was they who were arguing. Furiously. I heard Mr. Hollybrass accuse the captain of deliberately taking the *Seahawk* into the storm. Jaggery was enraged. I thought he

◄ Why had Charlotte said nothing before? What does Zachariah think of her silence?

◄ What does Charlotte think Jaggery has done?

◄ What is Charlotte surprised to learn?

◄ What did Zachariah see during the storm?

was about to strike the man. Then the first mate took himself off while the captain turned toward me. At first he didn't recognize me. Only swore . . . as I did. But then—"

"What did he do?"

"Nothing. Just stared in a wild sort of way. Mind, the storm was growing worse. But before he could do or say anything I headed for the foremast where I chanced to be where you needed me."

"Didn't you wonder when after the storm he did nothing?"

▶ Why might the captain not have done anything after seeing Zachariah during the storm?

"Charlotte, you yourself told me that when I helped you on the mast you thought me a ghost, an angel perhaps. Think of Jaggery. If ever a man had guilty deeds locked in his thoughts, deeds enough to raise the dead from seven seas, he would be the one.

"When—after the storm—he did nothing, I decided that *was* exactly what he thought: that I was an apparition. His leaving me here was proof enough. How else to explain it? And therefore I was safe."

I gazed at him through the bars, trying to grasp the full import of what he was saying. "Zachariah . . ." I said slowly, trying to sort out my tumbling thoughts, "during the trial he made a point of asking me what happened to you."

"And you answered . . . ?"

"To make sure he didn't know, I said that you had died. But Zachariah, if he *did* know you to be alive, he might also guess we *all* knew it. And might think—exactly as I did—that you killed Mr. Hollybrass. But he wouldn't say."

"So as to condemn you."

"Only with me gone, could he turn on you. He could not do it the other way around, for fear of my going to the authorities—as I threatened to do. Do you think he knows who really killed Mr. Hollybrass?"

"He might."

"But who?"

Zachariah grew thoughtful. "To kill a hand, during such a storm, when everyone is desperately needed, takes a kind of . . . madness," he said finally.

"Well then," I said. "Who does that leave?"

We looked at one another. And knew.

"The captain," I said. "It must have been he who killed Mr. Hollybrass."

▶ Who do Charlotte and Zachariah realize is the true killer?

"Charlotte," Zachariah protested, "Mr. Hollybrass was Jaggery's only friend . . ."

"Yes, people would think them friends. No one would believe it could be Captain Jaggery. But you told me they had never sailed together before. And I never saw much friendship between them. Did you?"

"No . . ."

"You said they argued," I continued. "I saw some of that too. In the storm, you even thought Captain Jaggery lifted a hand to strike him after Mr. Hollybrass made an accusation."

"Of deliberately sailing into the storm."

"Is that a serious charge?"

"The owners would be greatly alarmed. But to *kill* him . . ."

"Zachariah, he sees you. He knows you're alive. The crew, he realizes, must know it too. I'm a threat to him. So are you. And now, here's Mr. Hollybrass, another threat. But, let him murder Mr. Hollybrass and everyone will think you did the crime."

◄ How does the captain's plan rid him of all three of his troubles?

"But then, he accuses you," Zachariah said.

"And see how much he's managed!" I cried.

Zachariah stared into the dark. Then slowly he said, "The crew keeps silent to protect me, even as he hangs you."

To which I added, "And once I am gone, Zachariah, then . . . he'll deal with you."

Zachariah grew thoughtful. Finally I heard him whisper, "May the gods protect us . . ."

The excitement of our discovery ebbed. We sat in silence. In time the candle went out.

"What," I asked ruefully, "can we do about any of this?"

"Charlotte, we must force him to confess."

"He's too powerful."

"True, you'll not get any man to confess when he holds a gun and you've got none."

"What do you mean?"

"Charlotte, see what happened when we rose against him before. You've been in his quarters, haven't you? You must have seen that iron safe of his that's full of muskets. You're not likely to get into that. No one knows where he keeps the key."

◄ What role will Charlotte have in a new uprising against the captain?

I reached over and plucked at his arm. "Zachariah," I said, "I know where he keeps it."

Chapter Twenty

 scrambled from the brig and very quickly told Zachariah what had happened when I brought the information about the round robin to Captain Jaggery, how he removed a key from behind the portrait of his daughter and with it opened up the gun safe.

Zachariah grunted. "I never thought to look there."

"Did you look?"

▶ What would have happened if the crew had found the key before?

"To be sure. If we could have secured that key—and the guns—we would have taken him before. And I can promise you, it's still true."

I felt a surge of excitement. "Is there anyone who goes into his cabin now?" I asked.

"I don't know," Zachariah said. "But *you* could go."

"Me?"

"You know exactly where it is, don't you?"

"But I'm supposed to be here!"

"Exactly."

"Zachariah," I cried. "That would be insane. What if he caught me?"

▶ Why is there nothing to stop Charlotte from going to get the key?

"He could do no worse than he intends to do."

I saw the gruesome logic in that. "But even if I did get the key, then what?"

"If Jaggery had no muskets, the men could be rallied again."

"What if the crew gets their hands on the guns? What will they do?"

"I couldn't answer to that," he admitted.

"I don't want any more death," I said.

"Get the key to me, Charlotte. The rest will follow."

The <u>enormity</u> of the idea frightened me. "Why shouldn't you get it to begin with?" I wanted to know.

▶ Why shouldn't Zachariah try to get the key?

"If it's me he catches, Charlotte, he'll be free to get rid of both of us. If it should happen that you fail, it would still leave me a chance to try and act."

"*Try?*"

"Charlotte, it's all I can promise."

Words For Everyday Use

e • nor • mi • ty (e nôr′mə tē) *n.,* outrageousness

I considered his reasons. Then I said, "Zachariah, you told me that the crew has been coming down to bring you food.

"Yes."

"I won't do anything until you tell them that it wasn't you who killed Hollybrass. Nor me. And that we're certain it was Captain Jaggery himself. It will make it much safer for me to make the attempt."

"I see your point."

"When do they come?"

"When they can."

"Zachariah," I reminded him. "He's only given me twenty-four hours."

"Get back there then," he said, motioning to the brig and pulling himself up. "I'll try to find someone."

◀ What does Charlotte demand must happen before she tries to get the key?

I retreated into the cage. He adjusted the bars, and left a new candle within easy reach—as well as a tinder box. I heard him move away through the darkness until I lost sense of where he was.

There was this about the dark: It freed me from time and space. Cut off as I was, I could retreat into thoughts about all that had happened since my arrival at Liverpool with that odd Mr. Grummage. It seemed a million years ago, yet no time at all. I couldn't help but feel some pride in what I'd accomplished.

◀ How does Charlotte feel about what she has done since the ship left Liverpool?

Perhaps it was Zachariah's reference to my father, but for the first time in a long while I began to think of my true home, in Providence, Rhode Island. Though I'd only the vaguest memories of the house itself (I had left it when I was six), thoughts of my mother, my father, my brother and sister, were all very strong and clear.

With a start—for it is a curious fact that I had *not* truly considered my family for a time—I began to contemplate an accounting to them of all that had happened—if I lived. With great <u>vividness</u> I pictured myself relating my adventure, while they, grouped about, listened in <u>rapt</u>, adoring attention, astonished yet proud of me. At the mere anticipation, my heart swelled with pride.

◀ How does Charlotte anticipate her family will react to her adventures?

I was still basking in these dreams when I heard the sounds of someone approaching. Not knowing who it might be, I pushed myself to the back of the brig and waited. But then I heard: "Charlotte!"

Words For Everyday Use

viv • id • ness (viv′id nis) *n.*, striking realism

rapt (rapt) *adj.*, completely absorbed

It was Zachariah's voice.

"Give us light," he called in a whisper.

I scrambled forward, found the tinder box, and in moments had the candle lit. There was Zachariah. And with him was Keetch.

From the first moment I had seen Keetch—as I came aboard the *Seahawk*—I'd never cared for him. He was too nervous, uncertain. To see that he was the one Zachariah had brought was not the greatest comfort.

"Miss Doyle," Keetch said when he drew close, peering about in his agitated way, "I'm pleased to see you."

"And I you," I made myself reply.

What followed then was a strange council of war. Zachariah made it clear at the start that neither he nor I had murdered Mr. Hollybrass.

"But who did then?" Keetch asked, truly alarmed.

"Captain Jaggery," I said quickly.

"Why . . . what do you mean?" he demanded.

We offered our reasons.

Keetch listened intently, only occasionally looking up with startled eyes at me or Zachariah, yet nodding to it all. "Murder his own mate," he murmured at the end with a shake of his head.

"Do you have any doubts?" Zachariah asked.

"None about you," Keetch told him.

"And me?" I asked.

He seemed hesitant to speak.

"As I see it," I said, "the men didn't want to help me during the trial because you thought it was Zachariah who killed Mr. Hollybrass."

"True enough," Keetch said. "We talked about just that. I'll admit, I was one who said we owed more to Zachariah here than to you. Understand," he said, "where old loyalties lie."

I assured him that I did and insisted I laid no blame.

"As you know," Keetch continued, "I wasn't one of those who took to you in any partial way, not like Zachariah here. I'll confess too, I never wanted you aboard. You'll remember, I told you so when first you came."

I nodded.

"But you've proved me wrong more than once," he concluded. "So if my word means anything, you can now be sure no man will support your honor more than I." That said, he held out his hand to me.

I was relieved at Keetch's acceptance. Perhaps, I thought, I'd wronged him.

▶ *Who does Zachariah bring? How does Charlotte feel about seeing him?*

▶ *Why hadn't the crew stood up for Charlotte during the trial?*

▶ *What does Keetch promise?*

So then and there, he and I shook hands like old sailors. I felt a great weight drop from my soul.

The news Keetch brought was crucial, that we were—by the captain's reckoning—a few days' sail from Providence. Hanging me was therefore of the utmost urgency—which explained the captain's twenty-four hours.

Keetch readily agreed with Zachariah that if we could manage to keep the captain from his guns, never mind securing them for ourselves, another rising could be staged. He would vouch for that. "But," he warned, "he keeps those guns locked up and the key to himself."

"I know where he hides it," I said.

He looked around in surprise.

"Where?"

I told him.

"And would you try to get them?"

"Yes."

Keetch whistled softly. "Most times he keeps to his cabin," he said.

"All you need do is find some way to get him and hold him on deck," Zachariah said.

◄ What role will Keetch play in the plan?

"I'll be here and ready when you have," I put in. "Once you've detained him, I can secure the key to the gun cabinet."

"It shouldn't take her but a moment, Keetch," Zachariah pressed.

Keetch studied his hands for a long while. "It might be possible." He glanced upward. "What about the others?"

"You're going to have to spread the word that it was the captain who murdered Mr. Hollybrass, not me," Zachariah told him. "Not her either."

◄ What else must Keetch do?

Keetch nodded. "They're going to want to know what happens to that key once she's got it," he said.

I looked to Zachariah.

"She'll give it to me," he said. "I'll be in top cargo, waiting for it. And when I've got it that will be the time for you and me—" he nudged Keetch with an elbow—"to lead another rising."

Once again we waited on Keetch. The way he fidgeted it was easy to see that he was nervous about the plan. But that was natural. I was nervous too. Finally he said, "It would be the only way. Except it better not fail."

Zachariah turned to me. "There you are," he said. "We'll do it!"

On all this we shook hands, and I was soon, once again, alone in darkness.

► Why wasn't
Charlotte frightened?

It's odd perhaps, but I was not frightened. I assumed we could succeed with our plan. Oh, what a power of faith in justice had I then!

A few days from Providence . . . I smiled. I would return to the life I led with my family, but now in America, where, so I had been long taught to believe, greater freedom held sway. I sat for the better part of an hour thinking, not of what was about to happen, but of happy days ahead. . . .

I heard a sound. I started up, peering into the darkness.

Zachariah, quite breathless, appeared before me, "Charlotte," he called. "It's time!"

I crawled out from the brig. Zachariah had found a small lamp, one well-hooded. "This way," he whispered before I could ask him anything.

We moved down the hold toward the central cargo bay and its ladder. I looked up. It was quite dark above.

"What time is it?" I suddenly asked.

"Two bells into the midwatch."

► Why must the
plan be carried out in
the middle of the
night?

By shore reckoning that meant it would be one o'clock at night!

"Couldn't we do it by daylight?"

"Charlotte, you're scheduled to be hanged at dawn."

My stomach rolled. My legs grew shaky.

Zachariah put his hand on my arm as if he himself had caught my fear. "You'll do well," he said.

He closed down the lantern's hood to a mere slit and led the way up the ladder. I followed until we reached the top cargo. Once there, Zachariah signaled me toward the rear ladder. It would put me directly into the steerage before the captain's cabin.

"Where will the captain be?" I whispered.

"Keetch sent word that he's got him at the helm," Zachariah explained, his voice low. "He's managed to jam the wheel somehow, and called the captain for instruction. Roused him from his bed."

"How long will I have?"

"Take no more time than you need," was his reply.

"And the rest of the crew?"

"Word on that too. They all know, and are waiting. Go on now. I'll watch for you here."

I looked at him.

| Words
For
Everyday
Use	**rouse** (rouz) vt., wake from sleep

"Charlotte, it's this or the royal yard."

I crept aloft and soon was standing alone in the empty steerage, listening. The steady wash of waves, the bobbing and swaying of the ship, the creak and groan of timbers, all told me the *Seahawk* was plowing toward home in a brisk wind. By chance the door to my old cabin was open. As it swung to and fro it banged irregularly, rusty hinges rasping. When had I heard that sound before? What came into my mind was my first night aboard the ship, when I lay upon my bed feeling so abandoned! How frightened I'd been then! How little was there then to fear! I even remembered the voices I'd heard outside my door at that time. *Who had spoken?* I wondered, as though to keep myself from moving forward now. *What was said?*

Nervously, I glanced back over a shoulder through the steerage portal. While I could not see much, the soft glow that lay upon the deck told me that it must be a full or nearly full moon. I was glad of that. It meant there would be some light to see by inside the captain's cabin.

Yet, <u>inexplicably</u>, I remained standing there, wasting precious time, listening to my old door bang and creak, trying to rid myself of the fear that lay like heavy ballast[1] in the pit of my stomach: a notion that I had neglected to consider *something* about the voices I had heard that first night. The suspicion became rather like an invisible rope that restrained me. Try though I might I could not find how to unbind it.

A random plunge of the ship roused me to my business. Making sure the little lantern was well shielded, I moved to the door, put my hand to the handle, and pushed. It gave with ease.

The room lay open before me. Dimly I could make out its fine furnishings—even the chessboard with its pieces—exactly as I recollected them from my first visit. I lifted the lantern. There, seated at the table was Captain Jaggery. His eyes were upon me.

"Miss Doyle," he said, "how kind of you to visit. Do please step in."

◄ What does Zachariah mean?

◄ What does Charlotte try to remember as she stands outside the door to her old cabin?

◄ What is Charlotte unable to figure out?

◄ What does Charlotte see when she enters the captain's cabin?

---

1. **ballast.** Anything heavy carried in a ship for balance

| Words For Everyday Use | in • ex • pli • ca • bly (in eks´pli kə blē) *adv.*, without explanation |

e was waiting for me. All I could do was stare at him in disbelief.

"Miss Doyle," the captain said. "Would you be good enough to sit." He rose and held an upholstered seat out for me.

As the *Seahawk* rolled, the door behind me slammed shut. The sudden noise startled me from my daze.

▶ Why isn't the captain surprised to see Charlotte?

"You knew I was coming," I whispered, finding it impossible to raise my voice.

"Of course."

"How?"

There was a slight smile on his lips. Then he said, "Mr. Keetch."

"*Keetch?*" I echoed lamely.

▶ Of what else had the captain been informed?

"Exactly. Who, from the start, kept me well informed about the crew; how they kept other sailors from signing on, how they threatened passengers so they would not sail. He informed me about Cranick. About Zachariah. Yes, Miss Doyle, I know your friend is alive and has been hiding in the hold. I'm delighted that he keeps out of the way. No charge of murder shall be put to *me*, shall it?

"More to the point I know about what you are doing in my cabin now. It is the business of a ship's master, Miss Doyle, to know his ship and his crew. To keep everything in order. I told you that before. Apparently it still surprises."

I stood unmoving.

"Won't you sit?" he asked.

"What do you mean to do with me?" I asked.

"You've had your trial. Was it not fair?"

"I did not kill Mr. Hollybrass."

"Was the trial fair, Miss Doyle?"

"It was you who killed him," I burst out.

He remained silent for a long while. Then at last, he said, "Do you know why I despise you, Miss Doyle?" It was said evenly, without emotion. "Do you?"

"No," I admitted.

▶ Why does the captain despise Charlotte?

"The world of a ship, Miss Doyle, is a world not without quarrels," he began, "sometimes bitter quarrels. But it is, Miss Doyle, a world that does work according to its own order.

"Now when a voyage commences, all understand the rightful balance between commander and commanded. I can deal with the sailors, and they with me. I need them to run the *Seahawk*. Just as they need me to command her. So we live by a rough understanding, they and I. When this voyage began I had high hopes you would help me keep the crew in order with your ladylike ways.

"But you, Miss Doyle, you interfered with that order. You presumed to meddle where you had no right. Look at the way you acted! The way you've dressed! It doesn't matter that *you* are different, Miss Doyle. Don't flatter yourself. The difficulty is that your difference encourages *them* to question their places. And mine. The order of things.

"Miss Doyle, you ask me what I intend to do. I intend to—"

"You killed Hollybrass, didn't you?" I now demanded.

"I did."

"Why?"

◀ *What does the captain admit?*

"He threatened me," the captain said with a shake of his head. "And in the midst of that storm. It was <u>intolerable</u>."

"And then you decided to put the blame on me," I pressed. "To keep me from going to the authorities and telling them the truth about you."

"Who shall be blamed for this disastrous voyage?" he asked. "It cannot be me, can it? No, it must be someone from the outside. The unnatural one. To preserve order, Miss Doyle, sacrifices must always be made. You."

◀ *Why must Charlotte be blamed?*

"Am I a sacrifice?" I demanded.

"In all honesty, I wished you had broken your own neck falling from the rigging or on the bowsprit. You did not. As it stands we should reach Providence in a few days. It is crucial that when we make landfall I be firmly established as master.

"Mr. Hollybrass had to die. No one could possibly believe I would do such a thing. So, yes, since you are unnatural—proclaimed so, I hasten to remind you, by *all*—you shall be held responsible. Thus is our world set right again."

I still hadn't moved.

Ignoring me now, he proceeded to light some candles. A soft yellow glow filled the room.

"Look," he said.

Puzzled, I gazed about the cabin. I saw now what I had not seen before in the light of the moon. In the candlelight I could see that much of the furniture was cracked. Many legs

◀ *What does Charlotte now see in the captain's cabin?*

Words For Everyday Use

in • tol • er • a • ble (in täl´ər ə bəl) *adj.,* unbearable

had splints. Upholstery was water stained. Frames on the walls hung crookedly. Some had pictures missing. Maps and papers on the table were wrinkled or sadly torn. The tea service on the table was dented and tarnished, but arranged and presented as whole. The chess pieces were, I now realized, no more than salt and pepper shakers, broken cups, bent candlesticks.

I looked at him again. He was gazing at me as if nothing had happened.

"It was the storm that destroyed much of it," he said. "I have spent considerable time in setting the room to rights. Have I not done well? Order, Miss Doyle, order is all. Take away the light and . . ." He leaned over and blew the candles out. "You see—it's hard to notice the difference. Everything appears in order."

"You're . . . mad," I said, finally able to respond to the man.

"On the contrary, Miss Doyle, I am the soul of reason. And to prove my reasonableness I'm going to give you some choices.

"You came to my cabin, Miss Doyle, to steal the key to the guns. Is that not so?"

I didn't know what to say.

"You don't have to admit to it. I know it's so. Mr. Keetch has informed me about everything." Even as he spoke he reached into his jacket pocket and drew out a key.

"Here is the key you wanted," he said, tossing it so that it landed by my feet. "Take it up, Miss Doyle," he said. "Go to the cabinet. Take out any one of the muskets. All are loaded. I will sit here. You may carry out the plan you and Zachariah <u>concocted</u>. You must know that I will be murdered. But Miss Doyle, do not doubt for an instant that the world will learn your part in this. Do you think these sailors will keep quiet? No. Open that cabinet and you let out scandal. Horror. <u>Ruination</u>. Not just you. Your family. Your father. His firm.

"So before you do that, consider another choice." He walked to the far corner of his cabin and picked up what looked like a bundle of clothing. He dumped it at my feet. I saw by the light of my lantern that it was the garments I had set aside weeks ago—a lifetime ago, it seemed—for my dis-

> ▶ What choices does the captain offer Charlotte?

Words For Everyday Use	**con • coct** (kən käkt´) *vt.*, devise, plan **ru • in • a • tion** (rōō ə nā´shən) *n.*, being ruined

embarkation. White dress. Stockings. Shoes. Gloves. Bonnet. All in perfect order.

"Put these back on, Miss Doyle," he said. "Resume your place and station. Publicly <u>renounce</u> your ways, beg me for mercy before the crew, and I—you have my word—I will grant it. All will be restored to its proper balance. Like my cabin furnishings. A little dented and torn perhaps, but in the diminished light no one need know. All reputations saved.

"Of course, there is a third choice. You had your trial. A verdict was reached. You could accept that verdict and be hanged. I'll even invent a story for your family. Some . . . sickness. An accident. The hurricane. So yes, the hanging is one of your choices.

"Now what shall it be?" He clasped his hands, sat again in his chair and waited.

Out on the deck three bells rang.

"What if I don't accept any of them?"

He hesitated. "Miss Doyle, I thought I made it clear. There are no other choices."

◀ What does Charlotte choose?

"You're wrong," I said. And so saying, I turned and rushed out of his cabin, along the steerage and into the waist of the ship.

There was, as I had guessed, a full moon. It sat high in a sky of darkest blue, amidst shadowy scudding clouds. The sails on the forward mast were full, and fluttered with the tension of the wind. The sea hissed about the bow as the *Seahawk* rushed ahead.

In a line upon the forecastle deck the crew had gathered and were looking down at me. When I turned to look at the quarterdeck I saw Keetch there, not far from the splintered stump of the mainmast. Near him was Zachariah, his hands bound before him. It took but a moment for me to realize that our entire conspiracy had been overthrown and turned against us.

◀ What has happened to Zachariah? What does Charlotte realize?

I stepped forward. Behind me I heard Captain Jaggery at his door. I took a quick look; he had a pistol in his hand. As he emerged I moved hastily across the deck.

For a moment all stood still as if each were waiting for the other to move first.

It was Captain Jaggery who broke the silence. "There stands your shipmate," he proclaimed shrilly to the crew.

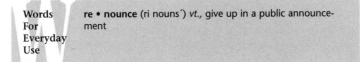

Words For Everyday Use

re • nounce (ri nouns´) *vt.*, give up in a public announcement

▶ What accusations does the captain make?

"She crept into my cabin and would have murdered me in my sleep if I'd not awakened and managed to wrest away this pistol. Not enough to have murdered Mr. Hollybrass! She would have murdered me. I tell you, she would murder you all!

"It was Zachariah there," the captain continued to <u>rant</u>, "hiding, pretending injury to keep from work, who let her out and set her on this murderous plot.

"She had her trial. She had her verdict, to which you all agreed. Only just now I gave her yet another way to release herself from the punishment of hanging. I begged her to put on her proper dress, and told her I would find the heart to forgive. This she refused."

"He's lying!" I called out. "He's trying to save himself. He's the one who killed Hollybrass. He's admitted it."

"She's the one who lies!" the captain cried, pointing his pistol now at me, now toward the crew, which made them visibly flinch. "The truth is she wants to take over the ship. Yes, she does. Would you stand for that? Do you wish to put into port and have this girl spread the slander that she, a *girl*, took command of this ship, took over each and every one of you and told you what to do?

▶ What does the captain claim Charlotte wants to do? Why does he think this reason will inspire the crew to side against her?

A *girl!* Would you ever be able to hold your heads up in any port in any part of the world? Think of the shame of that!"

I had begun to edge toward the steps to the forecastle deck, thinking the men there would stand behind me. But as I approached none moved forward. I stopped.

"You mustn't believe him!" I begged them.

"Don't be afraid of her," Captain Jaggery cried. "Look at her. She's nothing but an unnatural girl, a girl trying to act like a man. Trying to *be* a man. She can only harm you by living. Let her have her punishment."

▶ Does the crew support Charlotte?

I started up the forecastle steps. The men began to back away. Horrified, I paused. I sought out Barlow. Ewing. Grimes. Fisk. Each in turn seemed to shrink from my look. I turned back.

Captain Jaggery fingered the pistol in his hand. "Take her!" he commanded.

But that far they would not go. And the captain who saw this as soon as I now began to advance toward me himself.

I backed away from him until I was atop the forecastle

Words For Everyday Use	**rant** (rant) *vi.,* talk in a loud, wild way

deck. The line of crew had split, some to either side. "Help me!" I appealed to them again. But though they were deaf to Captain Jaggery they were equally deaf to me.

The captain, in careful pursuit, now slowly mounted the steps to the forecastle. I retreated into the bow, past the capstan, on a line with the cathead.[1] He kept coming. Against the moon, he seemed to be a faceless shadow, a shadow broken only by the daggerlike glitter of the pistol that caught the light of the moon. My heart hammered so I could hardly breathe. I looked for a way to escape but found none.

The bow seemed to dance under my feet. Frantically I looked behind me; there was little space now between me and the sea.

Still the captain closed in. I scrambled back high into the fore-peak. He stopped, braced his legs wide, extended his arm and pistol. I could see his hand tighten.

The bow plunged. The deck bucked. He fired all the same. The shot went wide and in a rage he flung the pistol at me.

I stumbled backward, tripped. He made a lunge at me, but I, reacting with more panic than reason, scrambled down onto the bowsprit itself, grabbing at the back rope to keep from falling.

◄ Where does Charlotte go to try to escape the captain?

Clinging desperately to the rope—for the ship plunged madly again—I kept edging further out on the bowsprit, all the while looking back at Captain Jaggery. In the next moment he scrambled after me.

I pushed past the trembling sails. Below, the sea rose and fell.

Vaguely, I sensed that the crew had rushed forward to watch what was happening.

There was no more back rope to hold to. And the captain continued to inch forward, intent on pushing me off. There were only a few feet between us. With a snarl he lunged at me with both hands.

◄ What happens when Captain Jaggery lunges after Charlotte?

Even as he did the *Seahawk* plunged. In that instant Captain Jaggery lost his footing. His arms flew wide. But he was teetering off balance and began to fall. One hand reached desperately out to me. With an <u>instinctive</u> gesture I jumped toward him. For a brief moment our fingers linked

---

1. **cathead.** Beam near the bow of a ship to which an anchor was hoisted

Words For Everyday Use

in • stinc • tive (in stiŋk´tiv) *adj.,* prompted by a natural tendency

and held. Then the ship plunged again and he tumbled into the waves. The ship seemed to rear up. For one brief interval Captain Jaggery rose from the sea, his arm gripped in the foaming beak of the figurehead. Then, as if tossing him off, the *Seahawk* leaped, and Captain Jaggery dropped into the roaring foam and passed beneath the ship, not to be seen again.

Weak, trembling, soaking wet, I made my way back along the bowsprit until I could climb into the forepeak.

The crew parted before me, no one saying a word. I stopped and turned, "Give me a knife," I said.

Grimes took one from his pocket.

I hurried across the deck to where Zachariah still stood. Keetch had fled his side. I cut the rope that bound Zachariah and then embraced him as he did me. Finally he walked to the quarterdeck rail. As if summoned, the crew gathered below.

> ▶ *Who does Zachariah say should be the new captain?*

"Shipmates," Zachariah cried. "It's needful that we have a captain. Not Keetch, for he was an informer and should be in the brig. But Miss Doyle here has done what we could not do. Let her be captain now."

Chapter Twenty-two

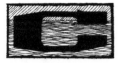aptain in name perhaps, but not in practice. I was too aware of all I had yet to learn for that. Besides, as Zachariah would acknowledge later, the fact that I was the daughter of an officer in the company that owned the *Seahawk* was no small factor in my formal <u>elevation</u>. It would preserve the niceties. But, though I was entered into the log as captain—I wrote it there myself—it was Zachariah who took true command. I insisted, and no one objected. The crew chose their mates—Fisk and Barlow—and assembled themselves into two watches, and managed well enough. Johnson was more than happy to return to the forecastle.

◄ *Why is Charlotte a good choice for captain? Who is the actual leader of the ship?*

Regarding Captain Jaggery, the log read simply. At the crew's urging I wrote that our noble captain had kept his post at the wheel during the hurricane, only to be swept away in the storm's final hour. Mr. Hollybrass was afforded the same heroic death. I have been skeptical of accounts of deceased heroes ever since.

◄ *What explanation of the captain's disappearance is given?*

Though Fisk and Barlow insisted I move into the captain's quarters, I continued to work watch and watch as before. In between I wrote furiously in my journal, wishing to set down everything. It was as if only by reliving the events in my own words could I believe what had happened.

Within twenty-four hours of Captain Jaggery's death, Morgan threw the line, pulled up a plug of black sand, tasted of it, and announced, "Block Island."[1] We would reach Providence—assuming the wind held—in no more than forty-eight hours. Indeed, twelve hours later, the mainland was sighted, a thin <u>undulating</u> ribbon of green-gray between sea and sky.

There was much rejoicing among the crew about this and their grand expectations once they were ashore. As for me, I found myself suddenly plunged into instant, and to me, inexplicable <u>melancholia</u>.

"What ails our Captain Doyle?" Zachariah asked, using the term he had taken to teasing me with. He'd discovered

---

1. **Block Island.** Island in southern Rhode Island

Words For Everyday Use

el • e • va • tion (el ə vā´shən) *n.*, high position

un • du • lat • ing (un´dyo͞o lāt iŋ) *adj.*, moving in waves; wavy

mel • an • cho • li • a (mel ən kô´lē ə) *n.*, mental disorder characterized by extreme depression of spirits

me up at the forepeak, <u>morosely</u> watching the sea and the coast toward which we were drawing ever closer.

I shook my head.

"It's not many a lass," he reminded me, "who boards a ship as passenger and eases into port as captain."

"Zachariah," I said, "what shall become of me?"

► What does Charlotte have to look forward to?

"Why, now, I shouldn't worry. You've told me your family is wealthy. A good life awaits you. And Charlotte, you've gained the firm friendship of many a jack here, not to speak of memories the young rarely have. It has been a voyage to remember."

"Where is your home?" I asked suddenly.

"The east coast of Africa."

"Were you ever a slave?"

"Not I," he said proudly.

"And did you want to become a sailor?"

That question he didn't answer right away. But when he did, he spoke in a less jovial tone. "I ran away from home," he said.

"Why?"

"I was young. The world was big. My home was small."

"Did you ever go back?"

He shook his head.

"Never longed to?"

"Oh yes, often. But I didn't know if I would be welcome. Or what I would find. Do you remember, Charlotte, what I first told you when you came aboard? That you, a girl, and I, an old black man, were unique to the sea?"

"Yes."

"The greater fact is, " he said, "I am unique everywhere."

"And I?"

► What does Zachariah warn Charlotte to do with care?

"Who can say now?" he answered. "I can only tell you this, Charlotte. A sailor chooses the wind that takes the ship from a safe port. Ah, yes, but once you're abroad, as you have seen, winds have a mind of their own. Be careful, Charlotte, careful of the wind you choose."

"Zachariah," I asked, "won't anyone—in Providence—ask what happened?"

"The thing we'll do," he replied, "is remind the owners that we managed to bring the *Seahawk* into port with their

---

Words For Everyday Use

mo • rose • ly (mə rōs´lē) *adv.*, gloomily

cargo intact. True, we lost captain and first mate, but they died, don't you see, doing their duty."

"Won't Keetch talk?"

"Too grateful that we spared his life. Beside, Jaggery had some hold on him. Blackmail. So Keetch is free of that too. "

"Cranick?"

"Never on board. I promise you Charlotte," he concluded, "the owners will be sorrowful for all the loss, but their tears won't be water enough to float a hat."

Almost two months after we left Liverpool, we entered Narraganset Bay[2] and slowly beat our way up to Providence. And on the morning of August 17, 1832, we warped into the India docks.

◀ How long has Charlotte been aboard the ship?

When I realized that we were going to dock I went to my cabin and excitedly dressed myself in the clothes I had kept for the occasion: bonnet over my mangled hair. Full if some-what ragged skirts. Shoes rather less than intact. Gloves more gray than white. To my surprise I felt so much pinched and confined I found it difficult to breathe. I glanced at my trunk where I had secreted my sailor's garb as a tattered memento. For a moment I considered changing back to that, but quickly reminded myself that it must—from then on—remain a memento.

◀ What does Charlotte do as the ship approaches Providence? How does she feel about this change?

As the ropes secured us, I looked upon the dock and—with a beating heart—saw my family among the waiting throng. There were my father and mother, brother and sister, all searching up for me. They were as I remembered them, prim, overdressed despite the dreadful summer heat.

My mother was in a full skirt the color of dark green with a maroon shawl about her shoulders and a bonnet covering most of her severely parted hair. My father, the very image of a man of property, was frock-coated, vested, top-hatted, his muttonchops[3] a gray bristle. My brother and sister were but little miniatures of them.

Truly, I was glad to see them. And yet, I found that I struggled to hold back tears.

Farewells to the crew were all too brief, carefully restrained. The real good-byes had been spoken the night before. Tears from Barlow, a gruff hug from Fisk, kisses to my cheeks from Ewing—"You're my mermaid now, lass," he whispered—an offer (with a sly grin) of a splicing knife from Grimes—refused—a round of rum toasted by Foley, topped out with three "Huzzahs!" from all. Then came the final mid-

◀ What kind of farewell does Charlotte get from the crew?

---

2. **Narraganset Bay.** Inlet of the Atlantic, extending into Rhode Island
3. **muttonchops.** Side whiskers shaped like a mutton chop, that is, narrow at the top and broad and rounded at the bottom

night watch with Zachariah—during which time he held my hand and I, unable to speak, struggled to keep my tumbling emotions within.

Now I marched down the gangway into the careful embrace of both my parents. Even my brother, Albert, and sister, Evelina, offered little more than sighlike kisses that barely breathed upon my face.

We settled into the family carriage.

"Why is Charlotte's dress so tattered?" Evelina asked.

"It was a difficult voyage, dearest," my mother answered for me.

▶ What does Charlotte's family notice about her?

"And her gloves are so dirty," Albert chimed in.

"Albert!" Papa reproved him.

But then, after we'd gone on apace in silence, my mother said, "Charlotte, your face is so very *brown.*"

"The sun was hot, Mama."

"I would have thought you'd stay in your cabin," she chided, "reading <u>edifying</u> tracts."

Only the clip-clop of the horses could be heard. I looked past the brim of my bonnet. I found my father's eyes hard upon me as if <u>plumbing</u> secrets. I cast down my eyes.

"A difficult voyage, my dear?" he asked at last. "You were dismasted."

"There was a terrible storm, Papa," I said, appealing to him with my eyes. "Even Fisk . . . the sailors called it one of the worst they'd ever experienced. We lost the captain. And the first mate."

"God in his mercy . . ." I heard Mama whisper.

"Well, yes, I'm sure," my father offered. "But one must be careful about the words we choose, Charlotte. It's well known that sailors have an unhealthy tendency toward exaggeration. I look forward to reading a more sober account in your journal. You did keep it as you were bidden, did you not?"

"Yes, Papa." My heart sank. I had completely forgotten he would want to see what I'd written.

"I'm greatly desirous of reading it." He wagged a finger at me playfully. "But mind, I shall be on the lookout for spelling mistakes!"

Then, thank heavens, Albert and Evelina insisted upon telling me about our fine house on Benevolent Street.

Words For Everyday Use

ed • i • fy • ing (ed´i fī iŋ) *adj.,* enlightening, building morality or spirituality

plumb (plum) *vt.,* discover the facts; fathom

It was bigger than I remembered. Great columns graced the doorway. Huge draped windows—like owl eyes—faced the street. Its full two stories put me in mind of an English fortress.

Then we were safely inside, standing in the large foyer before the grand stairway. It seemed immense to me. And dark. Cut off—after so many days—from sun and air.

With my father looking on, Mama gently removed my bonnet. When she saw my mangled hair, she gasped.

"Charlotte," she whispered. "What happened?"

"Lice," I heard myself saying. One of the few explanations I'd rehearsed.

She gasped again and before I could restrain her, took up my hands in pity. "Poor girl," she whispered. "Such awfulness." Even as she stood there, holding my hands, a strange look passed across her face. Slowly she turned my hands over, gazed at the palms, then touched them with her fingertips. "And your hands?" she asked in horror. "They are so . . . hard."

"I . . . I had to do my own washing, Mama."

"Dear Charlotte, I am so frightfully sorry."

"Mother," Papa suddenly said, "perhaps we should move on to our breakfast together." He offered me his arm. I took it gratefully.

We walked into the dining room. The table was laid with white cloth, fine china-plate and silver. Breaking from father I started to sit.

"Let your mother sit first, my dear," I heard him murmur.

As we began to eat, my father said, "Am I to understand, Charlotte, as the shipping agent informed me, that those other families, the ones who had promised to be with you during the voyage, never fulfilled their pledge."

"No, Papa," I answered. "They never came to the ship."

"How dreadfully lonely for you," my mother said, shaking her head sadly.

"Two months with no one to talk to!" Evelina exclaimed.

"Of course I talked, silly."

"But—to whom?" Albert asked in puzzlement.

"The men. The sailors."

"The men, Charlotte?" my mother said with a frown.

"Well, you see . . ."

"You mean the captain, do you not Charlotte?" my father suggested.

"Oh, no, not just him, Papa. You see, a ship is so small. . ."

Suddenly my father interjected, "We seem to be lacking butter."

◄ What explanation does Charlotte make for her cut hair? What else must she explain?

◄ What things does Charlotte say or do that surprise her family?

"I'll get it!" I said, pushing back my chair.

"Charlotte, sit!" my father barked. He turned to the maid who was waiting near by. "Mary, butter."

The maid curtsied and went out.

When I turned back around I found my sister staring at me.

"What is it?" I asked.

"I just thought of what you look like!" Evelina said.

"What?"

She wrinkled her nose. "An Indian!"

Albert laughed.

"Children!" my father cried. With much effort Albert and Evelina sat still.

"Charlotte," I heard my mother ask, "how *did* you pass your time?"

"Mama, you have no idea how much work there is on . . ."

My father abruptly took out his watch. "It's much later than I thought," he said. "Evelina and Albert have their lesson in the nursery. Miss Van Rogoff, their tutor, will be waiting. Children."

Now struggling to suppress their giggles, Albert and Evelina rose from their seats.

"You may go now," my father said to them.

Once they had gone, the room became very quiet. My mother was looking at me as if I were a stranger. My father's gaze was his most severe.

▶ How do Charlotte's parents react to what she has said?

"The sailors were very kind to me," I offered. "I could hardly be expected . . ."

"You must be fatigued," he cut in. "I think some rest would do you some good."

"I'm very awake Papa. I mean, I've grown used to very little sleep, and . . ."

"Charlotte," he insisted, "you are tired and wish to go to your room."

"But—"

"Charlotte, you mustn't contradict your father," my mother whispered.

I rose from my seat. "I don't know where my room is," I said.

"Mary," my father called. "Ask Bridget to come in."

Mary appeared in a moment with another maid, a girl not very much older than I.

"Bridget," my father said, "take Miss Charlotte to her room. Help her with her bathing and change of clothes."

"Yes, sir."

Bridget led the way. My room was on the right side of the house on the second floor. Its windows faced the rear garden where a trellis of roses were in <u>radiant</u> bloom. I stood at the windows, gazing down on the earth and flowers and told myself again and again, "This is home. This is home."

I heard a sound behind me. A man—yet another servant, I assumed—brought in my trunk and opened it. Then he left.

I went back to staring out the window.

"If you please, miss," I heard Bridget say, "your father said I was to bathe and dress you."

◄ Why won't Bridget call Charlotte by her name?

"Bridget, my name is not miss. It's Charlotte."

"I'll not be wanting to take the liberty, miss."

I turned to face her. "Even if I want you to?"

"I don't think the master would approve, miss."

"But if *I* asked you . . ."

"Not wishing to be impertinent, miss," Bridget said in a barely audible voice, "but it's master who pays my wages."

I looked into her eyes. Bridget looked down. I felt a pain gather about my heart. There was a soft knock on the door.

"Shall I answer it, miss?" Bridget whispered.

"Yes, please," I said with great weariness.

Bridget opened the door to the other maid, Mary.

Mary entered and curtsied. "Miss," she said to me, "master asks that Bridget take and destroy all your old clothing, miss. He also requests that I bring your journal down to him, miss."

I looked at the two of them, the timidity of their postures, the unwillingness to engage me with their eyes.

"Mary," I said. "That is your name, isn't it?"

"Yes, miss."

"Would you call me Charlotte if I asked you to. Be my friend?"

Mary stole a nervous glance at Bridget.

"Would you?"

"I shouldn't think so, miss."

"But . . . why?" I pleaded.

"Master wouldn't have it, miss. I should be <u>dismissed</u>."

I could not reply.

Then, after a moment Mary said, "I'll be happy to take the journal down now, miss."

"Shall I fetch it, miss?" Bridget asked me.

I went to the trunk, found the book, and gave it to Mary. She curtsied and without another word—and still avoiding

---

Words For Everyday Use

ra • di • ant (rā´dē ənt) *adj.,* showing well being

dis • miss (dis mis´) *vt.,* remove from a position of employment; fire

my look—stepped soundlessly from the room, shutting the door behind her. I went back to the window.

"Shall I assume that all the clothes in the trunk, miss, are old?" Bridget asked finally.

"What will happen to them?"

"Give them to the poor, I should think, miss. Mistress is very kind that way."

"There is one thing I must preserve," I had the wits to tell her. Hurriedly I removed my sailor's clothing.

"Are those to be *kept,* miss?" Bridget asked in puzzlement.

"I wish to show them to my parents," I lied.

"Very good, miss."

My trunk was unpacked. I bathed. How strange *that* was! The filth fairly floated off. I dressed, helped—or rather interfered with despite my protestations—by, Bridget. But instead of going downstairs I dismissed her, then sat on my bed, marveling at its softness.

In truth, I was trying to compose myself. I was afraid to go downstairs. A call, I knew, would come soon enough. But, as I sat there a memory came of my first moments upon the *Seahawk.* How alone I felt then. How alone I was now! "Oh, Zachariah," I whispered to myself. "Where are you? Why don't you come for me!"

It was my father's call that came—but not before two hours had passed. Mary returned with a request that I go directly to the parlor. With a madly beating heart I started down the broad, carpeted stairs, my hand caressing the highly polished balustrade.[4] Before the massive doors to the room I paused and drew breath. Then I knocked.

"Come in," I heard my father say. I entered.

My mother was seated in a chair; my father was by her side, standing with his legs slightly apart, as if bracing himself. A hand gripped one of his jacket lapels. The other hand rested protectively on Mama's shoulder. She stared down at the carpet.

"Charlotte," my father said, "please shut the door behind you."

I did so.

"Now come stand before us."

"Yes, Papa." I advanced to the place indicated by my father's pointed finger. Only then did I notice that the room—even for an August midday—was uncommonly warm. I glanced toward the fireplace and was startled to see a blaze there. It took me another moment to realize that my journal was being consumed by flames.

---

4. **balustrade.** Railing

► What does Charlotte keep from her trunk? What excuse does she give for keeping them?

► Why does Charlotte compare this moment to her first on the Seahawk?

► Why is the room uncommonly warm?

I made a move toward it.

"Stop!" my father cried. "Let it burn."

"But . . ."

"*To ash!*"

I turned to them in disbelief.

"Charlotte," my father began, "I have read your journal carefully. I have read some of it—*not all*—to your mother. I could say any number of things, but in fact will say only a few. When I have done we shall *not* speak of any of this again. Is that understood?"

◄ What demand does Mr. Doyle make about the journal?

"But . . ."

"Is it *understood*, Charlotte!"

"Yes, Papa."

"When I sent you to the Barrington School for Better Girls, I had been, I believed, reliably informed that it would provide you with an education consistent with your station in life, to say nothing of your expectations and ours for you. I was deceived. Somehow your teachers there filled your mind with the unfortunate capacity to invent the most outlandish, not to say *unnatural* tales."

◄ What does Charlotte's father believe about what she has written?

"Papa!" I tried to cut in.

"*Silence!*" he roared.

I closed my mouth.

"What you have written is rubbish of the worst taste. Stuff for penny dreadfuls! Beneath contempt. Justice, Charlotte, is poorly served when you speak ill of your betters such as poor Captain Jaggery. More to the point, Charlotte, your spelling is an absolute disgrace. Never have I seen such <u>abominations</u>. And the grammar . . . It is beyond *belief!*

"An American tutor, miss, shall instill a little order in your mind. But the spelling, Charlotte, the spelling . . ."

"Papa . . ."

"That is *all* we have to say on the subject, Charlotte. All we shall *ever* say! You may return to your room and you will wait there until you are summoned again."

I turned to go.

"Charlotte!"

I stopped but did not turn.

"You are forbidden—*forbidden*—to talk about your voyage to your brother and sister."

My wait to be called was a long one. The simple truth is I

Words
For
Everyday
Use

a • bom • i • na • tion (ə băm ə nāˊshən) *n.*, anything hateful and disgusting

► Where is Charlotte confined? What excuse is made for her absence?

► What does Charlotte do with the books she is given to read?

► How does Charlotte get a newspaper? Why does she want the newspaper?

was not allowed to leave my room. All meals were brought by Mary on a tray. I was permitted no callers, not even Albert or Evelina. "She's seriously ill," people were told. And no matter how much I tried, Bridget, the one person I saw with any regularity, would not yield to my efforts of friendship.

From my mother I received little comfort but many tears. From my father, a vast quantity of books that he deemed suitable for my <u>reclamation</u>. Not a word, not a question, to console me.

But I did not read. Instead I used the books, the blank pages, the margins, even the mostly empty titlepages, to set down secretly what had happened during the voyage. It was my way of fixing all the details in my mind forever.

One week had passed in this fashion when I thought to ask Bridget for a newspaper.

"I'll have to request it of master," she replied.

"Bridget," I told her, "for every day you bring a newspaper *without* informing my father I shall give you a gift."

Bridget gazed at me.

After a momentary search of my vanity table I selected a pearl-headed hairpin and held it up. "Like this," I said.

She complied with my request. Within a week I found what I was searching for under the listing of "Departures for Europe."

Brig *Seahawk,* to sail on September the ninth, by the morning's tide. Captain Roderick Fisk, master.

For the next few days I made such a show of concentrating hard on my books that I was finally permitted to have my evening meals with the family downstairs.

On September the eighth—surely one of the longest days I can remember—I informed everyone at table that I wished to be excused to continue the reading that was so occupying me.

"What are you studying, my dear?" my mother asked nervously.

"Dr. Dillard's essay on patience, Mama."

"How very gratifying," she said.

Later that evening I was informed that my father wished me to come to his study. I went down and knocked on his door.

Words For Everyday Use

rec • la • ma • tion (rek lə mā´shən) *n.,* process of reclaiming

"Enter!" he called.

He was sitting in his reading chair, an open book before him. He looked up, closed his book, and drew me forward with a gentle gesture of his hand.

"You are making progress, Charlotte," he said. "I wish to commend you. I do."

"Thank you, Papa."

"You are young, Charlotte," he told me. "The young are capable of absorbing many shocks and still maintaining an . . ." He searched for the proper words.

"An *orderly* life?" I offered.

He smiled the first smile I had seen in a long while. "Yes, exactly, Charlotte. *Orderly.* You give me much hope. You and I now understand each other perfectly. Good night, my dear girl. Good night." He took up his book again.

"Good night, Papa."

I bathed. I let Bridget supervise my going to bed.

By two o'clock in the morning all was perfectly still. I slipped out of bed and from the bottom drawer of my bureau took from beneath my paper-layered frocks the sailor's clothes that Zachariah had made me. I changed into them.

I opened the window to my room. It was child's play for me to climb down the trellis. I almost laughed! Within half an hour I was on the India docks, standing before the *Seahawk*, dark except for a lantern fore and aft. A new main-mast had been stepped.

As I watched from the shadow of some bales of goods, I saw someone on watch, pacing the quarterdeck. At one point he proceeded to the bell and rang out the time, four bells. Each clang sent shivers up and down my spine.

Boldly now, I walked up the gangplank.

"Who is that?" came a challenge.

I said nothing.

"Who is that?" came the demand again. Now I was certain of the voice.

"Zachariah?" I called, my voice choked.

"Charlotte!"

"I've decided to come home."

By morning's tide—and a southwest wind—the *Seahawk* sailed away. As it did I was clinging to the topgallant spar below a billowing royal yard. Something Zachariah told me filled my mind and excited my heart: "A sailor," he said, "chooses the wind that takes the ship from safe port . . . but winds have a mind of their own."

◄ What does Charlotte's father see as progress?

◄ How does Charlotte get out of her house?

◄ What does Charlotte say she has done?

◄ Why did Charlotte return to the Seahawk?

Responding to the Selection

Does Charlotte belong in Rhode Island with her family or on the ship?

Investigate, Inquire, and Imagine

Recall: GATHERING FACTS

1a. What is the main argument the captain makes at Charlotte's trial? What evidence does he use to support this argument?

2a. Who does Charlotte think is responsible for the murder of Hollybrass at first? Who does she finally realize is responsible? What does Charlotte remember when she stands outside her old cabin door?

3a. What do Charlotte's siblings think of her appearance? Why does Charlotte's father burn her journal?

Interpret: FINDING MEANING

1b. Is the captain's argument sound? Why doesn't the crew stand up for Charlotte?

2b. How does Charlotte realize she is incorrect about her first suspicion? How had Charlotte's suspicions been growing since she first came aboard?

3b. Would Charlotte have left her parents' house if her family had been more accepting of her experience? Explain your response.

Analyze: TAKING THINGS APART

4a. Compare and contrast Charlotte's character at the beginning and the end of the novel. Consider her appearance, her attitudes, her actions, and her relationships with others.

Synthesize: BRINGING THINGS TOGETHER

4b. At the beginning of the novel, Charlotte states, "At the time my name *was* Charlotte Doyle. And though I have kept the name, I am not—for reasons you will soon discover—the *same* Charlotte Doyle." Explain the meaning of this statement.

Evaluate: MAKING JUDGMENTS

5a. Assess the crew's failure to support Charlotte at her trial. Is their behavior justified by their reasons? Explain your response.

Extend: CONNECTING IDEAS

5b. Charlotte herself did not mention Zachariah at her trial. Do you think it is a good idea to keep quiet to protect somebody else? Why, or why not?

Understanding Literature

A **theme** is a central idea in a literary work. Identify three events or indications of the theme of justice in this novel. What statement is made about justice?

The **resolution** is the point at which the central conflict is ended, or resolved. What event marks the resolution in this novel?

Point of view is the vantage point from which a story is told. This novel is told from the first person point of view. That is, Charlotte tells her own story using words such as *I* and *we*. Summarize the story Charlotte has just told if it were told from the point of view of Zachariah, Charlotte's father, or Captain Jaggery.

APPENDIX

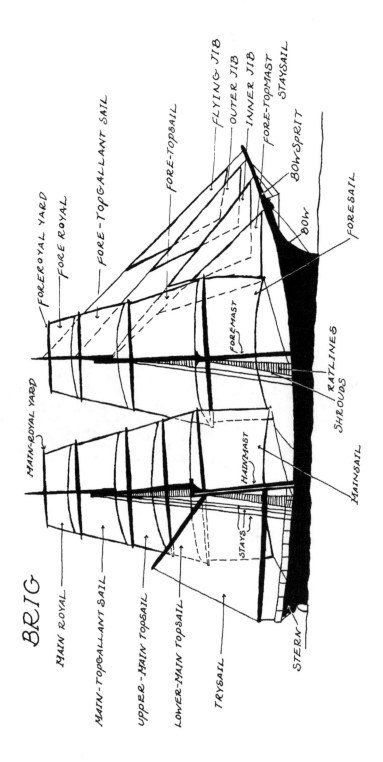

BRIG

FORE ROYAL YARD
FORE ROYAL
FORE-TOPGALLANT SAIL
FORE-TOPSAIL
FLYING-JIB
OUTER JIB
INNER JIB
FORE-TOPMAST STAYSAIL
BOWSPRIT
BOW
FORESAIL
FOREMAST
RATLINES
SHROUDS
MAIN-ROYAL YARD
MAINMAST
MAINSAIL
STAYS
MAIN ROYAL
MAIN-TOPGALLANT SAIL
UPPER-MAIN TOPSAIL
LOWER-MAIN TOPSAIL
TRYSAIL
STERN

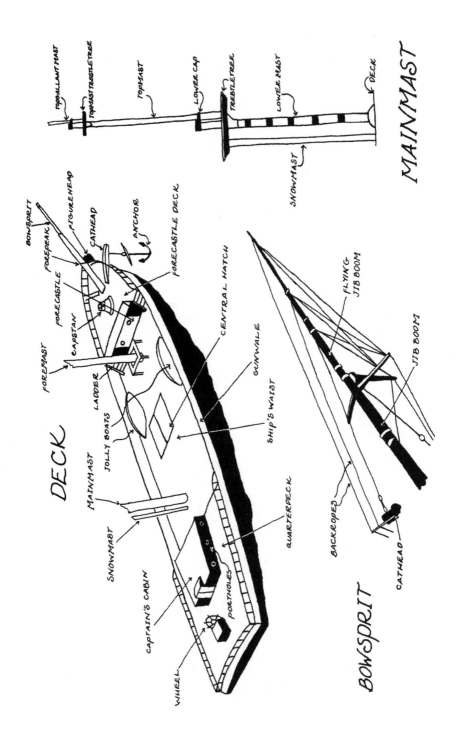

MAINMAST

TOPGALLANT MAST
TOPMAST TRESTLETREE
TOPMAST
LOWER CAP
TRESTLETREE
LOWER MAST
DECK
SNOWMAST

BOWSPRIT
FIGUREHEAD
FOREPEAK
CATHEAD
ANCHOR
FORECASTLE DECK
FORECASTLE
CAPSTAN
CENTRAL HATCH
FOREMAST
GUNWALE
LADDER
SHIP'S WAIST
JOLLY BOATS
MAINMAST
QUARTERDECK
SNOWMAST
CAPTAIN'S CABIN
PORTHOLES
WHEEL

DECK

FLYING-
JIB BOOM
JIB BOOM
BACKROPES
CATHEAD

BOWSPRIT

Ship's Time

On sailing ships crews were divided into teams so as to share all work. These teams were called watches. On the *Seahawk*, Mr. Hollybrass had the command of one watch, Mr. Keetch—then Mr. Johnson, as second mate—took charge of the second.

The day was broken up into time periods—also called watches—as follows:

> Midwatch ran from midnight to 4:00 A.M.;
> morning watch ran from 4:00 A.M. to 8:00 A.M.;
> forenoon watch ran from 8:00 A.M. to 12:00 noon;
> afternoon watch ran from 12:00 noon to 4:00 P.M.;
> first dog watch ran from 4:00 P.M. to 6:00 P.M.;
> second dog watch ran from 6:00 P.M. to 8:00 P.M.;
> night watch ran from 8:00 P.M. to midnight.

A typical day would have a sailor working alternate watches, a system called "watch and watch," in this fashion:

> Off during midwatch: midnight to 4:00 A.M.;
> work morning watch: 4:00 A.M. to 8:00 A.M.;
> off forenoon watch: 8:00 A.M. to 12:00 noon;
> work afternoon watch: 12:00 noon to 4:00 P.M.;
> off first dog watch: 4:00 P.M. to 6:00 P.M.;
> work second dog watch: 6:00 P.M. to 8:00 P.M.;
> off night watch: 8:00 P.M. to midnight.

This meant that on the following day the sailor's schedule would be:

> Work during midwatch: midnight to 4:00 A.M.;
> off morning watch: 4:00 A.M. to 8:00 A.M.;
> work forenoon watch: 8:00 A.M. to 12:00 noon;
> off afternoon watch: 12:00 noon to 4:00 P.M.;
> work first dog watch: 4:00 P.M. to 6:00 P.M.;
> off second dog watch: 6:00 P.M. to 8:00 P.M.;
> work night watch: 8:00 P.M. to midnight.

And so on . . .

This pattern of watch and watch meant that no sailor ever had more than four hours sleep at a time. Of course if there was need, such as a general resetting or overhaul of the sails—or a storm—all hands could be called, and they would report even if it was not their watch.

To keep track of time, the mates rang the ship's bell every half hour. They did it this way:

1 bell meant the first half hour after the watch began;

2 bells meant the second half hour;

3 bells meant the third half hour;

4 bells meant the fourth half hour;

5 bells meant the fifth half hour;

6 bells meant the sixth half hour;

7 bells meant the seventh half hour;

8 bells meant the eighth half hour and the end of the watch.

For example, if two bells rang out during the first dog watch, it would be, by land reckoning, 5:00 P.M.

Plot Analysis of *The True Confessions of Charlotte Doyle*

The following diagram, known as Freytag's Pyramid, illustrates the main plot of *The True Confessions of Charlotte Doyle*. For definitions and more information on the parts of a plot illustrated below, see the Handbook of Literary Terms on page 186.

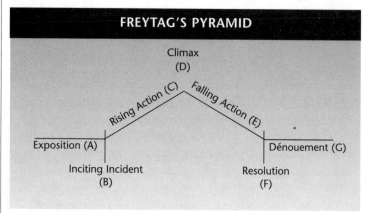

FREYTAG'S PYRAMID

Climax (D)

Rising Action (C)

Falling Action (E)

Exposition (A)

Dénouement (G)

Inciting Incident (B)

Resolution (F)

The parts of a plot are as follows:

The **exposition** is the part of a plot that provides background information about the characters, setting, or conflict.

The **inciting incident** is the event that introduces the central conflict.

The **rising action**, or complication, develops the conflict to a high point of intensity.

The **falling action** is all the events that follow the climax.

The **resolution** is the point at which the central conflict is ended, or resolved.

The **dénouement** is any material that follows the resolution and that ties up loose ends.

Exposition (A)

Charlotte explains how she is able to remember the events that she is about to recount. She explains why she is sailing on the *Seahawk*. She learns that the other families she expected as passengers will not be sailing on the ship. The disappearance of two porters and the comments of Keetch warn her not to sail on the ship. Charlotte decides she will not sail on the *Seahawk,* but discovers too late that the ship has already set sail.

Inciting Incident (B)

Zachariah gives Charlotte a knife and suggests that she may need it for her own safety. He also tells Charlotte of some of the history between the crew and Captain Jaggery. Shortly thereafter, Captain Jaggery warns Charlotte about the crew and tells her she must tell him everything she sees and hears, especially if she ever sees a "round robin."

Rising Action (C)

Charlotte watches Captain Jaggery work the crew hard, at some points harder than she thinks is necessary. At the same time, Charlotte begins to spend more time with the crew and to become friendly with them. While running an errand to help one of the crew, she discovers a round robin and a pistol in the crew's quarters. Charlotte discloses her discovery to Captain Jaggery who ends the mutiny by shooting the leader, Cranick, a former member of the crew and a stowaway on the ship. The captain also punishes Zachariah who refuses to throw Cranick overboard without a prayer. Charlotte grabs the whip to stop the punishment and accidentally whips the captain across the face. After the uprising, neither the captain nor the crew wants anything to do with Charlotte. Charlotte chooses the crew and asks to become one of them. She proves her worth by climbing to the top of the highest mast. Upon learning of Charlotte's decision, the captain removes any sense of protection or friendship he had previously offered her.

Climax (D)

The captain deliberately steers the ship into a hurricane. During the storm, the first mate is killed. Captain Jaggery accuses Charlotte of murder. She is tried, convicted, and sentenced to die.

Falling Action (E)

Charlotte and Zachariah realize that Captain Jaggery is the murderer and attempt a new plan to remove him from power.

Resolution (F)

Keetch informs the captain of the plan. Charlotte is offered a chance to give up her life as part of the crew and return to her life as a passenger. She refuses both and runs from the captain's cabin. As she climbs out on the bowsprit to get away from the captain, he follows and falls into the ocean.

Dénouement (G)

The crew makes Charlotte the new captain of the ship. They arrive safely in Providence where Charlotte is reunited with her family. They are surprised to see her sun- and work-hardened appearance. Charlotte's father reads her journal and is outraged. He burns the journal and sends her to her room. Charlotte waits until she reads that the *Seahawk* is about to set sail. Then she sneaks out of the house and chooses a life on the sea.

Creative Writing Activities

Creative Writing Activity A: Journal

Try keeping a daily journal for a week. Write about your experiences, your feelings, and your observations. Don't worry about grammar and spelling as you record your life in your journal initially. After a week, choose one day and polish the writing by cleaning up any errors.

Creative Writing Activity B: Review

What did you think of this novel? Would you recommend it to your peers? Why, or why not? Write a brief review of *The True Confessions of Charlotte Doyle* with the aim of convincing somebody else to read or not read the novel. Try not to give away too much of the story as you discuss it. If you have access to the Internet, you can add your review to the online reviews at www.avi-writer.com.

Creative Writing Activity C: Adventure Continuation

What will happen to Charlotte next? With your classmates, brainstorm a list of new challenges or difficulties Charlotte might encounter. Choose one and consider ways in which she might face this new experience. Write one chapter that tells about Charlotte's next adventure. You may choose to end the adventure on a suspenseful note as many of the chapters in the novel do.

Creative Writing Activity D: Editorial

Imagine you are a reporter who has heard how Captain Jaggery treated his crew. Write an editorial that either supports or speaks out against his actions. Use examples from the novel to support your claims. You may also include your ideas about justice. You may wish to include quotes from Charlotte, Captain Jaggery, or crew members.

Critical Writing Activities

Critical Writing Activity A: Class, Race, and Gender

In this novel, many distinctions are made based on class, race, and gender. In a brief essay, address one of these issues. You may wish to discuss the role Charlotte's gender plays in her trial, the effects of race on Charlotte's friendship with Zachariah, or the similarities or differences between class distinction on land and sea. To get started, reread the quotations in "Echoes" on page XIV.

Critical Writing Activity B: The Changing Character of Charlotte Doyle

How does Charlotte change throughout the course of the novel? Why is she no longer the same Charlotte Doyle she was when she started out on her voyage? Write an essay in which you address these questions. You may wish to begin by reviewing your responses to questions 4a and 4b after chapter 22 on page 166.

Critical Writing Activity C: Adventure and Suspense

The True Confessions of Charlotte Doyle is full of suspense and adventure. Examine how Avi uses suspense throughout this novel. You may wish to pay special attention to chapter endings and refer back to your responses to the Understanding Literature question on suspense after chapter 6 on page 44.

Critical Writing Activity D: Compare and Contrast

Charlotte tells Captain Jaggery that he reminds her of her father. Are the two men similar? Although the reader only meets Charlotte's father briefly at the end of the novel, we see how he treats Charlotte and how she perceives her father's character. Write an essay in which you compare and contrast the two men. You may wish to focus on their treatment of Charlotte.

Projects

Project A: Mock Trial

Hold your own trial of Charlotte Doyle. One student can play Charlotte, others can be Captain Jaggery and the members of the crew. Identify evidence for and against Charlotte. Let each side present his or her case. Then let the crew vote on Charlotte's fate. As an alternative, you might hold a mock trial for Captain Jaggery. Is he really the cruel captain his crew makes him out to be or is he simply trying to maintain control of the ship?

Project B: Model Ships

Create a model of the *Seahawk*. Use the ship diagrams in the appendix and the descriptions throughout the novel to create and identify the parts of the ship. Include the brig, the galley, the different masts, the figurehead, and other important parts of the ship.

Project C: Online Discussion

Did you enjoy this book? Do you have a question about Charlotte that you would like answered? Participate in an online discussion at www.avi-writer.com. Using the bulletin board at this site, you can start a strand about a topic that interests you or you can add to a discussion that has already been started.

Project D: Women Sailors

It is true that women sailors were not common in the 1800s when this novel is set, but there were some female sailors and even pirates. Research this subject and present your findings to the class. As an alternative, you might examine other activities that were not common for women at that time and some of the pioneers in those fields. Present your findings to your class.

Glossary

Pronunciation Key

Vowel Sounds

a	hat	ō	go	ʉ	burn
ā	play	ô	paw, born	ə	extra
ä	star	o͞o	book, put		under
e	then	o͞o͞o	blue, stew		civil
ē	me	oi	boy		honor
i	sit	ou	wow		bogus
ī	my	u	up		

Consonant Sounds

b	but	l	lip	t	sit
ch	watch	m	money	th	with
d	do	n	on	v	valley
f	fudge	ŋ	song, sink	w	work
g	go	p	pop	y	yell
h	hot	r	rod	z	pleasure
j	jump	s	see		
k	brick	sh	she		

a • bate (ə bāt´) *vi.*, lessen, diminish

a • bom • i • na • tion (ə bäm ə nā´shən) *n.*, anything hateful and disgusting

ac • cost (ə kôst´) *vt.*, greet in an unwelcome way

ac • rid (ak´rid) *adj.*, sharp, bitter, stinging, or irritating in taste or smell

ag • i • tat • ed (aj´i tāt id) *adj.*, perturbed, excited

al • be • it (ôl bē´it) *conj.*, even though

al • le • giance (ə lē´jəns) *n.*, obligation or loyalty to a leader or country

a • miss (ə mis´) *adv.*, in a wrong way

ap • pall • ing (ə pôl´iŋ) *adj.*, horrifying, causing dismay

ap • pease (ə pēz´) *vt.*, pacify or calm

ap • pre • hen • sive (ap rē hen´siv) *adj.*, anxious or fearful about the future, uneasy

ap • pre • hen • sive • ly (ap rē hen´siv lē) *adv.*, fearfully, uneasily

ar • dent (ärd´´nt) *adj.*, passionate, intensely enthusiastic

as • sault (ə sôlt´) *vt.*, attack

a • sun • der (ə sun´dər) *adv.*, apart or into pieces

au • dac • i • ty (ô das´ə tē) *n.*, shameless boldness

bask (bask) *vi.*, enjoy a warm or pleasant feeling from being in a certain situation

be • grudge (bē gruj´) *vt.*, give with ill will or reluctance

be • guil • ing (bē gīl´iŋ) *adj.,* charming or delightful

bla • tant (blāt´'nt) *adj.,* glaringly conspicuous or obtrusive

blithe • ly (blīth´lē) *adv.,* cheerfully, in a carefree way

bolt (bôlt) *vi.,* start suddenly and run away

brand • ish (bran´dish) *vt.,* wave, shake, or flourish

cen • sure (sen´shər) *n.,* strong disapproval

chas • ten (chās´ən) *vt.,* make purer, refine; punish

cher • ish (cher´ish) *vt.,* hold dear, appreciate

clam • ber (klam´bər) *vi.,* climb clumsily and with great effort

com • men • da • tion (käm ən dā´shən) *n.,* act of recommendation or praise, compliment

com • pel (kəm pəl´) *vt.,* force

com • pli • ance (kəm plī´əns) *n.,* giving in to a request or demand

com • plic • i • ty (kəm plis´ə tē) *n.,* state of being an accomplice

com • pose (kəm pōz´) *vt.,* put one's mind at ease, calm, allay

con • coct (kən käkt´) *vt.,* devise, plan

con • done (kən dōn´) *vt.,* forgive or pardon

con • fin • ing (kən fīn´iŋ) *adj.,* restricting

con • gen • ial (kən jēn´yəl) *adj.,* having the same tastes; agreeable

con • spir • a • cy (kən spir´ə sē) *n.,* plot; secret unlawful plan

con • tem • plate (kän´təm plāt) *vt.,* look at intently

con • tempt (kən tempt´) *n.,* attitude of one who looks down on somebody or something

con • tort (kən tôrt´) *vi.,* twist, distort violently

con • vul • sive • ly (kən vul´siv lē) *adv.,* shake involuntarily

co • pi • ous • ly (kō´pē əs lē) *adv.,* abundantly

cor • rupt (kə rupt´) *adj.,* contaminated, rotten

coun • te • nance (koun´tə nəns) *n.,* face

course (kôrs) *vi.,* move swiftly

cow (kou) *vt.,* intimidate, make submissive

curt • ly (kʉrt´lē) *adv.,* bluntly to the point of rudeness

de • co • rum (di kō´rəm) *n.,* propriety and good taste in behavior

de • crep • it (dē krep´it) *adj.,* weak, broken down by old age

del • e • gate (del´ə gāt) *vt.,* appoint as a representative

de • ri • sion (di rizh´ən) *n.,* contempt or ridicule

des • pi • ca • ble (des´pi kə bəl) *adj.,* deserving to be despised, not worthy of respect

des • pot (des´pət) *n.,* anyone in charge who acts like a tyrant

des • ti • tute (des´tə to͞ot) *adj.,* abandoned, forsakened, poverty-stricken

dex • ter • ous (deks´tər əs) *adj.,* showing skillful use of the hands or body

dis • dain (dis dān´) *n.,* aloof contempt or scorn

dis • mayed (dis mād´) *adj.,* filled with alarm or apprehension

dis • miss (dis mis´) *vt.,* remove from a position of employment; fire dis • traught (di strôt´) *adj.,* extremely troubled

doc • ile (däs´əl) *adj.,* easy to manage, obedient

dole • ful (dōl´fəl) *adj.,* full of sorrow, mournful

ear • nest • ness (ʉr´nist nəs) *n.,* seriousness

ebb (eb) *vi.,* weaken or lessen

ed • dy (ed´ē) *vt.,* move in a whirlpool-like motion

ed • i • fy • ing (ed´i fī iŋ) *adj.,* enlightening, building morality or spirituality

el • e • va • tion (el ə vā´shən) *n.,* high position

em • i • nent (em´ə nənt) *adj.,* distinguished, outstanding

e • mit (ē mit´) *vt.,* send out, give off

en • deav • or (en dev´ər) *vi.,* strive, make a solid attempt

en • gross (en grōs´) *vt.,* take the entire attention of, absorb

e • nor • mi • ty (e nôr´mə tē) *n.,* outrageousness

en • su • ing (en sŏŏ´iŋ) *adj.,* following, resultant

e • qua • nim • i • ty (ek wə nim´ə tē) *n.,* composure, evenness of mind

fas • tid • i • ous • ness (fas tid´ē əs nəs) *n.,* daintiness; state of being overrefined

fath • om (fath´əm) *vt.,* get to the bottom of

fes • ter (fes´tər) *vi.,* decay

fes • toon (fes tŏŏn´) *vt.,* adorn or hang with items in a loop or curve

flail • ing (flāl´iŋ) *adj.,* move in a striking or beating motion

flog (fläg) *vt.,* beat with a whip

flour • ish (flʉr´ish) *n.,* showy, wavy motion

forth • right • ness (fôrth´rīt nəs) *n.,* directness

gan • gly (gaŋ´glē) *adj.,* tall, thin, and awkward

gape (gāp) *vi.,* stare with open mouth

glow • er (glou´ər) *vt.,* scowl angrily

grave • ly (grāv´lē) *adv.,* seriously

griev • ous (grēv´əs) *adj.,* atrocious, very serious

gro • tesque (grō tesk´) *adj.,* fantastic, bizarre

gump • tion (gump´shən) *n.,* courage and initiative

gy • ra • tion (jī rā´shən) *n.,* circular or spiral motion

i • dle (id´´l) *adj.,* inactive, useless

im • pede (im pēd´) *vt.,* hinder, obstruct, or delay

im • per • ti • nence (im pʉrt´´n əns) *n.,* lack of respect

im • pla • ca • ble (im plā´kə bəl) *adj.,* cannot be appeased, relentless

im • pul • sive • ly (im pul´siv lē) *adv.,* suddenly, spontaneously

in • cred • u • lous (in krej´ŏŏ ləs) *adj.,* skeptical, unable to believe

in • cre • ment (in´krə mənt) *n.,* amount of an increase

in • dig • na • tion (in dig nā´shən) *n.,* anger or scorn in reaction to injustice

in • dis • tinct (in di stiŋkt´) *adj.,* not seen or heard clearly

in • ex • pli • ca • bly (in eks´pli kə blē) *adv.*, without explanation

in • stinc • tive (in stiŋk´tiv) *adj.*, prompted by a natural tendency

in • tol • er • a • ble (in täl´ər ə bəl) *adj.*, unbearable

in • tone (in tōn´) *vt.*, utter or recite

ire (īre) *n.*, anger

ir • rel • e • vance (ir rel´ə vəns) *n.*, uselessness

la • con • ic (la kän´ik) *adj.*, brief in speaking, using few words

lame • ly (lām´lē) *adv.*, weakly

lark (lärk) *n.*, merry time

lash (lash) *vt.*, tie or fasten with a rope

lit • a • ny (lit´'n ē) *n.*, repetitive listing

liv • id (liv´id) *adj.*, extremely angry

loath • some (lōth´səm) *adj.*, disgusting, detestable

lum • ber (lum´bər) *vi.*, move heavily or clumsily

ma • li • cious (mə lish´əs) *adj.*, spiteful; intentionally mischievous

mal • o • dor • ous (mal ō´dər əs) *adj.*, having a bad odor

ma • roon (mə rōōn´) *vt.*, stranded in a desolate place

mel • an • cho • li • a (mel ən kô´lē ə) *n.*, mental disorder characterized by extreme depression of spirits

men • a • cing (men´əs iŋ) *adj.*, threatening

met • a • mor • phose (met ə môr´fōz) *vt.*, transform

mock • ing • ly (mäk´iŋ lē) *adv.*, scornfully; with ridicule

mo • men • tous (mō men´təs) *adj.*, very important

mo • rose • ly (mə rōs´lē) *adv.*, gloomily

mor • ti • fy (môrt´ə fī) *vt.*, cause to feel shame or humiliation

mu • ti • ny (myōō´t'nē) *n.*, rise up against authority

naught (nôt) *n.*, nothing

nil (nil) *n.*, nothing

ob • liv • i • on (ə bliv´ē ən) *n.*, condition of being forgotten

om • i • nous (äm´ə nəs) *adj.*, threatening

pal • lor (pal´ər) *n.*, lack of color

pal • pa • ble (pal´pə bəl) *adj.*, tangible, perceived by the senses

par • tial (pär´shəl) *adj.*, favoring one person or thing more than another

per • ish (per´ish) *vi.*, die

per • me • ate (pʉr´mē āt) *vt.*, penetrate and spread throughout

per • pet • u • al (pər pech´ōō əl) *adj.*, continuing forever

per • plex • i • ty (pər pleks´ə tē) *n.*, bewilderment; confusion

per • va • sive (pər vā´siv) *adj.*, spread throughout

pin • ion (pin´yən) *vt.*, confine or shackle

plumb (plum) *vt.*, discover the facts; fathom

por • ten • tous • ly (pôr ten´təs lē) *adv.*, pompously; with awe or amazement

pre • sump • tu • ous (prē zump´chōō əs) *adj.*, too bold or forward

prey (prā) *vi.*, weigh heavily

prone (prōn) *adj.,* inclined to

proph • e • cy (präf´ə sē) *n.,* prediction

pro • trud • ing (prō trōōd´iŋ) *adj.,* jutting out, projecting

punc • til • i • ous (puŋk til´ē əs) *adj.,* very careful about every detail; exacting

quell (kwəl) *vt.,* quiet, put an end to

quiv • er (kwiv´ər) *vi.,* shake, tremble

ra • di • ant (rā´dē ənt) *adj.,* showing well being

rant (rant) *vi.,* talk in a loud, wild way

rapt (rapt) *adj.,* completely absorbed

rash (rash) *adj.,* reckless

rasp (rasp) *vt.,* scrape; make a grating sound

rau • cous (rô´kəs) *adj.,* loud and rowdy

re • bel • lion (ri bel´yən) *n.,* defiance to authority

rec • la • ma • tion (rek lə mā´shən) *n.,* process of reclaiming

re • coil (rē koil´) *vi.,* draw back; retreat in surprise, fear, or disgust

re • nounce (ri nouns´) *vt.,* give up in a public announcement

re • prieve (ri prēv´) *n.,* temporary relief

res • er • va • tion (rez ər vā´shən) *n.,* limiting condition or qualification

re • solve (ri zälv´) *n.,* firm determination, fixed purpose

res • ti • tu • tion (res tə tōō´shən) *n.,* giving back to rightful owner; reimbursement

rouse (rouz) *vt.,* wake from sleep

ruf • fi • an (ruf´ē ən) *n.,* hoodlum, lawless person

ru • in • a • tion (rōō ə nā´shən) *n.,* being ruined

sal • low (sal´ō) *adj.,* having a sickly, yellow complexion

sar • don • i • cal • ly (sär dän´ik lē) *adv.,* sarcastically, bitterly sneering

scorn • ful • ly (skôrn´fəl lē) *adv.,* with contempt or disdain

scru • ti • nize (skrōōt´´n īz) *vt.,* examine closely

sear (sir) *vt.,* burn

seeth • ing (sēth´iŋ) *adj.,* having and showing violent anger

shirk (shʉrk) *vt.,* neglect or evade doing work

slan • der • ous (slan´dər əs) *adj.,* damaging to another person's character

smug (smug) *adj.,* self-satisfied to an annoying degree

spec • u • late (spek´yōō lāt) *vi.,* consider various aspects of a subject

stam • mer (stam´ər) *vi.,* speak with pauses

stark (stärk) *adj.,* harsh, bleak

stint • ing (stint´iŋ) *adj.,* sparing

stout • ly (stout´lē) *adv.,* bravely

stu • pen • dous (stōō pen´dəs) *adj.,* overwhelming

sub • side (səb sīd´) *vi.,* become less active or intense

suc • cumb (sə kum´) *vt.,* yield, submit

sul • len • ness (sul´ən nis) *n.,* dullness and resentment

sup • pli • ca • tion (sup lə kā´shən) *n.*, humble prayer

sur • mise (sər mīz´) *n.*, guess

sus • tain (sə stān´) *vt.*, support, strengthen the spirits

taut (tôt) *adj.*, stretched tight

tor • rent (tôr´ənt) *n.*, flood or rush

tran • quil • i • ty (tran kwil´ə tē) *n.*, calmness, serenity

tran • spire (tran spīr´) *vt.*, happen, take place

treach • er • ous (trech´ər əs) *adj.*, untrustworthy or insecure

trep • i • da • tion (trep´ə dā´shən) *n.*, fearful uncertainty

un • du • lat • ing (un´dyo͞o lāt iŋ) *adj.*, moving in waves; wavy

un • im • peach • a • ble (un´im pē´chə bəl) *adj.*, that which cannot be doubted, questioned, or discredited

un • mer • ci • ful • ly (un mʉr´si fəl lē) *adv.*, relentlessly

un • rul • y (un ro͞ol´ē) *adj.*, hard to control

ven • ture (ven´chər) *vi.*, do or go at some risk

ver • i • ta • ble (ver´i tə bəl) *adj.*, actual

vex • a • tion (veks ā´shən) *n.*, being distressed

viv • id • ness (viv´id nis) *n.*, striking realism

wan • ing (wān´iŋ) *adj.*, grow less in extent

way • ward (wā´wərd) *adj.*, willful, disobedient

wont (wänt) *adj.*, accustomed

wrench • ing (rench´iŋ) *adj.*, suddenly pulling or twisting

wretch • ed (rech´id) *adj.*, miserable

Handbook of Literary Terms

Allusion. An **allusion** is a rhetorical technique in which reference is made to a person, event, object, or work from history or literature.

Adventure. **Adventure** is a genre of literature in which the main character faces many dangerous and exciting experiences. Based on the introduction to *The True Confessions of Charlotte Doyle,* identify some of the adventures Charlotte will face throughout the course of this novel. Make a prediction about how each will happen.

Conflict. A **conflict** is a struggle between two people or things in a literary work. A plot is formed around conflict. A conflict can be internal or external. A struggle that takes place between a character and some outside force such as another character, society, or nature is called an external conflict.

Description. A **description** gives a picture in words of a character, object, or scene. Descriptions make use of sensory details—words and phrases that describe how things look, sound, smell, taste, or feel.

Dialogue. **Dialogue** is conversation involving two or more people or characters. Plays are made up of dialogue and stage directions. Fictional works are made up of dialogue, narration, and description. In a play, dialogue appears after the names of characters.

Foreshadowing. **Foreshadowing** is the act of presenting materials that hint at events to occur later in a story.

Mood. **Mood,** or **atmosphere,** is the emotion created in the reader by a piece of writing. A writer creates a mood by using concrete details.

Motive. A **motive** is a reason for acting in a certain way.

Plot. A **plot** is a series of events related to a central *conflict,* or struggle. A plot usually involves the introduction of a conflict, its development, and its eventual resolution. The following terms are used to describe the parts of a plot:

- The **exposition,** or **introduction,** sets the tone or mood, introduces the characters and the setting, and provides necessary background information.
- The **inciting incident** is the event that introduces the central conflict.

- The **climax** is the high point of interest or suspense in the plot.
- The **crisis,** or **turning point,** often the same event as the climax, is the point in the plot where something happens to decide the future course of events and the eventual working out of the conflict.
- The **resolution** is the point at which the central conflict is ended, or resolved.
- The **dénouement** is any material that follows the resolution and that ties up loose ends. Some plots do not contain all of these parts. See *conflict.*

Point of View. Point of view is the vantage point from which a story is told. If a story is told from the first-person point of view, the narrator uses the pronouns I and we and is a part of or a witness to the action.

Resolution. The **resolution** is the point in a poem, story, or play in which the central conflict, or struggle, is ended.

Simile. A **simile** is a comparison using like or as.

Suspense. Suspense is a feeling of anxiousness or curiosity. Writers create suspense by raising questions in the reader's mind and by using details that create strong emotions.

Theme. A **theme** is a central idea in a literary work.